# Quilty
# as Charged

# Also Available by Maggie Bailey

*Seams Deadly*

# Quilty
# as Charged

## A MEASURE TWICE
## SEWING MYSTERY

## Maggie Bailey

**CROOKED LANE**

NEW YORK

Published in the United States by Crooked Lane Books, an imprint of The Quick Brown Fox & Company LLC.

Crooked Lane Books and its logo are trademarks of The Quick Brown Fox & Company LLC.

Library of Congress Catalog-in-Publication data available upon request.

ISBN (hardcover): 978-1-63910-799-5
ISBN (ebook): 978-1-63910-800-8

Cover design by Joe Burleson

Printed in the United States.

www.crookedlanebooks.com

Crooked Lane Books
34 West 27th St., 10th Floor
New York, NY 10001

First Edition: August 2024

10 9 8 7 6 5 4 3 2 1

To Jes:

My gremlin, my bestie, my home.
It is about time a book started with your
name. Love you heaps, too.

# Chapter One

**Friday**

It had to work. It was as simple as that. It had to work.

Lydia Barnes' fabric store, Measure Twice, was in the red. Bright red. Each day she worked at the store, located on the cute main square of Peridot, an even cuter North Georgia mountain town, trying to win new customers, and each night she stayed up, bleary-eyed, and worried it wouldn't be enough. Every night as she struggled to fall asleep, Lydia scrolled through her Instagram, overwhelmed by the budgeting she still had to finish. Then one night, there it was. An invitation to a sewing retreat on the coast of Oregon. The retreat offered three days of good company, good food, and a chance to sew new clothes and learn new sewing skills. It was expensive, really expensive, and it looked incredible. Lydia wished someone would do something like that near her. Then it hit her. *She* was that someone. And her idea was born: SEW RELAX-ING, a sewing retreat with the ladies of Measure Twice.

If she made it a monthly event, the added income would move the store from drowning to treading water, and right now, for Lydia, that was enough. She would have the local shoppers in Peridot, but she could also woo sewists from Atlanta, sewists who might want to start making day trips to a cute fabric shop in the mountains long after the weekend was over.

She had picked a weekend and started to plan, but now that it was actually happening, she felt overwhelmed. Three days. Three entire days away from the store. Three days with no in-store sales. Three days that had to run smoothly. Lydia looked around the shop. Since she had taken over ownership of Measure Twice six months ago, she had opened the store every day except Christmas and New Year's. Now she had to close it in order to save it.

Before she spiraled into all the things that could go wrong, and, honestly, she was really good at that, she needed to focus on the tasks at hand. She checked the display, made sure all the bolts of fabric were neatly tucked into the shelves. Then she double checked that the register was locked, since she'd already taken the money to the bank earlier in the day.

It was time to leave the store, to go up to her apartment, just above Measure Twice, and finish her preparations. She breathed in, deeply. The store smelled like a blend of laundry, old coffee from the breakroom, and dust, combining to make her favorite scent in the world.

The door's small bell jangled as she locked it, and she held on to the sound as she walked up to her apartment and faced the last of her to-do list.

Her fabric was already folded in bins and waiting by the front door. As always, Lydia did all fabric-related tasks before anything else. She glanced at the linen, the quilting cotton, and the soft, slinky rayon already washed and ironed and ready to be transformed. Still, a sewing retreat, her first-ever Sew Relaxing event, needed more than just fabric.

Lydia had also offered to bring food for the first full night. It was a no-brainer. She knew what she would bring: lasagna. If any good thing had come out of her laughably short marriage, it was her lasagna recipe. Never mind the failed attempts, the quiet dinners pushing gloppy pasta around on their wedding plates. All those burnt pans and mushy noodles had led to this: the best lasagna. So, she set to it.

The turkey sausage browned in her cast-iron skillet while she mixed the egg, Parmesan, mozzarella, and ricotta together in a mixing bowl. Then crushed tomatoes and spices went in with the sausage as the wide, ribbon-like noodles went into a pot of boiling, salted water. Lydia wasn't coordinated, but she could dance this one recipe with her eyes closed. The sauce finished as she tipped the noodles into the colander. She rubbed three small baking tins with olive oil and started the layering. Sauce, noodles, cheese, sauce, noodles again. Whenever she lost count or got distracted, Lydia added more cheese. More cheese, she believed, covered a multitude of sins.

Even if the retreat didn't go exactly as planned, how mad could anyone be eating delicious lasagna on a chilly February night in the mountains? Although, it felt like jinxing herself to say no one in that group would be mad, so she looked at the planning sheet one more time and walked herself through the attendees.

Fran. Of course, Fran was "going." It was her house, the Laurels, on Cherry Log Mountain that would host the event. She had insisted. Fran had also already offered to provide three sewing machines *and* make dinner the second night. Since Lydia had bought the store from her, Fran had been determined to help Lydia make a success out of Measure Twice's new chapter. Sometimes Lydia thought of Fran as her fairy godmother. A fairy godmother in unflattering, high-waisted, pleated jeans, but a fairy godmother, nonetheless.

Just to balance out Fran, Clark was coming. He would be bringing no extra supplies to share and no food for the group. He would probably show up with his own stash of food for only him. Clark ran a small organic and upscale food store, the Pampered Pantry, on the Peridot town square, a few stores down from Measure Twice. No doubt he would be well stocked with seaweed chips and chia seeds. On top of that, he'd said he might be late. But the specific request part of the form? That Clark had filled out with gusto. Clark lived for specific requests. No gluten. No soy-based gluten substitute. Only alternative down pillows. The list went on.

Next on the list: The M's. Martha and Mary would be there, of course. One almost always guaranteed the other. They weren't sisters—Lydia had already asked them, and they had said "NO," in unison, appearing equally shocked by the brashness of her inquiry. But they might as well have been twins. The women, both in their late 70s at the youngest (even Lydia knew that question would definitely be too brash) dressed alike, talked alike, and were almost always in each other's company. Both were laughably polite, and completely exhausting. Sometimes, as a Northern transplant in her new small-town Southern home, Lydia thought of the M's as the living personification of the saying, "Bless your heart." They knew their way around a backhanded compliment better than anyone. Who else would run a church charity shop called Blessed Again and turn away so many donations with a sweetly said, "Honey, why don't you just keep that darling little knickknack for yourself?"

At least Lydia could count on Heather to be a steadying influence. She hadn't required Heather to come on the retreat, but if she were being honest with herself, she was relieved when the young woman had suggested it. Young woman. Was that how she thought of people now?

Candy-apple red hair cut right at her jawline, and a penchant for denim overalls cut pretty darn short, paired with combat boots, Heather always stood out of the crowd at Measure Twice. Lydia knew she needed Heather, needed her social media savvy, her creative approach to programming, and her more-than-honest opinion when Lydia showed her what fabrics and notions she wanted to order next. A twenty-five-year-old with a clear sense of what was cool, Heather was invaluable.

Toiletries packed, Lydia looked in her meager closet. Black leggings? Check. Sewing-related T-shirts? Check. Rainbow-colored hand-knit socks? Check. Add some underwear and Lydia was ready to be SEW RELAXED. She zipped up the duffel bag full of barely folded clothes and tried to breathe a sigh of relief. Who else was coming? Who was she forgetting?

Then she remembered Cynde, of course, with a hastily added *plus one* after her name. Cynde, a court stenographer with a penchant for long anecdotes, was apparently bringing a work friend. Cynde was a regular at the shop, since the courthouse sat in the middle of Peridot's town square, and she was always game to try a new class or buy a new kit. She promised Lydia that Amy, her friend, was the same and would be nothing but added value. Cynde might be well into her fifties, but she made friends and gossiped as well as any teenager Lydia had ever met. Since Amy was driving up from Atlanta, Lydia hoped the new addition could help spread the Measure Twice gospel among her friends, whoever they were.

The weekend, if she were being honest, was mostly about saving the store, but there were other goals, too, one of which was to teach the group how to make garments. Everyone coming knew how to sew, most knew how to knit, and some, like Cynde, could turn out a quilt with astonishing speed. She had already led them through making a simple shirt, and now she wanted to challenge them with a slightly more difficult project: a coat.

Lydia really loved to sew clothes. In the mood for a pink shirt with sushi on it? Boom. A blue linen pinafore-style dress covered in gold constellations? To be honest, Lydia had already made one of those, using her trusted York Pinafore Pattern from Helen's Closet and some Miss Matatabi fabric shipped all the way from Japan. Sewing clothes meant the only limit was your imagination. Well, that and your patience.

Like a lot of sewists, Lydia had fallen in love with the recent trend of "quilt coats." Some sewists used secondhand quilts, while some fast fashion shops just used fabric that looked like it had been quilted but wasn't. She knew the M's would consider it sacrilege to cut into old quilts for the sake of a jacket, but she hoped she could convince the group to love the garment by quilting fabric specifically for the project. All it would take was a lining fabric, cotton quilting batting, and an outer fabric. At the retreat, she would show them how to quilt the layers together for the sake of a garment rather than a blanket.

Lydia checked her final bin. Pattern weights. Rotary cutters. Dress shears, hefty and able to glide through any fabric. Batting to add warmth and bulk to the coats. Bias tape. Pins. Tailor's chalk. She was ready. She needed to breathe. Then she heard it, the off-key chime of her doorbell.

She looked out her front window. Cynde's old beat-up tan Honda minivan was parked outside the shop. Fran owned the apartment, but Lydia had been renting it for the last six months or so and had come to think of it as her home. Living right above Measure Twice had a lot of advantages, and Lydia was glad she almost never had to give people directions these days.

Lydia still needed to settle her cat in with her neighbor, Jeff, who lived in the next apartment over. Her cat, Baby Lobster, wasn't a great traveler, and Clark had some seriously negative opinions about cat dander, so it was easier to leave her behind. She just needed to get the supplies sorted with Cynde and her friend.

"Something smells *good*," Cynde declared as she walked into the small apartment the moment Lydia opened the door. Cynde was wearing one of her classic outfits, as Lydia thought of them, this time a matching set of linen top with autumnal leaves appliqued around the hem and linen pants with leaves around each pant leg. She always looked comfortable, but Cynde always looked a little what Lydia's mom would call snazzy, as well.

Interestingly, Amy looked far more buttoned up. A nondescript white button-down topped what could only be described as black slacks. Who wore slacks when they didn't have to? Cynde didn't immediately introduce Amy, which surprised Lydia. And even more noticeable was the fact that, while both women looked at Lydia, they steadfastly refused to look at each other. Had there been a fight on the way over? Lydia needed this retreat to work, and it already felt like it was slipping toward disaster. Cynde's next comment brought Lydia back from her imagined troubles.

"Oh, Lydia, you can't be serious," Cynde chided, gesturing to the save-the-date card propped against the toaster in the kitchen. "Why on earth," she continued, "would they invite you? And why on earth would you keep the invitation?"

Amy looked back and forth between Cynde and Lydia, clearly hoping one of them would offer further explanation. Lydia just fussed with her supplies, blushing a deeper and deeper pink.

Lydia could still see it perfectly: her diet lemonade spilled and spreading across the floor. All that good ice ruined. Lydia could see her own shoes, fancy wedge espadrilles she had worn to try to fit in at the Junior League that Graham had encouraged her to attend. Her funny stories of snotty women and silly agenda points died on her lips. Her handsome husband, Graham, in their bed. Naked. Her former teaching assistant, Emma-Grace, in their bed. Naked.

Cynde held up the card. The invitation was Pinterest perfect and featured a photo of the smiling couple. Lydia looked again at the glamour shot of the happy couple, wearing matching plaid shirts in an apple orchard. "Graham and Emma-Grace are getting married!" read the card, with the loopy white calligraphy that seemed ubiquitous lately. What a name: Emma-Grace.

"This is Lydia's ex-husband," Cynde said, jabbing a finger at the smiling face of Graham in the orchard. "And this is the woman he had an affair with!" Cynde continued, jabbing Emma-Grace next. "For some reason I cannot figure out, they have invited Lydia, of all people, to their wedding! Lydia," Cynde turned her attention from Amy back to her, "why on earth have you kept this ridiculous invitation?"

The invitation was part of Emma-Grace's desperate attempt to rewrite history, convince herself that Graham's first marriage had ended in a conscious uncoupling rather than a blistering screaming match soaked in lemonade. But that didn't mean Lydia wasn't tempted to attend. Still, she was not about to admit she fantasized about attending the wedding as a successful shop owner, dressed in one of her own creations, with a gorgeous mystery man on her arm. The shop was failing, she hadn't done any of her own sewing in weeks, and her dog, Charlie, was the only man in her life these days. Instead, she offered, "It's just a save-the-date. And I don't think I'm actually going to go."

Amy looked unconvinced and Lydia didn't blame her. She hadn't even convinced herself.

Cynde dropped the card, moved toward the covered lasagna pans, and sighed, looking longingly at them, adding, "Do you need a taste tester for these?"

"Cynde, we already had dinner," Amy countered, more seriously than Lydia thought was warranted.

Lydia could guess what they had eaten, since Cynde was still holding the large Styrofoam cup of what was sure to be sweet tea. A drive-through, fried-chicken sandwich wasn't the worst way to start a road trip, in Lydia's opinion.

"That's the lasagna I made for the first dinner tomorrow." Lydia tucked the hot pans into a warm dish carrier. "Cynde, would you mind?" She struggled to zip the bag and then passed it to Cynde. "If you could take this down to the car? I just need to drop Baby

Lobster off with my neighbor who is cat-sitting, and then I'll meet you down at the van. Sound good?"

"Baby what?" Amy asked, clearly concerned that the woman leading this sewing retreat was a few donuts short of a dozen.

"Baby Lobster is my cat," Lydia explained, realizing any chance of a good first impression was lost at this point. "I adopted her last summer. If I am being honest, the name got my attention first, but her awesome personality really won me over."

At this proclamation, all three women turned to see the calico cat grooming herself on the back of the couch with a clear air of superiority.

"She warms up once she gets to know you, I swear," Lydia added, sensing Amy's unspoken disbelief. "Besides, I don't know how much Cynde has told you, but it was Baby Lobster that saved my life when . . . when everything happened here."

Before Lydia explained the two murders that happened in Peridot this past summer, Cynde cut her off, grabbing the lasagnas and calling out, "We're on it!" as she headed to the door. Amy reluctantly picked up the sewing supplies, and the two women headed back down to the street. Lydia was grateful for the interruption. Now she just needed to drop off her cat, grab her own duffle bag, and Charlie's gear, and head down to the van. Easy.

Leaving Charlie behind for the moment, she picked up Baby Lobster and headed over to her neighbor, Jeff's, apartment.

Jeff answered the door so quickly, Lydia wondered if he had been standing just behind it, waiting for her to arrive. As soon as Jeff opened the door, Baby Lobster leapt from Lydia's arms and darted over to Jeff's couch, making herself at home, while also studiously ignoring Jeff himself.

# Quilty as Charged

Lydia couldn't blame the cat. Jeff was perfectly nice. And Lydia hoped if she kept telling herself that, she would finally believe it.

Behind Jeff, she could see his trains. That is what Jeff did, buy and sell toy trains. He really, really loved trains. And Italian silk button-down shirts. And hugging Lydia for just a little too long.

Today the shirt was a garish purple vertical stripe, but it was only unbuttoned two buttons down. That was how Lydia gauged Jeff's moods, and two buttons down meant he was in a good mood but not too good. Lydia needed to get going, but Jeff clearly wanted to chat. She caved.

"How's business, Jeff? I can't tell you how much I appreciate you looking after Baby Lobster."

"Business is brisk, Lydia, thanks for asking. I just had an online auction for this beauty. I'm sending it off to its new home tomorrow," he added, gesturing to the train he lovingly cradled in his hands. Placing the train on a stand, he picked up something and held it out toward her.

"Here, why not take a business card with you on that retreat thing. Maybe someone on the retreat will have a train to sell." Jeff passed her the heavy card stock business card that read *Jeff's Trains*, his business buying and reselling model trains from his home. "And why don't you give me the address of where you're headed, Lydia?"

"Huh? The address? Why would you need the address? I mean," Lydia was torn between feeling confused as to why he would want to know and not wanting to offend him so much that he rescinded the offer to watch Baby Lobster.

Jeff smiled, seemingly unaware of her discomfort, and replied, "Just to be safe. You can't be too careful. And I know how much Baby Lobster means to you."

Was he planning on coming up to the retreat? Was he going to fake some cat emergency and show up at the Laurels? Jeff put down the train and opened his arms to give Lydia a hug. She scolded herself, yet again, for assuming the worst, and leaned in for the hug.

Jeff wrapped her tightly in his arms, enveloping her in the scent of what she guessed was Drakkar Noir with a faint whiff of mildew. Mid-hug, Jeff slid one arm down her side, resting his hand above her hip and squeezed what she could only think of as her love handle. Lydia bit back a squeak of surprise, and stepped back, breaking the hug.

"Thanks again for looking after Baby Lobster. I'll be back midday on Monday and come get her then," Lydia offered weakly. Jeff just smiled.

She turned to head to her apartment but could still hear Jeff say quietly, "Anything for you, Lydia."

As soon as she got back to her apartment, she took a minute to smooth her shirt over her hips and give a little shake to her whole body. Ugh. Lydia grabbed her duffle bag and tucked Charlie's supplies under her free arm. Leaving the apartment, she whistled for her dog to follow and then wrestled the door shut and locked it. Fran's apartment—well, her apartment now—was convenient, but it wasn't exactly modern, and the front door lock required elbow grease and a certain amount of optimism to get locked correctly.

It was slow going down the stairs, but soon, with the gear stored in the back, Charlie lounging and looking out the window, and all three ladies more than a little red and breathless, the minivan headed out of Peridot's town square and out to Cherry Log Mountain.

"Lydia, meet Amy. Amy, meet Lydia, officially," Cynde said as she guided the old van onto the road.

Poor Amy already knew about Lydia's failed marriage, the attempt on her life last year, and her weirdly named cat, but there was nowhere to go but up. Lydia waved as she settled into her seat in the middle row of the old minivan. "Hi, Amy! So glad you can join us this weekend."

Truth be told, Cynde hadn't told her much about Amy, just that she had a friend she wanted to bring on the retreat. Amy would apparently drive up to Peridot and then they would carpool over in Cynde's van, pick up Lydia, and make a fun trip of it up to the Laurels. Lydia, never one to look a gift horse in the mouth, had immediately agreed to the idea. Faced with an hour in the car together, however, Lydia realized she knew almost nothing about Amy, who now knew so much about her. Well, Lydia was too much of an anxious extrovert not to rectify the situation with needlessly personal questions.

"So, Amy, how long have you and Cynde been friends?" Lydia started with a softball.

Frustratingly, Cynde answered before Amy could. "Oh, we met back in college. First comp class she sat down right next to me."

Lydia briefly registered that this conflicted with Cynde's earlier claim that Amy was a work friend but then told herself, "It could be that both are true," and reminded herself to stop being so nosy. Amy still hadn't spoken.

Once they hit the highway, it was almost comforting to realize that Cynde's minivan was never going to be pulling to the left, flying down the fast lane. In fact, it stayed just one lane over, trucking along just above the speed limit. Lydia relaxed and put her head against the window and watched the Beamers stream past, listening for the occasional roar of a motorcycle weaving back and forth between lanes.

Lydia tried again to kick-start a conversation.

"Cynde, did you see that Shenanigans is having a comedy night next month? What do you say to a girls' night out? Drinks on me," Lydia offered, wanting to make Cynde smile and more than a little hoping it would actually happen. It would do Lydia good to get out of her sweatpants and off of her couch every now and then.

Cynde took the bait, responding, "First round is on you, then. *And* the second round if the comedy stinks!"

They were joking, but Lydia noticed again how quiet and silent Amy seemed in the dark front seat of the minivan while they planned. Was Lydia just imagining the tension in the air? Or had she hurt Amy's feelings? Should she invite Amy to her only-probably outing? She let it go but remained a little worried that she had already gotten off to a bad start with Cynde's friend. One bad attitude could really impact the retreat, since it was such a small group. Plus, it wasn't just the dynamics of the retreat that had Lydia worried.

Fran had also seemed off lately. Almost fragile. She had moved out to the Laurels full time and was coming into the shop less and less. Did she regret renting her Peridot apartment out to Lydia? Was Fran going to quit the little town completely? Lydia forced herself to concentrate on the drive.

"How about some music for the ride?" Cynde offered. Unsurprisingly, Cynde still had a CD player, and, since it was her car, she played DJ, quickly selecting an Indigo Girls CD.

Lydia loved their harmonies and was pleased with the choice, immediately feeling more optimistic.

If Lydia had expected that to be the background for a new conversation, she was sorely disappointed. Amy nodded and stared out the window into the dark, winter evening. Lydia struggled to not feel miffed, but the silence felt awkward, so she tried a different approach.

"Cynde, how is work going these days?" It wasn't the most creative question, but it was something.

"Court? It's okay, nothing too exciting to report. Amy has been up at the Peridot Courthouse part-time, so it's been fun to have a friend around."

So, Amy *was* a work friend.

Cynde continued, "That's actually how she met . . ."

Cynde was interrupted by a loud thwack of something hitting the front of the van. Whatever hit them wasn't large enough to knock the van off course, but it startled the women and Charlie. He began to whine anxiously, while Lydia scanned the dark, trying to see what they had hit.

"What *was* that?" Lydia asked Cynde from the backseat. "A deer?"

"Couldn't have been a deer, we would have seen it in the head-lights. And it would have done way more damage. Maybe there was some sort of trash on the road? I'll check the grill as soon as we get to a gas station. I don't really want to just pull over on the side of the road."

Lydia liked that plan. The route to the Laurels mostly followed Highway 52, but it was getting emptier as the night went on and certainly wasn't well lit. Better to check the car somewhere that felt more like civilization. How bad could it be?

# Chapter Two

L ydia's new worries were interrupted by the sharp turn of the minivan as Cynde pulled into a gas station. Thank goodness. Lydia inhaled sharply at the shock of the cold air as she rolled back the old minivan door. Cynde followed suit and they both stood in front of the van, gawking at the sight before them.

Feathers. So many feathers.

"We hit a bird?" Lydia asked, incredulous.

"Well, Lydia. I doubt he had a heart attack, dropped from the sky, and just happened to hit my van on his way back to earth," Cynde replied, laughing.

Lydia laughed, too, admitting, "Okay, that is a fair point. What sort of bird did we hit? And how?"

"My guess? A wild turkey. We must have hit it before I even saw it in the road. Listen, can you not say anything to Amy? She's super squeamish. She'll eat meat, but she doesn't even like to cook it. I don't think it would be good for her to see . . ." she gestured at the feathers sticking straight out of her headlights. "Maybe you could offer to get her a snack? So, she can just, you know, stay put?"

"Sure thing, Cynde," Lydia replied as she turned back to the van.

First, she clipped Charlie's leash on and took him for a quick potty break. With Charlie and his empty bladder happily back in the warm van, she headed to the passenger side window. "Hey, Amy. I'm going in to grab a snack. What can I get you?"

"Just a water. Thanks. Lydia," Amy replied. It was stilted, but it was start.

Inside the gas station, Lydia bought what she always went for, a weird combination of who she was as a teenager and how she was trying to eat as a forty-year-old: pretzel-and-cheese Combos paired with a sparkling water. She added a bottle of regular water for Amy and a big bag of Smartfood and a Diet Dr. Pepper for Cynde. Was Amy actively trying to not enjoy the trip? Lydia stopped herself. Maybe Amy was allergic to Combos. It would all work out if she just stopped overthinking.

She walked back to the van to see Cynde, in a pair of gardening gloves, pulling out as many feathers as she could wrestle from the impact site. Cynde stuffed the handfuls of feathers into the garbage can next to the gas pump as she filled up the van, occasionally shouting to Amy that the tank wasn't quite full yet. Whatever was going on between the two women, that was a deep friendship. Roadkill turkey feathers were beyond the pale as far as Lydia was concerned.

Seeing Lydia with the snacks, Cynde gave it one last go, then threw the gloves in the trash after the feathers. The front of the van still looked rough, but it was dark enough Amy might not notice when they got to the Laurels.

Back in the van, Cynde turned up the Indigo Girls, Lydia distributed the snacks, and each woman sank into her own thoughts.

A tight corner swerve woke Lydia up and she was embarrassed to find she'd fallen asleep still holding her Combos, mouth hanging slack. Cynde was talking, and Lydia had no idea how or where the conversation had gone. She tried to jump in as if she hadn't dozed off.

"So, remind me, who else is coming?" Cynde asked, deftly handling the road as it grew curvier and curvier.

"Just the usual crew: us, Fran, Heather from the store, Clark, and Martha and Mary," Lydia answered, yawning and looking out at the dark wintery landscape sliding past. Lydia thought it didn't get much cozier than sewing in a cabin with a nice fire going. Charlie, her mutt still flopped in the back of the minivan, was going to love it. Not too much farther to go now.

Since they had decided this would be a "device-free" retreat, and since Cynde's minivan did not have anything resembling GPS, Lydia had printed out Fran's step-by-step directions.

Cynde had put Amy in charge, and she held the printout out in the front of her in the passenger seat, clearly anxious to navigate correctly. Her hands clenched the wrinkled paper as she peered closer at the directions.

"Turn right on Cherry . . .," her voice trailed off. "Oh, listen, I can't read this. It's pitch-black in here. Cynde, I'm going to need a light," and without waiting for Cynde to answer, she flipped down the passenger-side visor and held the directions up to the weak light above the mirror.

"Okay, so it's a left turn here . . . here here here here here!" Amy yelped as Cynde almost passed the turn they needed to make.

"Hold on a second; I need to look at the directions," Amy said. Cynde complied, stopping the minivan right under a sign in the shape of a bright pink pig.

"Holloway's pink pig, yeah, okay, this is on the sheet, so keep going straight for about half a mile. Then it says to turn right at Hillside House. What is that?"

But Amy's question was answered almost as soon as she asked it. The minivan's headlights illuminated a wooden sign that read: "Hillside House: Changing Lives and Healing Hearts." Lydia read the sign out loud as they passed and looked at the large, slightly dilapidated house behind it.

Lydia loves houses like this one, old Southern houses with wrap-around porches and intricate eaves. Behind the house was a rolling, unkempt yard that stretched up the mountainside and was lost to the darkness of the evening.

"Is that a church?" Lydia wondered. It didn't look like a church, but since moving to the South, Lydia had learned that something didn't need to look like her idea of a church to be a church. Especially when it came to strip malls.

To Lydia's surprise, Amy answered quickly and confidently, explaining, "No, that's a rehab center. Just opened up last year."

Lydia wanted to ask Amy why she knew about a random rehab center in an old house on Cherry Log Mountain, but she also wanted to see what Amy would say next. Her curiosity won out, so she stayed quiet and waited.

Amy continued, "They do really good work there. People don't realize just how needed centers like these are," her voice tight.

Was Amy angry?

Cynde drove on into the dark, and it was impossible to tell if they were going the right way. They just had to trust that Fran's directions would be clear enough. "Left here," Amy declared, her voice still tight, and Cynde took the first left onto the interestingly named Goose Island Road. Lydia realized that they were about to drive across a set of railroad tracks, so just like she had as a kid, Lydia lifted her feet as the rickety minivan made its way over the tracks and they went farther into the woods. Now they'd have good luck. Surely. At this point, there wasn't even a line dividing the lanes on the road.

Amy spoke up again. "Okay, I think in one more mile we're going to be taking another left on Whispering Pine Lane. I wish your friend Fran could've given us some more landmarks to look out for." Amy's voice seemed to catch on the word "Fran," as if she were saying something distasteful. No, Lydia had to be projecting. She was nervous about whatever conversation it was that Fran wanted to have, and it had her reading things into normal conversation. Did Amy and Fran even know each other?

Lydia wanted to point out that it didn't look like there were a lot of landmarks to choose from at this point, but she didn't want to upset Amy further. Now there were yellow signs saying DANGER CURVE AHEAD as the road turned into more of a gravel switchback working its way up the mountainside. Then she couldn't see any more road signs. Instead, the dirt road was sprinkled with handmade signs painted with house names that winked back at their headlights. Some were pretty boring: Smiths, Johnsons, and the like. But Lydia smiled as she read the more creative names: GETAWAY CABIN, SLEEPY RETREAT, BOB'S HIDEAWAY. That said, there were enough large, bright orange NO TRESPASSING signs to keep her from feeling that any sign, no matter how cute, was an invitation to head down one of the driveways.

She decided that she would stop looking out the window when she started to feel a little bit of vertigo. Not for the first time, Lydia was grateful it wasn't a Northern winter, as the road got more and more treacherous and the curves sharper and sharper until she wasn't even sure she could call it a road anymore, just a glorified shared driveway.

Not only was Lydia relieved that she didn't have Northern weather to contend with, but she was also glad to see that the residents of Cherry Log were not night owls, so Cynde could continue steering her minivan like a boat down the center of the drive into the night to the sounds of soft folk music.

"How long 'til my soul gets it right? Can any human being ever reach that kind of light?" Lydia sang along to the lilting harmonies.

Lydia was about to comment that "Galileo" by the Indigo Girls reminded her of long car rides in high school and awkward crushes, when they turned the last sharp sweep of the gravel driveway and the house came into view. The Laurels. Fran had talked about it, of course. However, for once, Lydia's imagination hadn't done justice to the reality.

Fran had always insisted that the cabin was well past its glory days. But if that was really the case, Lydia thought, those must have been some serious glory days.

Fran was generous about inviting Lydia up to the house, but somehow the time had gotten away from her, consumed with getting the shop on financially firmer ground and getting to know her new town. But when Fran talked about the "cabin," as in Fran saying, "We should hold the retreat up at my cabin!" Lydia had pictured something small and cozy, like a log cabin from a storybook. The Laurels was *not* that kind of cabin. Even in the dark, Lydia could tell she was looking at something very different, something she could only describe as a "mountain house." As in, "We spend our summers at our mountain house and the winters at our beach house," said by someone wearing too much pink and green. Someone like Emma-Grace.

For a moment, Lydia worried she should have worn slacks.

The others in the house must have seen the minivan arrive, since the door opened immediately. Light spilled out the open front door, warm and orange in the cold winter night. She couldn't see Fran's face clearly, since she was silhouetted by the light, but somehow Lydia knew her friend was smiling. *See*, she chided herself. *Nothing to worry about.*

"Finally! Y'all were making me a little nervous. Everybody else is already here!" And with that, Fran turned and gestured them into the house.

Lydia unbuckled and then heaved the minivan door open, rolling it along its old track. The noise of the door, like an enormous can being opened, woke Charlie, and he padded out onto the gravel driveway.

Cynde was already out of the car, bringing in first the fabric, then the supplies, and then her own and Amy's bags. Lydia swung her duffle bag over her shoulder and grabbed the food bag with two hands.

She'd come back for Charlie's things later. Knowing her pup, he'd prefer the foot of whatever bed Fran assigned to Lydia, anyway.

When she walked in the front door, at first, all she could see were the windows that made up the opposite wall. They reached two stories and positively dominated the whole house. It was breathtaking.

Then she remembered the lasagnas in her hand.

"Fran, wow. This is beautiful. Could I just get these suckers into the fridge?" she asked, holding up the bag that smelled strongly of garlic and sausage, even with the insulated sides.

Fran laughed. "Those 'suckers,'" she said, chastising Lydia's somewhat crude word choice, "can go right into the icebox. Let me show you. Cynde and Amy, come on in. I'm so glad you both are here."

For a moment, Lydia wondered how Fran knew Amy, but realized she must have told Fran about her in their retreat planning. This entire time, Lydia had been standing more or less in the doorway and looking toward the enormous main living room that was clearly the heart of the house. On the right side of the room, perpendicular to the windows, rose a huge, freestanding stone chimney. It served as the unofficial room divider, as Lydia could see that Fran was moving around the fireplace to the kitchen that ran along the right side of the house. She followed suit and realized the house didn't have a formal dining room. Instead, a huge pine table dominated the kitchen, within easy access of the living room. She had thought, as her eyes followed Fran, that the kitchen was the same length as the living room, but upon entering, she realized there was a small, separate room at the end of the kitchen.

Fran followed Lydia's gaze and explained, "The icebox is just here. It's not much of a kitchen, but my dad made this table himself." As she said that, Fran ran her hand down the smooth wood. "And that's what we call the summer room," she said, explaining the little box of a room that sat at the bottom end of the kitchen. "When the weather is nice, you can swap out the glass windows for screens and have your morning coffee out there. Not much use in February, but it really is one of my favorite spots in the house."

Her rescue dog, Charlie, had peed as soon as he got out of the minivan, and now he came into the kitchen and curled up under the pine table. Lydia was glad to see Clark was in the living room, explaining something or other about winter driving safety to the rest of their motley crew, giving her a moment alone with Fran.

As Lydia put the lasagna away, she told Fran, "Fran, I think you undersold the Laurels just a tad . . . it's . . . well, it is spectacular."

Fran smiled. "It's really the mountains that are spectacular, as you say; the house just does a good job of showing them off. My great-grandfather bought the place. But it was my grandfather who really made the house what it is. The windows. The fireplace. He had real vision when it came to houses. Did you know I'm an only child?" Fran asked.

Lydia nodded, remembering an old conversation with Fran when she had learned that fact among many others. There was a sparseness to Fran's life that she wanted to ask her friend about, but she didn't want to ruin the mood, so she just waited, and Fran continued.

"The thing is, my parents were only children, too. Both of them. So, I didn't have any first cousins growing up. My second cousins used to come stay in the summer," Lydia raised her eyebrows, "second cousins being when their grandparents are siblings," Fran explained, "but their families all left the area, and soon the house became more about the family you make out of your friends. Both my parents are gone now, but it would make them happy to see you all here. Plus, my daddy would have loved that lasagna," Fran offered, clearly trying to lighten the mood a little.

Seeing that Lydia was done putting away the food, Fran steered them back into the main room. Just as Fran came to stand in front of the fireplace, facing the large couch and an assortment of deep, comfortable armchairs scattered around the hearth, a loud, sonorous BONG filled the air.

Amy started. Mary and Martha looked at each other, pleased, as if some unspoken expectation had been met, and Clark just looked frantically around the room. The group followed his gaze and they all saw the clock at the same time: an elegant, imposing grandfather clock at the foot of the stairs chiming out the hours.

Lydia found herself counting along, quietly under her breath: "Six, seven, eight, nine, ten." And then the lack of the sound was as startling as the first striking tone had been. Lydia thought for a moment that she could see Clark owning a grandfather clock. He had that sort of style—classic but a little quirky. His clothes were always well fitted, always high quality, but he also took time to sew for himself, things that were more modern. She looked at his outfit tonight: slightly tapered dark brown corduroy trousers, unassuming loafers, and a simple crewneck sweater. Any preppy man in the South would wear that outfit, except Clark's sweater was lavender. Just a little hip, just a little unexpected. Like an antique grandfather clock that had a moon painted on its face, a moon with a cheeky grin. Lydia started to daydream about embroidering a moon face like the one on the clock, when she was brought back to the conversation.

Heather had spoken up for the first time since Lydia had arrived. Lydia knew she was there since she had seen Heather's bright red Camry in the drive, but it was still surprising to actually hear her flat, somehow effortlessly cool, voice pronounce, "I love grandfather clocks. That is so rad." Lydia stashed away the idea for the embroidery for later. It was a good sign that Heather thought it was "rad" as well. Realizing they were all gathered around the clock, Lydia expected Fran to give them their room assignments so they could head to bed. Before Fran could say anything, however, Clark cleared his throat.

"HEPA?"

"God bless you?" Lydia replied.

"No, HEPA, as in high-efficiency particulate air. Does the house have a HEPA air filter, Lydia?" Clark's smile tightened into a grimace.

"Oh, well, Clark, I don't imagine it does. The Laurels is a pretty old house." Lydia forced herself to keep smiling.

"Fine. I brought one from home just in case. Next week is an important week for me, Lydia, so I need to get good rest this weekend. I've already told you," he added in response to her raised eyebrow, "the committee will be deciding on the new chair of the board for the botanical garden. Once they make the announcement, I'm sure there will be photo ops and what have you. I can't look red and stuffy. Next week is going to be huge for me. I need my sleep. And I need clean air." With that, Clark turned to Fran.

"Listen, Fran, the house is gorgeous, but when exactly are we getting to bed?" he demanded to know.

Fran looked abashed, "Of course, of course, let me show you to your rooms. They all have names on them, from when my cousins and I were kids. Silly, but I can't bring myself to change them. So. The house has three floors, since the basement is finished and opens out to the back lawn. Why don't I give you all a tour and assign the bedrooms as we go?"

Before anyone could answer, Fran had turned to the staircase opposite the massive fireplace and started to climb.

The staircase ended in a long hallway with three doors on one side and a balcony overlooking the stately living room below on the other side.

Fran paused and opened the first door to reveal a bedroom appointed with two twin beds separated by a small table. Opposite the door was another, smaller door, that Lydia guessed must lead out to a balcony. The dark made it impossible to see the details, but Lydia imagined two chairs, ready for morning coffee while watching mist rise from the mountains. Each bed had a blue quilt, patterned with classic log cabin squares. Lydia looked over Fran's shoulder and saw a sign, clearly made by a child, that read, THE BLUE ROOM.

Fran followed her gaze. "Well, I did say the rooms have silly names. Our grandmother made all the quilts in the Laurels, and we just got in the habit of referring to the rooms by their colors. Cynde—and Amy?" she added, looking at the only newcomer in the group. "This is your room," and with that she motioned the group back out of the bedroom and down the hall.

"The bathroom is next and has a shower, but y'all will have to take turns, and then the last room up here is . . ."

And Fran opened the last door to reveal the mirror image of the first bedroom. Two twin beds. A table between them. Another door leading to a balcony hidden in darkness. But gone were the classic blue quilts of the first room. These beds were covered in crazy improvisations of every color in the rainbow, mixed with pieces of patterns, polka dots, and even though she couldn't get next to the bed on the left, Lydia thought she saw a polar bear peeking out of one patch in the dizzying display.

"This is the Rainbow Room," Fran explained, laughing as she said the name. "Heather, sweetheart, I had you in mind for this room."

The room had two beds like before, but both were covered in bright, scrappy quilts, and colorful art filled the walls. Fran was clearly trying to make Heather feel as comfortable as possible, the only "youngster" at the retreat.

Normally, Lydia would have expected Heather to adore the crazy brightness of the room. But Heather just nodded and set her things down quietly in the room, staying behind as the tour continued.

Once they were back on the main floor, Fran continued.

"Clark, darling, you have almost the whole downstairs to yourself. There is a bedroom, a bathroom with a clawfoot tub, and even a small fridge and coffee machine," Fran offered, hopefully, as she gestured to the staircase that led down to the lower level.

"Right. Well. I brought my diffuser and white noise machine, so I will just head out and grab those," Clark retorted, seemingly already disappointed in his sleeping arrangements. As he huffed toward the door, he asked bitingly, "And pray tell, Fran, what color is my room?"

Fran remained unruffled by his smirk and simply replied, "Oh, the downstairs is the newest part of the house, so no silly names for you. Just a king-sized bed and new flooring."

Clark at least had the decency to look a little abashed as he opened the door and stepped into the ink-dark night to gather his things.

Fran added, "The Library is also on the lower level. That is where I set up the tables for the first session. Because the house is built on a slope, the Library does have a few windows, even though it's nothing like the view up here. Still, it's a good-sized space, and I could lock all my sewing things away when I used to rent out the house."

Lydia had forgotten that Fran had been renting out the Laurels for most of the year before she decided to move out to the mountain full time. As if reading her mind, Fran continued, "The renting had been going pretty well, and it certainly helped offset the costs of the place. I found the whole Air ABC thing"—Lydia saw Heather flinch at the misnomer—"a little too daunting, so I've actually had the caretaker handle all of that. Mr. Williams did a great job, and he still handles any crisis that comes up. He lives in the only house higher up the mountain than the Laurels. Most of us on the mountain employ him to keep an eye on things, maintain the properties, and such."

Fran turned toward Lydia. "In fact, Lydia, since you're hosting this weekend, I should mention that his name and number are taped to the icebox. In case you need anything, he really is a jack-of-all-trades," she continued, always the consummate host. Clark was running his varied accoutrements downstairs, and Heather, Cynde, and Amy were all busy settling upstairs. Lydia yawned.

Fran was left at the foot of the stairs, looking at Lydia, Mary, and Martha. Suddenly, Lydia panicked. She tried to keep her face neutral as she realized she had no idea where she was sleeping. She hadn't demanded a room of her own, like Clark had. She had assumed, well, what exactly had she assumed? Was she about to be assigned two roommates who smelled of Elizabeth Arden perfume and dry-cleaning chemicals? Crud. It was hard to imagine the M's even sleeping. Sleeping was like eating; you never talked about it in polite company, and sometimes Lydia doubted the women did either at all.

"The first room here, on the left," Fran continued, pointing to a hallway of rooms that ran on the opposite side of the house

29

from the kitchen, with the living room and its enormous fireplace sandwiched between them. "I thought the M . . . I mean, Mary and Martha, I thought you ladies would like this room, the Yellow Room." And true to form, Fran opened yet another door to reveal yet another set of twin beds covered in intricate pale-yellow quilts.

This time, however, on the table between the beds, there was a lamp just like in the other rooms, but also something else: a lovely blue-and-white pottery bowl filled with jelly beans. Before Lydia could take it in, Mary had entered the room, crossed to the table, and cupped a handful of jelly beans.

It was just like Fran to think of the jelly beans. Lydia amended her earlier thoughts about the M's. They didn't eat . . . much. But Mary definitely ate jelly beans. Nothing fancy. No gourmet flavors. Just regular jelly beans. Lydia had never seen Mary buy them; they were just *there*. In her coat pocket. Her purse. A little cup next to her sewing machine during classes. When Lydia thought of vices, she rarely included candy, but she was sure that Mary considered jelly beans a personal weakness, perhaps even a spiritual failing. Leave it to Fran to place a little bowl of jelly beans in their room.

"There is a Jack-and-Jill bathroom between your room and Lydia's room," Fran explained. Walking past the aforementioned bathroom, Lydia opened the door to "her" room, the Flower Room. Fran stayed at the doorway, explaining, "My room is right next door, if you need anything. I figure you must be beat. I'm . . . I'm really glad you're here, Lydia."

Lydia realized that was it. Everyone was going to bed.

But then Fran had turned serious and said, "Lydia, there are some things we need to discuss."

"Great. What else do we need to check off the list to get ready for the first session?" Lydia answered lightly.

"No, not retreat things. Bigger things. I think it's time that you. . . ." Fran's generally happy face twisted, the corners of her mouth pulled down. She suddenly looked so much older.

Lydia felt her stomach clench. She knew it. Something was wrong with her friend. What was Fran about to say?

"Well, now isn't the time. But let's make sure we get some time together this weekend, just the two of us. Maybe a walk on the mountain. It's important," Fran finished, still frowning.

"We'll find the time. I promise," Lydia replied, trying, and failing, to smile.

Fran nodded and started to walk past the Flower Room toward her own bedroom, the last in the hallway.

"Fran!" Lydia felt a little embarrassed to be raising her voice in the peaceful hallway, "Don't you need to lock the front door?"

Fran smiled, wearily, and replied, "Lydia, we are at the top of a mountain in the middle of the winter. There is no need to lock the door. I promise." And with that, Fran stepped into her own room and shut the door.

Lydia had no real choice than to do the same herself. After she quickly brushed her teeth and washed her face, she threw on her PJs, which were probably too similar to her daytime clothes, and snuggled into the bed. Charlie quickly jumped up to curl up at her feet, and she turned off the bedside lamp.

First, she tried breathing slowly, in and out. Then, she tried counting backwards from one hundred. Finally, she gave in and let herself picture Emma-Grace in terrible, tacky wedding dresses that were poorly sewn and terribly altered. It worked, but just as she started to fall asleep, Lydia heard a great BANG! Charlie yelped and jumped out of the bed, Lydia threw back the flowery quilt and raced to her door. When she stepped into the hallway, already a little breathless, she bumped right into Fran.

Lydia jumped back and let out a somewhat embarrassing squeak.

"What on earth was that?" she asked, aware that her voice sounded far too high and strained.

Before Fran could answer, they heard another crash, as if someone were out on the porch, drunk as a skunk, and trying to wash some dishes.

"See, Fran," she said stridently, "THAT is why you lock your door!"

"That," Fran said, "is a bear."

"Excuse me?" Lydia countered.

"A bear. A black bear would be my guess. I told Clark, if he had trash, he had to dispose of it correctly, and knowing him, he probably just threw some unfinished organic turkey jerky straight into the trash can. You can't do that up here. Bears have a great sense of smell, and they will go right for your trash if they think they can get a treat. Everything else has been tied up properly, so hopefully Mrs. Bear will just move right along."

"Right. A bear. Just a massive bear. Nothing to see here," Lydia retorted feebly.

"Lydia, we really are safe up here, I promise. Just don't let Charlie out to pee in the middle of the night. Now get some sleep. I'm making homemade cinnamon rolls in the morning." Fran said the last bit with a smile. She knew Lydia's weaknesses all too well.

"Okay, you hear that, Charlie? Back to bed, and no peeing till morning!" The friends smiled at each other and walked back to their rooms.

A bear. Sure. Nothing weird about that. Lydia tried to concentrate on the promise of cinnamon rolls. If there were anything better in life than the innermost curl of a cinnamon roll, she had yet to discover it.

Charlie hopped back on the bed and was soon fast asleep, snuffling and dreaming of fat, slow squirrels. Lydia needed to be asleep herself. They had a huge day planned for tomorrow. She couldn't scroll through Instagram to plan new projects since she was the one who had declared it a "device-free" weekend. Breathing deeply, she tried to walk herself through the dream fabric store of her imagination, tried to picture which sumptuous, imaginary Liberty silk she was going to buy. But that conversation Fran wanted to have felt like a bear in her mind, crashing around, making a mess of the fabric. Making a mess of everything.

# Chapter Three

**Saturday**

Charlie had gotten out of the house and run into the dark. She couldn't see him, but she could hear his tags clinking on his collar as he headed into the woods. It was still the dead of the night, and Lydia kept calling out to her dog. Fran had warned her. Fran had told her. How had Charlie gotten out of the house? Who had let him out? What if there were a bear? Her heart caught in her throat, and she called again.

Charlie barked. Lydia sat up, frantic. The bear.

No, there was no bear. She was still in bed. She was in the Flower Room, and Charlie was perfectly safe. Lydia, however, was cold. She tried to shake off the remnants of the nightmare, reminding herself that everything was fine, but she found herself clenching her jaw. The feeling of betrayal, that someone had sent Charlie out into the dark on purpose, lingered like a hangover. The morning was gray and overcast, so she got dressed quickly and headed into the living room with two objectives: let Charlie out and get some coffee. After that she could deal with running the retreat, talking to Fran, and saving the store. No big deal.

Lydia walked into the living room to find the fire already lit, even though it was barely 8 AM. To her left, the enormous windows that made up the back wall of the room were clearly displayed. Three huge rectangles of windowpanes were topped with two halves of a pyramid, also in clear, shining glass. She had sensed the splendor of the windows the night before, but now there was no doubt. They served as the focal point of the whole living room, a large room filled with leather furniture, that in turn seemed to be the heart of the house.

Mountains, ranging from green to deep blue, stretching out toward the horizon, are what she imagined would normally be framed in those windows. But a fog had set in, and Lydia was worried that the good weather they'd had for the drive up wouldn't last. She opened the back door and Charlie quickly took care of his business.

With Charlie back beside her, she didn't linger to look out at the encroaching mist, because the tantalizing smell of cinnamon beckoned her on into the kitchen. Fran had made homemade cinnamon rolls. FAIRY GODMOTHER. Laced with the scent of cinnamon was the scent of freshly brewed coffee. She felt the bad dream slipping back into the shadows and decided to give Charlie a treat as well.

In the corner of the kitchen closest to the living room, Lydia set up his bowls of dried kibble and water. But then, knowing she was about to have cinnamon rolls and Charlie would be jealous, she put the peanut butter-filled chew toy she'd brought from home next to his breakfast.

Charlie wolfed down his food and turned his attention to the peanut butter, wagging his tail as he contorted himself in his effort to reach every bit of goodness.

Lydia thought she heard a disapproving sigh as Charlie rolled and wiggled. Of course.

The M's were already there, hair perfectly coiffed. Lydia had no idea how they managed it, settling for a messy top bun herself. Cynde and Amy were at the table as well, picking at cinnamon rolls. Then Heather came in and sat down next to Clark, completing the group. Unless Lydia was really losing it, she could have sworn she heard Clark harrumph and shift slightly away from the young woman. When Clark stood up to refill his coffee cup and then sat back down at the other end of the table, between the M's, Lydia realized she was right. Something was off between the two of them. She looked at her still slightly blue cuticles from the shibori dyeing class fiasco last month. Now was not the time to stir up drama. Although another spot of trouble was already brewing. Mary adjusted her blouse and sat up a little straighter at the table.

"Heather, darling," Mary said and then stopped speaking. Then she looked at the young woman expectantly. The rest of the group looked from Mary to Heather and back again. "Heather," Mary repeated, with a firm tone.

"Yes, Mary?" Heather replied, her voice lifting at the end.

"You are at the table, Heather," Mary replied, still curt but a little more encouraging.

"Can I get you something, Mary?" Heather asked, politely but with a tinge of frustration.

"I don't need a thing, darling. But." Finally, Mary broke the stalemate by gesturing at Heather's face.

Lydia was the first to realize what Mary was trying so hard to imply.

"Heather, your hat," Lydia clarified.

"My hat?" Heather raised a hand and touched the hat she was wearing, a canvas snap back she had made at the store. "I made it from a kit, Mary. Would you like to buy the kit? We offer a class at Measure Twice."

Mary said nothing, frowning.

Lydia continued, "Heather, you don't, well, you shouldn't, I mean I think Mary would like . . ." She took a deep breath. "Heather, would you mind taking your hat off when we are at the table?"

Mary and Martha finally smiled.

"What? Seriously? Oh fine," and with that Heather ungraciously removed the hat, and ran her fingers through her bright red hair to try to salvage her look. Lydia heard Heather mumble, "You have got to be kidding me," but she was pretty sure the M's missed it. Otherwise, they would have commented on the sass of it, surely. Lydia had to stop herself from chiding the young woman, her old teacher instincts coming to the fore. The M's were old-fashioned, but they were also devoted and loyal friends. Lydia bit her tongue.

The other three women simply stared at each other.

Fortunately, Fran was busy telling the group about Cherry Log and the Laurels. The small drama passed by more or less unnoticed by the others as Fran talked about the hiking trails that wrapped around the mountain like tendrils of ivy.

As she picked up her third cinnamon roll of the morning and began to enjoy it, Cynde interjected, "Fran, you are a wizard in the kitchen. I know you gave me this recipe, but no matter how many times I try to bake them at home, they never turn out like yours!" With that, Cynde stuffed the remaining roll in her mouth and closed her eyes, signaling her cinnamon roll bliss.

Anticipating that Fran would make her famous breakfast treat, Clark had brought his own version of a cinnamon roll from home. Lydia looked at his plate. No frosting. No swirl of pastry. He had what looked like a rust-colored rock in front of him. She was sure it was healthy, but she smiled as she thought to herself, *at what cost?* You could break a tooth on that kind of healthy.

As if sensing her disdain from across the table, Clark began a litany of questions.

"We're here. We all drove up that death trap of a mountain road last night. I was just wondering, at what point is this going to be 'Sew Relaxing'?" he asked, adding the finger quotes for extra emphasis.

For once, Lydia had anticipated this line of complaint. She was prepared. Lydia loved itineraries. It was a holdover from her days as a junior high teacher. There was something so satisfying about well-written instructions. It was no surprise she had taken to garment sewing so quickly. Good patterns were clear and engaging, just like a perfect lesson plan. She reached into the tote bag she had carried into the kitchen and pulled out a stack of paper. The totes had been a promotional idea for Measure Twice, and she kept finding them all over her apartment as well as the store. At least they were handy. She passed around the sheets. As Cynde grabbed hers, she began to read aloud:

## SEW RELAXING

Sewing retreat with the ladies of Measure Twice
Presidents' Day Weekend in the Blue Ridge Mountains

### Day One: Saturday

- Breakfast
- Session 1: Cutting out your pattern and quilting your fabric
- Lunch
- Personal time
- Dinner
- Group game/fireside s'mores

### Day Two: Sunday

- Breakfast
- Session 2: Bias binding and closures
- Lunch
- Handsewing session/personal time
- Dinner

### Day Three: Monday

- Breakfast
- Fashion show of newly made quilt coats
- Leave for Peridot between noon and 2 PM
- Optional meet-up for lunch at Frank's Pizza in Peridot

Clark, unsurprisingly, was the first to comment on the itinerary, "Personal time? Are you serious? What am I supposed to do for fun on a mountain in February?"

Lydia, having anticipated this as well, had a ready list of suggestions, which she proceeded to rattle off. "Well, you might want to nap, or go for a walk, or watch a movie on the old TV in the corner of the living room. Or you could read a book? Do some hand-sewing, maybe some English Paper Piecing? If I remember correctly, you don't know how to knit, but some others might want to knit by the fire." Lydia finished her list with a smile.

"Besides, Clark, we're just about to start our first session! Fran is already down in the Library setting up the sewing stations. Everybody should go grab their fabric and head downstairs. Fran will show you where to sit," she declared, and with that, Lydia ushered them out of the kitchen. She stacked the dishes to deal with later and poured herself another mug of black coffee. She had a feeling she was going to need it.

She couldn't be happier that she had a chance to challenge her little retreat group to sew something a little more complicated. Fran had insisted, when they first came up with the idea, that they lead the workshops together. It would put the old-timers at ease, she had said. And their skills were complementary, Fran had insisted. She had implied but not actually stated the obvious: Lydia had a bad habit of starting her bias binding on the wrong side of the fabric. Not exactly the best look for a workshop leader, let alone the store owner.

She headed down to the basement to find Fran in the Library, where she was laying out the patterns and lining up the scissors. Lydia got out the rings of bobbins and set up the rack of thread.

# Quilty as Charged

The watery daylight struggled to fill the room, but sewing didn't need good weather. None of Lydia's favorite hobbies did.

Since quilt coats were enjoying a renaissance, Lydia had plenty of patterns to choose from for the group. In the end, she had picked three and let each participant pick from that selection: Muna and Broad's Grainger Jacket, Megan Neilson's Hovea Jacket, and Friday Patterns' Ilford Jacket. Clark picked the Ilford, Cynde, Amy, and Fran all went for the Grainger, and Lydia, Heather, and the M's each did a version of the Hovea.

Lydia's least favorite part of sewing was cutting out the pattern pieces, so she had prepped that for each sewist. Thankfully, the jacket edges could all be bound with bias binding, which made for a clean finish and would cut down on machines needed. No sergers required for this pattern. With that in mind, in addition to all the needed supplies, Lydia had also brought her own personal stash of handmade bias binding, a riotous mass of pink and orange and even yellow. The brighter the better was her theory when it came to details.

She looked around the room. All the sewists had made their way to the Library, most, like Lydia, still clutching their mugs of coffee.

"Okay, everyone. I already cut out your patterns, so the first thing I need you to do is take out your fabric and press it using the irons Fran has already set up around the room. Because this is a quilted jacket, each pattern piece will be cut out of your liner fabric, your outer fabric, and your batting. It takes a little longer, but trust me, it will be worth it!"

Lydia watched as all the members of the retreat shook out their fabric choices, all as unique as each sewist. The pattern worked with basically any pairing of fabric, as long as the outer fabric was a bit heavier, like a canvas or denim, which was one of the reasons Lydia had chosen it. True to her vibrant personality, Cynde's cotton lining had llamas in holiday regalia. Next to her at the same foldout table, Amy had clearly raided Cynde's fabric stash. She was nervously smoothing and folding a bright blue cotton covered in sweet, scattered white-and-blue whales. Lydia recognized the Cotton + Steel Kujira & Star fabric, and she thought again that Cynde must really care about Amy. Lydia had some hoarded pieces of that happy fabric herself, and she wouldn't part with them easily.

The M's had chosen gingham, blue for Mary and yellow for Martha. For the inner lining, they had simply decided on the other's cotton, which meant the jackets would be inverse versions of each other. Neither jacket would be very weather resistant, but then again, the Ms would probably only wear them in the consignment shop anyway.

Clark chose a waxed canvas in a deep olive that he intended to line with a muted Liberty Tana Lawn. That was Clark, classic, but then a little something more . . .

Heather's outer layer was a plain black denim, but Lydia knew for a fact that it was high-end Japanese denim, something Measure Twice had yet to even attempt to stock. For a lining, she had chosen a slinky rayon with a marbled pattern, swirling different shades of red and mauve.

Lydia walked around the room, helping her friends layer their pattern pieces, talking Clark through how to quilt across the layers of outer fabric, cotton batting, and inner lining, passing Heather a few pins as she worked. Quilt jackets were more time consuming, but also more rewarding, a better fit for a full weekend rather than a single class. Lydia imagined people complimenting the jackets, hearing about the retreat, getting interested. Regular retreats meant she could charge for the patterns, fabric, supplies, teaching time, and accommodations. Maybe she could even source some vintage quilts from Blessed Again, the church consignment shop run by the M's. That would create some buzz, surely? And buzz could mean keeping the store afloat.

The room was so quiet that she finally realized the obvious: It was raining. Hard. But she wasn't worried about that. If anything, rain was the natural companion of sewists. Why feel bad about not hiking when the weather is bad? It pretty much forces you to sew. Or at least that was Lydia's logic.

In the comfortable quiet, she also realized she was hungry. Really hungry. Her ex-husband used to forget to eat, which baffled Lydia. Forget to eat? Not only was she almost always at least a little hungry, she loved thinking about her next meal, just like she loved looking up restaurant menus online before she went out to eat. Planning was half the fun.

As she opened her mouth to declare it was lunchtime, she saw Amy's fabric. The best way to describe it was to say it looked like the machine had eaten her happy blue whales when she had attempted to quilt the back panel. Devoured them, even.

Lydia took a deep breath, plastered on the biggest smile she could manage, and approached Amy's machine. Maybe it was just some tangled thread? Or her bobbin had run out? A run-of-the-mill sewing emergency. Lydia looked at her still slightly blue hands and thought about just how badly wrong a craft lesson could go. All of her fears were validated when she realized that Amy had somehow crammed her fabric *into* her machine. The mistake was so weird, and so hard to solve, Lydia was actually kind of impressed. Amy, sadly, wasn't taking it in stride and looked dangerously close to tears. Lydia wanted to ask her, *why are you here? You certainly don't seem to enjoy sewing.* Because the truth was, anyone who sewed on a regular basis was used to mistakes. That was what the seam ripper was for!

But Amy just looked like she was in pain. "Your machine get a little jammed?" Lydia offered, trying to calm Amy down. She just nodded and gulped for air. Leaning over, Lydia tugged at the whale fabric, but it was thoroughly enmeshed in the machine. "Okay, I think I just need to get a screwdriver, and we will have you sorted out in no time. Why don't you head up to lunch while I get this fixed? Then you can pick this back up once you've had some food and maybe some sweet tea?" Amy slumped and smiled like she had just been granted some sort of reprieve.

"I have some aspirin in my toiletry bag upstairs, if you want to grab some," Lydia added.

"I never touch the stuff," Amy countered as she walked to the stairs. Lydia sighed. She was not making much progress with that situation. Maybe she would sit next to Amy at lunch. Unlikely, but she would try.

"Okay, everybody, great job with session one! Please make sure to turn off your machines, turn off the irons, and tidy your sewing space," Lydia directed the rest of the sewists as if they were summer campers.

One by one, the members of the group started to head upstairs, while Lydia got out her small screwdriver and set to work on Amy's machine. It only took a second to release the layers of fabric and batting from where they had gotten snarled in tangled bobbin thread.

She rethreaded the machine and quickly used a seam ripper to clean up the fabric so Amy could keep working on the back of her jacket after lunch, and then she headed upstairs.

Fran was already in the kitchen when Lydia walked in. As soon as she saw her, Fran let out her breath in a noisy exhale. Lydia was still buzzing. The first session had exceeded her expectations. It was going to work. It was actually going to work. She was already planning the next retreat. What about a capsule wardrobe weekend? Or occasion wear: Come and sew your Easter outfit! Lydia could suddenly see herself sitting in front of budget software, watching the numbers actually work for once. But when Fran turned to her, Lydia realized Fran was not in the same headspace at all. "Lydia, I know this has been a rocky transition."

"Between cutting and the sewing? I thought it was fine?" Lydia said, letting her voice rise into a question.

"No, I mean with the store. Measure Twice. I thought I was ready to sell, I needed to sell, but it was harder than I anticipated. I know I'm not always the best at hiding my emotions"—Lydia stifled a laugh, thinking of Fran's deep frown lines that were often put to good use—"but I'm really glad the store is yours now."

Lydia noticed, not for the first time, how thin Fran had become lately. Were they finally going to have the conversation she had been dreading?

"It was hard to sell the shop, but I see now it was the right decision. Adding a long-arm quilting service was never going to be enough. It was hard to let go, but now I understand. I haven't really lost anything. I've gained you. And I'm grateful. It all just worked so perfectly, you moving to Peridot, renting you the apartment above the store, helping you run this retreat. But you need to realize . . ." Fran looked at her hands. But before she could finish the sentence, her words were drowned out by the sound of a car revving and speeding through the gravel driveway. But everyone was in the house. Who was in the car? Who was in Fran's driveway. And what had made them so angry?

# Chapter Four

Who could possibly be tearing through the driveway like an angry teenager? No one made it to the Laurels by accident. The house sat at the very end of a dead-end road. At the top of a mountain. In Cherry Log, which was hardly a bustling metropolis on the best of days.

Who even knew they were there? Lydia felt her stomach tighten as her neighbor, Jeff, came to mind. Was Baby Lobster hurt? Lost? But if something were wrong, why not call? And why did the driver seem so angry? Then she thought of the way Jeff had insisted on knowing where she was staying, how he had squeezed her side and said he would do anything for her. Did he have some delusional idea of coming to see her? Surprising her? If that was the case, why didn't he come inside? Maybe he had changed his mind at the last minute? Gotten cold feet?

Although, Jeff didn't seem the type to ever get cold feet, since he never took a hint. He would just keep talking and talking as she tried to close the door to her apartment and put her groceries away.

Then she heard the front door close and Clark shout from the entryway, "Did you hear that? I just went to get my crafting support gloves from my trunk and a car practically burned through the driveway! And this rain is *freezing*!" She could hear Clark muttering as he dried off in front of the fireplace, and she turned to her friend, telling herself the Jeff theory was too far-fetched. Her neighbor was awkward, not sinister. Definitely.

"What was that about, Fran?" she asked, desperate for a good explanation. "And don't try to tell me that North Georgia bears can drive," she added weakly.

"This happened yesterday, before y'all arrived, actually," Fran admitted quietly to Lydia. "Same thing—just a car angrily turning in the driveway."

"Do you have any idea who it might be?" Lydia asked, relieved to think that her Jeff theory hardly held water now.

"It's probably nothing. But . . . well I do have this one neighbor. It's complicated, Lydia, but the short version is that the community up here on the mountain, well, we didn't all exactly see eye to eye when it came to Hillside."

"Hillside?"

"The rehab center at the bottom of the mountain. You passed it last night, but it was dark, so . . ."

"Right! The house with the huge porch," Lydia chimed in, relieved to have some handle on the increasingly confusing situation.

"That's the one. Well, there was quite a saga when it came to Hillside. You see, the house, we used to call it Dalton House, it was one of the first built on the mountain. The original agreement for Cherry Log, with those first houses, gave the other owners say when a property went up for sale. It had never been an issue, because all the houses just stayed in the family, but the Dalton heirs wanted to sell . . . so. Some folks wanted the house to become Hillside, some of us wanted a nature center. Tempers got a little frayed, I am ashamed to admit. I thought a nature center was a better path forward, and I think the whole thing led to some bad blood, I suppose. People can be a little shortsighted when it comes to personal attachment to a place, and a few of my neighbors might be a little disgruntled. It is certainly annoying but nothing to really worry about, I'm sure. Really, shame on them for being so immature."

Lydia liked that explanation. It had nothing to do with the store, and it really wasn't a big deal. She still hadn't talked to Fran about whatever was on her mind. Maybe she could bring it up now? But just then, the M's entered the kitchen and offered their own, unique perspective.

"You mean to say that was a *home* we passed last evening," Martha queried, as the M's joined them in the kitchen to help with lunch.

Mary nodded sagely, as if to say, *Well, that explains it.*

Fran headed the M's off at the pass, saying, "You know what, maybe it was just someone who got lost. Or a local kid with too much time on his hands. Nothing to worry about." Though Fran knew Lydia more or less made an Olympic sport out of worrying.

"Right. Right. Of course. Fran, I'm not worried. But you know what? I am hungry! Let's get lunch set up."

"You go ahead with that. I'm pretty tired. I'm gonna lie down for a tick but I will be rested and ready to go soon. We'll have that talk later. Please, don't worry!" Fran said, as she headed toward her room.

"Sounds like a plan!" Lydia responded, helping the M's with their various dishes and plates, trying to keep her worrying on the back burner of her mind. Against her better judgment, Lydia had put the M's in charge of lunch. Why did some food seem so typical of a generation? Lydia closed her eyes and imagined what was waiting in their carefully packed Tupperware containers: butter saltines, deviled eggs, chicken salad, white toast, and *maybe* some grapes? A deep breath, a few steps, and Lydia could only mentally congratulate herself on partial success.

Deviled eggs? Check. Even sprinkled with paprika and displayed on one of those weirdly specific deviled egg platters. How was that a market? Where were those plates even sold? Probably the same place where Mary and Martha got the pimento cheese, chicken salad, and butter saltines that filled in the rest of the meal. Lydia shuddered. She loathed deviled eggs. Passionately. Especially deviled eggs like the ones on the table now, the yolk mixture in the center slightly green. Exactly how fresh were those eggs, she wondered.

"Oh, *yum*, ladies! You have outdone yourselves!" Lydia lied with a smile plastered on her face. At least the rest of the group seemed eager to get plates and help themselves.

Lydia didn't take a plate this time, though. Instead, she busied herself by the sink and hoped the M's didn't notice that she kept a fair distance between herself and the eggs. She took longer than needed to stir the iced tea in the pitcher, to bring glasses to the table. The room was buzzing, though, as the others got food and sat down at the long wooden table. Mary and Martha tried to say grace, but people kept getting up for more food or leaving the kitchen to get something from somewhere else in the house.

It was too chaotic, but Martha soldiered on, saying more to herself than anyone else, "Bless us, O God. Bless our food and our drink. Since you redeemed us so dearly and delivered us from evil, as you gave us a share in this food so may you give us a share in eternal life. Amen."

Lydia flinched. Deliver us from evil? She knew it was a part of the Lord's Prayer, but it was jarring to hear it, here, in the rainy tableau of the meal. A sewing retreat was about the furthest thing from evil that Lydia could imagine. The other sewists either hadn't heard or weren't concerned by the strident nature of the blessing.

However, they did seem a little concerned by the green-ish tint of the deviled eggs. Lydia surveyed the plates and notice quite a few disassembled but not exactly eaten eggs.

But as Lydia listened to the talk at the table, she was relieved to hear excitement about the pattern. She really wanted to hook them on garment sewing. And maybe she actually was?

Clark explained his grand plans for his pattern hack to add internal pockets to the jacket, and Lydia could hear the words "innovative" and "daring" drift over the sounds of cutlery on plates.

When everyone had "finished" eating, they took their plates to the sink and then started to rummage around the kitchen for something sweet. The rainy weather made it feel like time for dessert, even though they had only technically planned to do desserts after the dinners. There had to be something they could eat now. Lydia was about to go ask Fran where she kept the chocolate. Then she heard it. Something that sounded like a knife stuck in bike spokes. What on earth? Then she looked across the kitchen to the sink, at the M's, who were cleaning up the dishes.

Mary looked panicked. Martha looked downright appalled. One too many deviled eggs down the garbage disposal, and now all that could be heard was a strangled gurgling. A clogged garbage disposal was one thing. A clogged garbage disposal full of not-so-fresh deviled eggs was another thing entirely.

Too many deviled eggs down the garbage disposal. Lydia hadn't even imagined that scenario in her litany of worries about the retreat. No amount of pom-pom trim would be able to distract them from that smell. Lydia cast her eyes around the kitchen, desperately looking for the information sheet Fran had shown her upon arrival.

When it rains, it pours. Where on earth did that expression come from? Lydia felt the truth of it as she pulled the contact sheet off the side of the fridge and heard the sleet hit the roof. It was a magical sound, like a great song had ended but the drum was still going, just inside the house. But even though it sounded soothing, Lydia knew deep down that sleet on a mountain was not ideal. The whole "phone-free" gimmick had sounded good, but she desperately wished for her iPhone in that moment. She wanted to swipe up, check the weather, and see a bright yellow sun predicted for the next morning. It would be easier to enjoy the stormy weather if she could promise herself it would soon pass. But she couldn't check the weather, and the sleet only fell harder and harder.

She knew she had to keep the windows shut against the sleet. Which meant shutting the smell *in*. Where was that number? While she rummaged through pages of the contact list, Clark started off again, acting as the retreat's official narrator. "Oh, my word. That smells to high heaven. Lydia, what on earth are you doing? You know what? This is what I meant when I said not bringing phones was a foolish idea. We simply cannot spend the weekend with that smell!"

Lydia was not about to admit to Clark that she had been think-ing the exact same thing. "Well, Clark. Thank you for your input. Fran actually has a caretaker for the Laurels, and his cabin is on the mountain. His number is on here somewhere, and I am sure he can sort us out in no time." With that, she brandished the contact list at Clark.

Instead of agreeing, Clark turned to start a whispered side conversation with Cynde's friend, Amy. Lydia took a deep breath, then immediately regretted it. That smell. One problem at a time. At least she had finally hit upon the scrawled phone number she needed: Mr. Williams. She picked up the old landline and called the number for the caretaker, Mr. Williams, and thankfully he answered immediately.

Lydia really didn't know how to concisely explain their pre-dicament, nor did she want to scare him off, so she simply asked him to come over and help with "an issue."

He sounded Southern and old fashioned, but at least he agreed to come over. Oh, lord, that was just what she needed, a Mr. Wil-liams. He probably knew more about the wood fireplace than the new garbage disposal. But she had plenty of pimento cheese if she needed to bribe him into helping. And Martha at least could use the distraction of what she imagined would be a well-weathered gentleman of a certain age.

What Lydia really needed was Fran. She turned to walk toward Fran's room. *No. Let Fran sleep.* She could handle this deviled egg crisis herself. It was the least she could do for the woman who had led her into a whole new life. Before she could second guess, or even third guess, herself, she heard knocking at the door. That would be the old caretaker, ready to dismiss their sink disaster with some easy fix they should have thought of themselves. When she opened the front door, however, she immediately regretted her assumptions.

Mr. Williams, as the sheet posted on the fridge referred to him, quickly held out his hand and said, "Auden Williams."

Without waiting for Lydia to reply, he stepped into the house and out of the now-freezing rain. Lydia took in the new arrival: He was tall, at least six feet tall, and young, at least under forty, and he was . . . named Auden.

Lydia paused. "Auden? Like the poet? The one who wrote the poem with that horse scratching its butt against the tree?"

If the caretaker's name had created a pause in the background conversation, Lydia's reply silenced the room. She looked down to see her hands still held up in an old pose from her teaching days, eagerly reaching out for a student's reply. Why, she asked herself, were her hands always so embarrassing?

"Do you mean 'Musée Des Beaux Arts'?" Auden asked. Now the room was silent *and* frozen. Seeing that Lydia had all but short-circuited, Auden kept talking, his voice low and rough and just Southern enough that he probably never got asked where he was from. "Yep, that Auden. That's what happens when your dad is a community college professor. You get a dorky name and grow up listening to poetry while you eat your pancakes."

Lydia had finally put her hands down, but now they floated by her thighs in a terrible attempt at looking natural. Plus, she still hadn't remembered how to speak.

Auden, seeing her startled expression, kept going. "Anyway, y'all called about a problem with the property? I'm the caretaker; that's my cabin right up the hill. How can I help?"

Luckily, Mary sprang to life and told him what had happened. "Martha here put too many deviled eggs down the pig!"

Mary's proclamation got the whole room's attention. Auden looked more than uncomfortable; he looked a little scared. "The pig? What pig?" he asked Mary. Mary looked at Auden like he had lost his mind. The silence seemed to expand, filling the room as thoroughly as the scent of those eggs. "The pig. The garbage disposal we called you to fix," she clarified, gesturing at the sink, her voice dripping in disdain.

"Oh, right, my grandma called it that. Yeah, let me take a look," Auden replied, without noticing how offended Mary was at being seen as a contemporary of his unnamed grandmother. Auden rolled up his sleeves, walked over to the sink, and flipped the switch for the garbage disposal.

It emitted the same metallic death rattle and the same noxious smell of ground eggs as before. He turned it off and wrinkled his nose in distaste. Then, in a move that surprised and honestly scared Lydia a bit, he stuck his bare hand down the drain. She heard quieter metallic clicking. And then with a sigh of triumph, Auden pulled out a thoroughly bent fork from within the disposal.

"Problem solved. Though I'm not sure what you can do about this fork," he added, while washing his hands a few times while the disposal ran, eating up the last of the ungodly eggs. "Okay, well, if there's nothing else?" Auden asked, looking directly at Lydia. Goodness, he was handsome. The silence dragged out.

Auden, a little disconcerted by Lydia's dreamy gaze, asked, "Are y'all prepared for the storm?"

Ever since she had started sewing, Lydia would categorize people by thinking about what she would sew for them. As soon as she saw Auden Williams, her sewing brain went into overdrive. It would need to be something useful. A vest? Something with snaps and pockets? Maybe Merchant & Mills had a good pattern. She could stock it in the store. Auden had a hint of tan, even in January, so she started to flip through fabric swatches in her mind; what would go best with his dark brown hair? His green eyes?

"Oh, my God," Lydia thought. She had just been standing there, staring at him, this whole time. Lydia willed her cheeks to stop burning. Then she willed herself to have a better wardrobe. Leggings? A T-shirt that says "Wine. Sew. Repeat"? Why didn't it ever occur to her to dress like an adult? Well, to be fair, she tried. The Graham Years. She shook her head, pressed her hands to her face, and tried to concentrate on the question. "The storm?" she said, trying to get a grip on herself.

"Have you even checked the forecast?" Clark whined. Lydia looked at her socks, let the mismatched rainbows calm her down, took a deep breath, and repeated for what seemed the millionth time, "We aren't meant to be using phones this weekend, Clark; that was one of the main ideas behind the retreat, remember? SEW RELAXING? Ring any bells?" Lydia asked, knowing he had read the packet and just didn't care enough to remember.

Auden just looked back and forth between the two of them as if watching the least athletic tennis volley in the history of all time.

"Mr. Williams, would you mind checking the weather on your phone for us? We were bamboozled into leaving our phones at home," Clark added to his request.

Bamboozled? Who said that anymore? Besides, she had done no such thing. They had all thought it would be a good idea to leave their phones at home. Hadn't they?

"Call me Auden, please. And I'm afraid I don't have a cell phone. The mountain doesn't have great reception, so I've never found it worth the trouble. I have a landline back in my cottage, as you know, since you called me," he clarified.

"Fine. You don't need a phone to check the forecast," Clark replied, still holding on to a bit of his whiny tone. With that he gestured at the old, battered television in the corner of the living room.

"Why does it matter, Clark?" she retorted. "We have sewing machines, cookies, more lasagna than we could possibly eat. A storm might actually make the whole weekend that much cozier!"

"Cozy? Lydia, have you even looked at the sky? There is a storm coming our way, and I don't think I am alone in saying there is nothing 'cozy' about a storm." Clark turned to the rest of the room with his final comment, bolstered by Mary and Martha's nodding.

Of course, Clark hit a gold mine shopping his anxiety to the M's. They lived for natural disasters. Natural disasters and anything that required amazing amounts of pity. Lydia couldn't count the number of times they had walked into the store, nodding in sync, as they'd asked, "Oh did you hear, it's just so horrible," and then gone on to detail some minor tragedy with a look that resembled glee more than pity. A winter storm was like Halloween candy to a toddler. They were horrified, of course, but they were also thrilled.

"Oh, Lydia. A storm? In the mountains? Do we have an emergency plan?" Lydia couldn't tell if Martha had said that or Mary, they were nodding so violently, gesturing to Clark as their heads bobbed up and down. Lydia almost burst out laughing imagining a pair of old biddy bobbleheads with catchphrases like "Who would have thought?" and "Have you ever heard such a thing?" and then a final "What will the family do now?"

Clark turned on the new arrival, "You must be able to turn that old relic on, surely?"

Auden looked a bit like a deer in headlights. A handsome deer, a deer in Carhartt's that were worn and almost begged to be touched, a deer . . . okay, no, he was just startled. But Lydia couldn't help thinking of the animals in Bambi when they all fall in love. What had the rabbit called it? Twitterpated? Yep, she was twitterpated.

Auden, meanwhile, found himself with the unmitigated attention of Mary, Martha, Clark, and Amy. Heather and Cynde were at least pretending not to panic. Lydia made a mental note to thank them both later.

Lydia felt the anxiety roll off of Amy in waves as Auden fiddled with the old dials. First static, but now the local news. And for once, Clark was right. The local newscaster was in full "big news" mode.

It wasn't just a cozy, blustery winter storm. It was an ice storm, a no-power, can't-drive sort of ice storm. Business closings scrolled across the bottom of the screen. That didn't scare Lydia. But then the church closings started. As far as Cherry Log was concerned, only an act of God could close His house. And that looked exactly like what they were going to get.

Lydia turned to take stock of the room as buzzwords drifted past: *winter storm warning, travel advisory, black ice likely. Areas most likely to be affected, power outages predicted for.* . . . She could swear Mary and Martha were smiling. Auden, on the other hand, was definitely frowning. "Um, Lydia, is it? We better get ready. If we get ice, we'll lose power and we might even lose the telephone line. I tried to tell Fran that February could be tricky on the mountain." He said all of this in an almost whisper, but everyone heard, and all eyes were on Lydia. "You are all going to need to stay in the house."

Now everyone looked outside. There was only one word for it: ominous. The soft rain that had made her feel so cozy was shifting as they watched. Now it hissed, the icy sleet crashing against the tin roof. The room filled with its low static, and while it was hard to see, Lydia could imagine the effect. In the strange, bright dusk, ice was coating each branch, each twig. The world would be crystal in no time. First, she thought, *Tomorrow morning will be so beautiful*. Then she thought, *We're trapped*.

*This is*, Lydia added to herself, *well above my pay grade*.

"No need to worry, everyone," she said as soothingly as she could manage. "Mr. Williams, I mean Auden, I mean, uh, will you stay and help us get the house ready for the storm?"

"I'd be happy to get y'all set up for the storm and answer any other questions you have. Could I have a word with Fran?" Auden replied.

"You sure can have a word with Fran. Let me just go give her a holler," Lydia replied.

Cynde stared at her, clearly baffled by the weirdly stiff manner Lydia had adopted. Had nothing changed from grade school? Cute boys made everything awkward.

Lydia plowed on, "Okay, team." She flinched at her own fake cheeriness. "Auden here is going to help us batten down the hatches, and I am going to go fill Fran in on all the excitement."

Fran would have a plan. Fran always had a plan. She would laugh at Lydia's worried face, tell her this was far from the first ice storm she had dealt with, and organize a hand-sewing class, all in one seamless gesture. Lydia walked down the hallway and reached Fran's room. The door was closed.

That made sense. Their group could be loud, and Fran had probably shut the door when egg-gate had gone down. So, Lydia knocked, gently at first, and then with increasing force. Nothing. Fran must still be asleep. She knocked as hard as she could and called out, "Fran? Fran, I'm worried. So, I'm, I'm going to come in now." Lydia tried to sound upbeat as she said it.

Hoping she wasn't being too rude, she stepped into Fran's room. It was just so . . . Fran. She had her own sewing machine set up in one corner to work on her current projects when they weren't all in class. Lydia looked at the fabric fed through the machine, it was a scrap quilt slowly coming to life, the next few squares already lined up for chain piecing, the fast-sewing method Fran used when quilting.

She kept staring at the fabric because she could not will herself to look at Fran. She refused to see what was already clear. Fran was dead.

# Chapter Five

She didn't look peaceful. Wasn't death always described as peaceful? At least, that is what she remembered from the British murder mysteries she had binged as her marriage fell apart. And that is what they had said about her grandfather, when he died at ninety while holding his wife's hand. Not Fran. Fran looked scared. Or, well, at least, this weird mannequin of Fran in front of her looked that way.

Because Fran was dead.

Fran's right cheek rested against the desk, while the left side of her head was a bloody mess, leaving no doubt as to whether her dear friend would ever wake up. And leaving no doubt as to whether this was some terrible accident. It wasn't. It was murder.

On the floor below the desk was a small, black iron, covered in blood. A sad iron, Fran had called it. Told Lydia women used to warm them in an open fire and then snatch them out to iron shirts with, in the days before electricity. Fran had found it at Blessed Again, been thrilled to have the antique with a melodramatic name, planned to use it as a paperweight. Fran told her it was from an old word for heavy, not depressed. Fran told her . . .

Fran wouldn't tell her anything ever again.

Lydia knew better than to touch the body. But it didn't matter; she couldn't get her feet to move. She couldn't make her voice work. She just looked. A cup of coffee on the side table in one of Fran's beautiful blue and white mugs. The pin cushion Fran had made that looked like a little mushroom. Fran's simple gold chain bracelet that she never took off. The blood spreading down her arm onto the fabric pieces scattered across the table.

As soon as her eyes refocused on the blood, she stepped backwards, out of the room, and then shut the door and leaned it against it. She still hadn't made a sound. But her brain had kicked into overdrive. Fran was dead. And the storm had started.

Lydia shook her head and tried to breathe. But she felt frozen, rooted to the spot. She could still perfectly picture the first time she had met Fran.

Lydia wanted to stay with that Fran—not the Fran behind the closed door. She had to tell the group. After that? Lydia remembered last summer. The two murders in Peridot. She knew what to do when you found a dead body. She hated that she knew. They would call 911, talk to the police, leave the house, and Lydia would go home with Charlie, pick up Baby Lobster from Jeff, and cry for the rest of her life. She just needed to move.

Somehow, she forced herself to walk back to the main room, where the group was still arguing about the ice storm and Mary had started to quietly cry from the stress of it all. Suddenly the house went dark, but before Lydia could start cursing the universe with language the M's would certainly disapprove of, a loud hum kicked in and the lights turned back on.

"That will be the generator," Auden explained to the group, adding, "most houses up here have one."

Lydia breathed a small thank you to the generator and prepared to tell her friends the worst possible news: "Everyone, let's go sit in the living room. I need to talk to y'all."

Just as she was about to explain, Clark interrupted. "Is this about dinner? Because if . . .?"

Lydia wanted to give him a sled and tell him to go get McDonald's at the bottom of the mountain, wish him luck, and kick him down the road.

"No, this isn't about dinner. I mean, no, listen, you need to sit down. You all need to sit down."

No one moved.

"Fran is dead."

Lydia had been more or less repeating those words on an endless loop to herself ever since she'd walked into Fran's bedroom but saying them out loud was different. She wanted to puke. She wanted to puke, take a bath, get in bed, and wake to find out that it was still Friday night in her apartment, Fran's apartment. Lasagna unmade. This time she checks the weather report, calls Fran, cancels the retreat, and spends the weekend with Charlie and Baby Lobster on the couch, balancing her spreadsheets and watching *The Great British Bake Off*. Right now, that sounded like heaven.

"She, well, she's in her room. And she's dead. And she was murdered."

*That's one way to do it,* she thought to herself, flinching. No wonder Graham had thought she lacked "finesse." No wonder her high school drama teacher had said she was "about as subtle as a heart attack." Thank goodness she hadn't tried to be a doctor, or a minister. Or even a makeup sales lady at Ulta. But she was avoiding the scene right in front of her.

Mary had never stopped crying, but now it grew much louder. Martha started tearing up, if a little dryly. Clark had buckled down to the couch like someone had let the air out of him. Heather was ghost white, a shade which looked even weirder next to her bright red hair. Lydia looked for Cynde, expecting the kinder, older woman to have reached out to the slip of a girl, but that was the biggest surprise of all: Cynde.

She wasn't just crying, which would have been shock enough. Lydia couldn't think of a single time she had seen Cynde crying. But crying implies some beauty to it, a little graceful melancholy.

There was nothing pretty in what Cynde was doing. She had turned her back to the rest of the group and sounded like a diver about to drown. Huge hiccups were interspersed with sobs. It sounded violent. It looked a little violent. And Lydia knew, the minute she heard that cry, that Cynde had absolutely no control over the sounds she was making. This. This was real grief. And Lydia had no idea where it was coming from.

The crying was harsh enough to wake Charlie, who had been snoring his way through the drama thus far. He slowly made his way to Cynde, sitting right next to her, the tip of his nose resting on her shoe. Charlie had gotten Lydia through her divorce. Somehow, he knew just how close a bereft person wanted him to be.

Amy was standing a little aside from the spectacle of Cynde's grief, gently rubbing her friend's back.

The only person who seemed more or less steady was Auden. He'd only worked with Fran on the house, and if Lydia had to guess, steady was probably his default.

"I don't believe you." Lydia was still in shock, so it took her a moment to even process who had spoken. It was Clark, of course. Of course.

"Um, what? Well. What?" Lydia felt like she was the garbage disposal, and someone had just stuck a fork in her. Or maybe she felt like the fork.

"I. Do. Not. Believe. You." Clark responded, rallying from his earlier confusion.

Lydia spoke now just to Clark. "Listen, Clark, you are in shock. Fran is dead. And it is awful."

Clark stared at her, unmoved, so she walked with him to Fran's room, leaving the rest of the group in the living room, sinking in their grief.

Stepping in front of her, Clark opened the door and stepped into Fran's room. Lydia looked again at the wrecked side of her dear friend's face, the bloodied, simple iron on the floor. Clark started cursing, something Lydia had never heard from him, and darted from the room. As she closed the door, he stumbled to the bathroom, and she heard him retching.

Enough. That was the only word Lydia could think. Enough. It was time to call the police. She went back into the living room, planning to tell the group she would make the call when, for the second time on that terrible day, a loud, frightening noise stopped her in her tracks. Not a fork in a disposal. A boom, followed by a strange lack of noise.

The room got too quiet. Too dark.

Auden spoke into the anxious stillness, explaining, "That must have been the generator. I told Fran that she should have had it replaced. It was old and the strain must have . . . well . . ." Auden held up his hands and gestured at the darkness around them: the old television dead, the lights all out.

Thankfully, Auden seemed more or less unperturbed by the loss of power. He walked into the front hallway, opened a closet door, and came back with four large flashlights and one electric lantern. He turned the lantern on and sat it in the middle of the room on the coffee table. Then he placed the four flashlights next to it.

Everyone was waiting for Lydia address the latest catastrophe, but she realized now the phone lines would be down as well. She simply did not have a plan.

*　*　*

Auden reached down and added two new logs to the fire. Once they caught, he turned his attention to the doors. Walking the perimeter of the first floor, he checked each door's lock. While the group sat in the living room, dazed, Auden disappeared downstairs, presumably to check the doors down there as well. Back upstairs, and apparently satisfied all the doors were locked, Auden moved into the kitchen.

Lydia watched him check the burners on the stove, and she was relieved to see them flare up in the growing darkness of the kitchen. Then Auden picked up the landline phone from the wall, an old plastic cream-colored phone with large buttons—buttons that should have been bright white. He listened to the receiver, grimaced, and put it back. When he stepped back out to the fireplace and started to give directions, Lydia almost laughed in relief. Finally, someone else could be in charge of this nightmare.

"The phone line is down and so is the generator. We can't do anything until we get power back; it's too dangerous to try to get down the mountain and into town for help. I think we all need to stay here in the main room with the lantern and wait until the power comes back. That is our best bet to stay safe."

For a moment, Lydia felt safe. Or at least, safer. They had a plan. The group seemed to agree, and one by one they started to look at each other across the rough circle of furniture by the light of the lantern. Everyone was sitting, seemingly ready for the next set of instructions. No, Lydia corrected herself, everyone was sitting down except Clark.

Clark was never one to follow the rules. Well, he followed his own rules. No gluten before noon. No white wines from below the equator. That sort of thing. But faced with the advice not to leave the house, Clark assumed, as he usually did, that the rules did not apply to him.

Grabbing his worn Barbour jacket, Clark declared, "This is ridiculous. I saw the body. No one slams their head into an iron by accident—which means this is murder. Which means," his voice went up in pitch, "that someone in this house is a murderer. I, for one, am not staying to find out who!"

Mary wrung her hands while Auden tried to repeat his previous warning, "Listen. We're at the top of the ridge. There isn't a house within five miles and the gravel roads are nothing but ice. That's where trees haven't fallen down and blocked them off completely. There's no way you can get traction on the road, and even if miraculously you did, where would you go? These are vacation homes up here. I know because I look after them. Not a lot of folks come up this time of year because, um . . ." With that, Auden gestured to the sleet spattering against the main windows overlooking the valley.

"Who even are you? You could be the murderer. You could be lying about people not being in their houses; there could even be a house right down the road. This is ridiculous," Clark countered. Lydia started to wonder if this was becoming Clark's catch phrase. And to be fair, it was ridiculous, but it was also true. Casting one last glare around the room, Clark threw open the door and stormed out, slamming the door closed again behind him.

Lydia heard it before she saw it. And the worst part of her hoped he looked like Goofy slipping on a banana peel. There was a shriek, a thud, and a low moan. No one said a word, when Clark, wet and slightly limping, came back in, hung up his coat, and sat down silently in front of the fire, his hair still wet with rain and clumps of ice.

Something like a laugh bubbled in her throat, something that almost sounded like a sob. Lydia wanted to laugh at Clark, she wanted to laugh so hard it hurt. It hurt not to, so she quickly started to speak. "I think Auden is right. Let's stay together. I'm sure we'll have power back soon and we'll call the police. This is the best way to stay safe," Lydia stumbled along, because it was unclear who in the room, besides Auden, could even form a sentence at this point.

"Besides," Cynde offered, speaking for the first time, "we don't know it was someone in the house." Clark started to tell her she was being absurd, but she spoke right over his attempts, "Remember that car that drove by so loudly before lunch? It practically rattled my teeth, they drove so fast. Maybe, maybe," she repeated, warming to her theory, "maybe it was that person, someone who was mad at Fran, someone none of us has even met."

Mary and Martha looked visibly relieved by this new theory. It fit perfectly with their comments from breakfast. A rogue hooligan was to blame. *What a tragedy*, they could say, adding phrases like *Well, what can you expect* and *It was only a matter of time.*

Martha commented sagely, "What has this country come to when you aren't even safe in your own home?" The moral decline of the country was a favorite topic for the M's. Lydia was happy to let them wax poetic though because she needed time to come up with a plan.

It was clear they couldn't leave the house. Even if the theory of an outsider as the murderer was correct, they still had two main problems, as far as Lydia could figure. How were they going to stay safe? And what were they going to do with . . . Fran? Lydia couldn't bring herself to call her dear friend "the dead body." But the fact remained. Fran was dead and she was still in the house. There would be no quick call to the ambulance, no kind and effective professionals to deal with the situation. Lydia had never expected to miss Sergeant Simpson from Peridot, but now she would have given anything to see the man and his sturdy mustache walk into the room. She banished the comforting but impossible thought. Martha was still holding court, and the rest of the group seemed too stunned to interrupt. All except for Auden.

She made eye contact with him, and he walked across the room toward her. Gesturing to the kitchen, she asked him, "Could I talk with you for a second?"

Auden nodded and they went into the kitchen and pulled out chairs at the long wooden table.

They sat in silence for a long moment.

Lydia took a deep breath and blurted out, "What do we do about Fran?"

Auden looked up; his eyes widened in surprised. Clearly, he had been expecting Lydia to seek solace, maybe cry on his shoulder.

"Fran is dead. We can't get out of this house. Where are we going to put her?"

Again, the silence stretched out.

Shaking his head as if waking from a bad dream, Auden finally answered, "Well, I'm guessing you mean in case Fran . . . in case the body . . .?" Auden wrinkled his nose and Lydia nodded. "Well, the 'good news,'" and at this point Auden actually made quotation marks with his fingers, "is that the generator just died, so the house isn't going to be that warm. We'll lock her door. This is a bad storm, but it can't last that long. Hopefully within forty-eight hours we'll be able to get the police up here. Better to just leave things as they are. I'm sure that's what the police would say if we could talk to them."

"That makes sense. Thanks," and before Auden could get up from the table, she barreled on, panic starting to crack in her voice, "What are we going to do about the murderer?" Lydia knew, even though she wished with her whole heart that she didn't, that one murder might mean there was a second murder to come. Had Fran ever told Auden about what happened in Peridot last summer? When two people had been murdered and the murderer then tried to kill Lydia herself. He probably read about it in the paper.

"Whoever hurt, well, killed, Fran—how do we know they don't want to hurt someone else? Auden, how on earth are we going to stay safe?"

Lydia felt the tears at the edge of her eyes, but she blinked them back. When this was over, she would let herself cry for a few days straight. She would get Charlie and Baby Lobster on her couch in Peridot and then she would order too much pizza from Frank's and eat all of it while watching reruns of *The Office*, even though she had already seen every single available episode more than a few times. She would cry and cuddle and eat. She just needed to get through this storm. Correction: She just needed to get through this storm *alive*.

It was clear that Auden had been thinking about the same problem.

"I know that your friends think some random person did this, but I'm not so sure. Listen, I trust you, Lydia. Do you trust me?"

Lydia didn't answer Auden immediately. She knew he was right. They couldn't rule out the chance that someone in the house had murdered Fran. Did she trust him?

Someone had killed Fran, and it had to have happened before or during the Great Deviled Egg Debacle. Lydia had had her eyes on Auden from the moment he walked into the Laurels until she went to Fran's room and discovered the murder. It was hard not to look at Auden, if she were being honest.

"I do trust you. But what are we going to do?"

"In some ways, the storm is actually helpful. If the others are right, and it was someone who drove up on the mountain to hurt Fran, I don't think they're hiding somewhere on the road in their car in this weather. That means we probably aren't in immediate danger. Not from someone outside the house," he added, gravely. "But I think we both know that might not really be the problem . . ."

Lydia nodded and replied, "It's just not that likely, is it? Some random person drives up here, murders Fran, and manages to get away unseen right before a storm hits? The murderer," Lydia stopped and swallowed hard, "the murderer is probably still in the house."

"Here's what I think we should do . . .," Auden offered, snapping into planning mode. Lydia wondered if he had been in the military. Why was he on this mountain, anyway? Didn't he want a regular job in a town with a bar and with women he could ask out and . . . But Auden was still talking, and she needed to pay attention.

". . . and since the doors to the bedrooms all lock from the inside, that takes care of the nighttime. Sound good?" Auden cocked his head to the side, waiting for Lydia's approval. She stared at him, clearly lost. Sighing, he repeated himself, "So, like I just said, I think we need stay in groups of at least three at all times. And then at night everyone can lock their rooms."

Lydia bit her lip, "That makes sense. It does. But, um, where are you going to sleep?"

She knew it was a legitimate question, so why could she feel her cheeks turning red?

Thankfully Auden responded as if it were a completely normal concern and told her, "I thought about that. I'm going to sleep on the couch in the living room. If there is a threat outside this house, someone needs to be on guard."

"But how are you going. . . ." Lydia's protest died on her lips as Auden leaned close and whispered to her. She tried not to notice that he smelled like soap and pine needles. That he didn't have a beard but could still use a shave. Just enough stubble on his face. . . .

"Fran keeps an unloaded rifle in the front hall closet."

The words hit Lydia like a bucket of cold water. Fran had told her that. Before. How had she forgotten?

"And I always have extra shells in my coat pocket when I come down to the Laurels." At that he moved his hand in his jacket pocket and she heard the sound of metal clinking against metal. Lydia wondered for a moment why he would make a habit of carrying ammunition, but her overwhelmed brain couldn't seem to follow the thought.

"Once everyone is asleep tonight, I'm going to load the rifle and keep it under the couch I'm sleeping on. Just to be safe. But Lydia," Auden paused, and Lydia realized he was still whispering, "this is why I asked if you trusted me. I trust you. But I don't think we should tell the others about the gun."

He was right. If someone in that house had killed Fran, the last thing they needed to do was make it common knowledge there was a gun in the house. And she did trust him. Right?

Auden would help her find the murderer and maybe, just maybe, it would have nothing to do with Measure Twice and her store could still be saved. Otherwise, a sewist was the killer. Her store was doomed. And Auden just happened to have pockets full of bullets.

# Chapter Six

Lydia told the group about the plan: to stay in groups of at least three and lock their bedrooms at night. She didn't say a word about the gun. Clark looked unconvinced but, given his recent humbling on the ice-slick driveway, he decided not to fight her on it. The grandfather clock sounded again, and the room was silent as they all counted along: one, two, three. Three o'clock. Far too early for dinner. But without power, they couldn't sew. Even if anyone had been able to concentrate well enough to operate a sewing machine. Still, they needed some sort of task. Grief had taken over the room, and Lydia worried for her friends. She worried for herself.

"Auden, do you need our help getting ready for the storm?" Lydia asked, hoping there was some menial task left to do.

"Actually, yeah, there are a few things. If y'all feel up to it, I could use the help." Auden knew just how to rope the M's in. They would be ready to rescue him, no matter how overwhelmed they felt.

"Let's see. Amy, Cynde, and Heather, it would be great if you could bring in more firewood, since I want to make sure it stays dry. We'll need to keep the fire going until the power comes back on. Clark, in a minute, can you head down to the basement with me? We need to wrap the pipes in towels to try to keep them from freezing and bursting. I know I said groups of three, but there are only eight of us. Are you okay with just me?"

Clark nodded, much to Lydia's relief. Auden continued, clearly comfortable giving directions, "When you ladies are done with the firewood, I know Fran has flashlights in the kitchen. She keeps, kept, she . . . the flashlights are in the skinny cabinet next to the fridge. And I know there are batteries in the kitchen. I'm just not sure where. Can you get the flashlights and find some batteries? I want as many as we can find, just to be safe. And we need them before it gets too dark."

"Totally. On it," and with that Heather stood up and followed Amy and Cynde as they went to get their jackets.

That left Lydia, Mary, and Martha still in the living room without a plan. Lydia had no idea what Auden would ask the M's to do; they could hardly be expected to move firewood.

"Mary, Martha, I have a particular request for you both, something I would only entrust to you," Auden said, crouching down a bit while talking to the two seated women. Dang. He was good at this. Both women perked up immediately, leaning toward Auden.

"When we get the power back, the first thing we will do is call the police. When the police get here, they are going to want a clear sense of what has happened. Really clear. Both of you clearly have a great eye for detail," he paused as the women nodded, "so I want you two to do the most important task. Write down a clear account of what has happened here. That way, we can give that straight to the police. Do you think you could do that for me, ladies?"

"Mr. Williams," Mary replied.

"Please, call me Auden."

"Auden, you are absolutely correct. The police will need a clear accounting of this tragedy. Rest assured Martha and I will record just that," Mary finished. Then she turned to look at Lydia, the only member of the group without a task.

Auden followed Mary's gaze.

"Mr. Williams, Auden, what should Lydia do?" Mary asked, as if Lydia were a child that needed a minder.

"Why doesn't Lydia serve as your scribe, that way you and Martha can really concentrate on remembering the events clearly? If that's okay with you, Lydia?" He smiled at her as he asked.

"Sounds great, I'll just grab a pad of paper from over . . ."

She was interrupted by Clark returning with an armful of towels. He jerked his head toward the stairs to the bottom level of the house, "Ready, Auden?"

Auden nodded and went to the stairs, meeting up with Clark, as Lydia crossed back to the couch, armed with a pad of paper and a pen.

The M's had seemed invigorated in Auden's presence, but when Lydia sat down, she noticed again how frail and tired they seemed. If the task was going to work in distracting them, they needed a little pick-me-up first.

"S'mores," Lydia said aloud.

"More of what, darling?" Martha asked.

"No. S'mores. You know, the treat? Made with graham crackers and marshmallows and chocolate?"

The M's stared back without a hint of comprehension. Of course. They had probably never been camping.

"S'mores are a dessert you can make over a fire. This is going to be hard work, so I thought we could use a little sustenance. Give me one moment, ladies." And with that she headed toward the kitchen, where Heather was meant to be looking for batteries.

But she wasn't. Heather was slouched at the kitchen table in the growing dark, muttering to herself. Lydia hesitated, listening.

"Why couldn't she? Why couldn't she just?" Heather repeated over and over, head in her hands.

Poor girl. Lydia didn't really understand what Heather was talking about, she knew grief left everyone reeling. She was probably wondering why Fran couldn't have just survived the attack. Lydia had wondered that, too.

"Heather? Sorry to intrude, I just need to grab some things," she said, embarrassed to interrupt the scene before her. Lydia grabbed the bag of s'mores supplies she had left near the stove and turned to leave the kitchen.

Heather didn't respond. She just stopped talking, wiped her face, and laid her head on the table, cradled in her arms.

Lydia went to the fireplace and got the s'mores started, placing a few marshmallows on one of the sticks she'd packed. Moving the fire screen to toast the marshmallows, she tried to get the M's started on their task.

"Where do you think we should start?" she asked, turning the stick to get the marshmallows a nice, even, golden color.

"Clearly we start with when we arrived," Mary answered.

"Surely we start with this morning," Martha countered.

Lydia slid the marshmallows off the stick, sandwiching them with chocolate between two graham crackers. She passed one gooey combo to each of the M's. Then she assembled one for herself and sat in an armchair, enjoying the more or less immediate sugar buzz.

"The police won't care about when we got here," Martha continued, "they are going to want to know what happened to Fran. We start with this morning."

"If they only care about what happened to Fran, then we may as well start with lunch." Both women looked distracted, remembering the garbage disposal mishap they had brought on the house only hours earlier, even though it now seemed like a different lifetime to Lydia.

Martha took a dainty, unconvinced, bite of her s'more and then set it aside, saying, "This is ridiculous." She crossed her arms, lips pressed together in a thin line.

"If you're going to be difficult . . ." Mary left the sentence unfinished and crossed her arms, mirroring her friend.

How had the task gone sideways so quickly? Lydia was going to have nothing to show Auden when he finished wrapping the pipes.

Lydia finished the last bite of her s'more and decided to try a different approach. "Mary, Martha, I was thinking. The police, when they come, hopefully soon, won't know anything about Fran. Maybe you could each share some of your memories of Fran since you both knew her so well; and I can write them down, to give the police a little context?"

"That does make a certain amount of sense, Lydia, dear," Martha acquiesced. They all paused to hear the grandfather clock ring out four sonorous bongs.

"Fran lived in Peridot her whole life. She never married, never had any children. She owned and ran Measure Twice for twenty years before selling to you, Lydia. She wasn't a church-goer, even though of course we always invited her to services," Martha added, not bothering to hide the judgment in her voice.

"Um, okay, that's great. Very informative," Lydia encouraged, as she jotted down the details, "But I'm sure they want to know more about the type of person she was."

Silence. Lydia could hear Heather opening cabinets in the kitchen and Cynde and Amy moving firewood onto the summer porch, out of the storm. She didn't have much written down. Why was this so hard?

"What type of person Fran was?" Mary answered. "Certainly. She was a businesswoman. A good baker. A decent knitter." Silence, again.

"She had a green thumb," Martha added, gesturing to the potted plant on the table beside the couch, her untouched s'more next to the plant.

"Of course! Her plants!" Mary stood. "With the power out, the plants will get cold. We should bring them to the living room, to be near the fire."

"Of course," Martha agreed, standing as well. "Come along, Lydia, dear, we will need your help carrying the plants." And with that, the M's set off to gather the various houseplants scattered about the Laurels.

As Lydia carried plants to the living room under their close direction, she tried to tell herself the M's hadn't exactly refused to say anything nice about Fran. They hadn't exactly refused to make a timeline of events leading up to the murder. Somehow, neither task had been accomplished. Lydia had so many things she could say about Fran, so many wonderful things about the woman who had changed her life, her fairy godmother. She had expected the

M's to feel the same. They didn't talk of Fran as they collected the plants, accompanied only by the sound of the storm still raging outside.

Carrying some sort of fern, the last of the wayward plants, Lydia almost ran into Clark, disheveled and sour-faced. The grandfather clock rang out five, and Lydia realized, in the midst of all the chaos, she was starving. She'd already eaten what was left of the M's s'mores when they weren't looking. But she was still ravenous. In an ice storm. Without power.

# Chapter Seven

Clark seemed to read her mind. He ran a hand through his hair, straightened his sweater, and demanded, "Five o'clock? The pipes are wrapped. I'm exhausted. What are we going to do about dinner? The fridge has lost power. All that food is going to spoil! I, for one, have no interest in adding food poisoning to this nightmare."

Clark's complaints had brought the others into the living room. They all looked to Lydia. Lydia looked to Auden. Auden, thankfully, continued to gently steer the group, explaining. "The oven will still work, since it's connected to the gas line, not the power. And you're right, Clark, we should eat whatever we can now. Though, most of the time, they get whatever tree fell off of the line and power comes back pretty quickly."

With that, he led the group to the large, old, and scarred wooden table that ran the length of the kitchen, placing the electric lantern he'd found in the middle of the table. Heather had arranged the flashlights in the center of the table, so the room felt almost well-lit. Or at least as well-lit as a dark restaurant. Auden walked over to the long counter with Lydia and grabbed an armload of blue plates for the group. Mary followed behind him and got the cutlery and napkins.

Cynde managed to muster enough energy to get two bottles of red wine she'd brought and open them before she sat at the table. With Auden, and without Fran, the table was a distorted echo of lunch earlier that day, when deviled eggs in the sink had seemed like an emergency.

After he had placed the lantern in the middle of the table, Auden even thought to turn on the oven to heat up the lasagna.

The group slowly settled in at the table, pouring drinks and finding napkins while Lydia busied herself getting dinner ready. Lydia put the lasagna pans in the oven and got the garlic bread, still wrapped in foil, set on top of the burner. Everything felt like it was underwater. Time moved both far too slowly and far too quickly. She had a terrible suspicion it was only about five minutes past five, but without a watch on (an iWatch—she'd left it at home), and out of sight of the grandfather clock, she couldn't be sure. Then she realized she didn't want to know what time it was. What were they going to do, anyway? She looked at the pale faces in front of her and thought back to just that morning. She had been so nervous about the itinerary. Or the night before, getting ready in her apartment, trying to time the lasagna just right.

Why had she ever cared about lasagna? It seemed laughable now. But they did need to eat, and the food was finally ready, so she started serving pieces, layers of cheese and pasta and sausage. On autopilot, she added a piece of garlic bread to each plate, even Clark's. Even more surprisingly, as the plates circled the table, Clark reached out and grabbed the bread and ate it, finished the whole piece without even putting it down. Later, Lydia would remember that moment, the moment where shock and grief made gluten a forgotten concern. In fact, bread seemed like the only answer. For Clark and for all of them.

She had been worried, because she always worried, that she had made far too much lasagna. But the pans were quickly emptied.

Lydia was so tired that she looked down at her plate, decided to be honest with herself, and just scooped the hot, cheesy goodness straight on to the crusty, buttery garlic bread. Normally she would have worried what the M's would have said about her table manners. Just a few hours ago she would have worried about looking like a total slob in front of "Mr. Williams." Now, she wanted all the comfort that comfort food could possibly offer.

Figuring that dessert was the hardest course to mess up, they had given the first night's dessert to Clark. How could someone care so much about health food yet care so little about food that tasted good? He had tried to convince her the cacao wafers he sold at the Pampered Pantry were delicious. He only tried that trick once. At home, in her cozy apartment, she made sure to have fancy dark chocolate in her freezer at all times.

Tonight, even though they had demolished the lasagna, it was clear the group wanted dessert. Grief had made them ravenous. They turned to Clark and he shrugged and opened a paper grocery bag he had slid under his chair. The Pampered Pantry was Clark's whole life—well, that and his bid to chair the new Peridot Botanical Garden. Lydia had to hand it to him, he had at least brought a lot of options. There were the dreaded cacao wafers, but there were also all sorts of fancy, imported cookies and small, sweet treats.

Quickly, what had seemed like a silly amount of dessert was gone. The adrenaline of Fran's death coupled with the loss of power had at first filled the group with purpose. But, hunger banished, that purpose finally abandoned them. They stared at each other, rudderless in the waves of loss and fear and confusion. Lydia knew something had to be done. She lifted the water glass she had filled with red wine and said, more bravely than she felt, "A toast. To Fran."

Everyone raised their glasses. The M's had made their typical gin and tonics, which were G and T's in name only, since there was so little tonic involved. They must have brought their own gin, since Fran didn't keep any hard liquor in the house. Heather had a craft beer she must have brought with her as well. Auden, Amy, and Cynde had followed Lydia's lead with red wine. And, of course, Clark wasn't drinking. He'd never given a reason, but she had also never seen him have a drink. Looking at her wine, she finally spoke.

"To Fran, thank you for Measure Twice. For changing my life. And for showing me the power of second chances and new beginnings." It was cliché. But that was the thing with clichés; they were so often true.

Cynde, no longer crying but still splotchy and red eyed, raised her wine and added, "To Fran, thank you for always making me feel at home." She brought her glass to her lips and drank it all in one gulp. Just as Lydia was wondering if she had ever really seen Cynde drink before, Cynde grabbed the wine bottle and refilled her glass. Lydia hadn't brought any wine, so she started to think they might soon run out. Maybe they could raid the M's stash of gin if it got bad enough.

Auden stood and raised his glass of red wine: "Fran, you always trusted me. I'm going to miss you," he said and then he sat back down.

Clark followed suit, without standing, and raised his glass of water, "To Fran, at least you were honest," and he set his glass down without taking even a small sip. Lydia had never actually asked Clark how old he was, but she had always pegged him as only a few years older than herself. But in that moment, he looked much older. Older and tired. And possibly angry? No, Lydia assured herself, that was just grief, surely.

Mary rose primly to her feet, smoothing her pencil skirt with one hand and holding her low glass of gin in the other. "To Fran. . . ." Lydia waited for the rest of the toast, expecting something heartfelt, if a little stilted, but nothing came. Mary sat down. The whole room shifted their attention to Martha. Martha was certainly sassier than her friend. But she was still seventy-something and Southern. That had to count for something. It didn't. Martha raised her glass, clinked Mary's, and continued sitting in complete silence. Just like before.

The silence grew. Finally, Heather stood up. Her bright red hair looked even more shockingly vibrant tonight against her pale face. She pulled her short cut-off denim skirt down, as if aware for the first time that it was a little too short for some people in the room. Multiple stacked silver rings glinted on her hands. She couldn't stop spinning them. Then she picked up her fancy IPA and quietly muttered, "To Fran. You were the mother I never had."

Lydia had been right. Both bottles of wine were empty. Plus, she had no idea how much gin the M's had drunk because their glasses never seemed to empty. Heather looked bereft, and Lydia started to doubt the whole idea of toasts. "Okay, everyone, that was lovely. Why don't we take a little time and meet up in the living room for EPP in about twenty minutes? Clark, can you and Mary and Martha stick together? Heather, Amy, and Cynde, can you three? I'll stay behind and clean up. I insist." With that she shooed the group out after they stacked their plates at the sink.

Auden lingered behind after the sewists took their flashlights and headed to get supplies. Without needing to be asked, Auden found a dishcloth and dried as Lydia washed. At first, they just went about the work in silence. It wasn't strained or tense, just quiet.

Eventually he asked, "EPP?"

"Oh, right, sorry, English paper piecing," Lydia clarified.

"English paper piecing?" Auden prodded.

"Oh, right, *sorry*. Um, so, sewing? Right, we mostly use sewing machines. Obviously. But you can also sew by hand. And one way of sewing by hand is called English paper piecing, or EPP," Lydia clarified. "I could, I could teach you if you're interested?"

"Well," Auden offered, "I am staying here tonight. So why not learn how to sew?"

"Great. I'll go get you some fabric. I always travel with extra kits," but as Lydia turned to leave, Auden lightly grabbed her shoulder. It didn't feel right to love how that felt, but she did.

"Thanks," Auden said, barely above a whisper. "Maybe I should come with you?"

Even though she knew he just meant to be safe, Lydia could feel a blush spreading up her neck as she imagined walking into her room with Auden. Then she imagined him seeing the disaster she had made of her room with her loose definition of "unpacking."

"I really think I'll be okay, and I promise to be quick. I'll meet you by the fireplace in just a minute," and with that lame assurance, Lydia headed down the hallway to her bedroom to get the EPP supplies, only to bump into Clark.

"Oh, I was just, you know, the powder room."

Lydia nodded and went to move past him into her room.

But instead of heading back to the living room, or even heading downstairs to get his hand sewing, Clark moved closer, blocking her path, and then he whispered conspiratorially, "What do you really know about this Auden Williams?"

Lydia tried to back up in the narrow hallway. "The same as you. He's the caretaker; he's helping us through the storm. That's it."

*And he likes lasagna*, she thought to herself. *And he's gorgeous. And he must be younger than me, but maybe not by that much. . . .*

Clark cut into her daydreaming. "Exactly! Did you ask to see his driver's license?"

"What?" she sputtered. "You wanted me to card the handyman?"

But Clark kept going without breaking stride. "So, we don't know who he is, he shows up right before we lose power, and then someone kills Fran! It all fits. I don't care how nice he seems, eating dinner and making toasts. He's clearly a murderer."

Lydia felt a strange desire to correct Clark and tell him that no one that cute could possibly be bad news, but she stifled it. After all, she couldn't pretend that the thought hadn't also occurred to her when Auden had asked if she trusted him. Clark was right; the timing was weird. But he had been at the sink the whole time. In fact, Auden was the only person that needed Fran alive, since she was his boss, in a way. She trusted Auden, and she could already tell Clark was going to make trouble. Lydia grimaced.

Clark took the frown as disagreement and plowed on, determined to convince her. "Listen," he continued, "I'm not saying our little group is perfect. Lord knows, Cynde talks too much and Heather is just plain weird. And Mary and Martha certainly haven't kept up with the times." Lydia flinched to think what his description of her would be. "But we know each other. *We* didn't do this. This has nothing to do with us. It has to be an outsider. And if it wasn't that Auden fellow, well, I think we should talk about Amy."

Amy? If Lydia was being honest with herself, she had more or less dismissed Amy from her list. The woman couldn't thread a bobbin, but Lydia was supposed to believe she was a cold-blooded killer?

"Um, Amy? Really, Clark. Amy doesn't even know us. I mean, I don't think she even likes sewing. What could she possibly have to do with all of this?" Lydia asked, making no attempt to hide her incredulity.

"That is exactly my point!" Clark declared triumphantly. "What is she doing here? Why come on a sewing retreat if you're practically phobic about sewing machines? What if she has some secret past, some secret connection to Fran? What if the whole confused, helpless act is just that, an act?" He pressed his lips together smugly.

Lydia had to admit there was a weird logic to his theory. What was Amy doing there? No, the real question was why Lydia was standing in the hallway, whispering with Clark? This was still her retreat, and the rest of the group deserved better. Besides, did she even trust Clark? Right now, she only trusted Auden. Weren't they supposed to stay in groups of three? That hadn't lasted long. Why hadn't she let Auden accompany her? She didn't even have her dog, Charlie, who at that moment was still in the kitchen, frustrated that he hadn't managed to steal any lasagna scraps.

It was time to take back control of the evening. She needed to end this conversation. "Clark, you are being ridiculous. And the best thing we can do right now is stay together. I am going to get my sewing and head to the living room. See you there." With that she brushed past him and went into her room, snapping the door shut just in case he didn't get the hint.

She hadn't been lying to Auden. Lydia really did always have extra fabric. Grabbing her EPP kit, she picked up some extra materials as well. The group would be waiting in the living room. It was important to stay together. But she couldn't shake the feeling that she wasn't safe. Why were the toasts so tense? Why was Clark accusing people? The house felt full of unspoken secrets, and Lydia just wanted to hide under her flower-covered quilt.

But she couldn't.

The group had settled in around the fire. Auden made sure the electric lanterns and flashlights were spread out to light the room enough that they could each see their own work. In another world, it would have felt quaint. Clark was already stitching away at his EPP, intently focused on his hand sewing. Mary and Martha were consulting a drawing they had made of their project, one holding the paper while the other picked up and discarded possible hexies.

Cynde was sharing memories of Fran with Heather, while Amy just looked lost. And Auden was still standing, as if guarding their little group from some unknown menace. Well, she supposed he was.

"Amy, would you like an EPP kit? I brought extras. And Cynde can certainly show you how it works. It is not nearly as complicated as it looks." Lydia passed her a Ziploc bag of materials as she asked. Amy took the bag but didn't otherwise respond.

"Auden, here's one for you." She gestured for him to sit down. He was too tall for her to teach while standing up. He was really tall. Tall and dreamy and. . . . *Stop it*, Lydia reprimanded herself. Sitting down next to Auden on the sectional, she pulled out a half-finished flower composed of one central fabric hexagon surrounded by a hexagon petal attached to three of the sides. "You're making flowers?" Auden asked.

"Well, you don't have to make flowers, but that is a great place to start with EPP. The shapes, we call them hexies, are really versatile and easy to sew. Let me show you the steps and then you can decide if you want to try it."

Lydia got out some hexagon-shaped pieces of paper and some scrap fabric. "So, first thing first, you need to cut out a hexagon from your fabric that's bigger than your paper one. The fabric is going to fold over the edges." With that she traced a hexagon-shaped ruler onto her fabric and cut it out. "Then you fold the fabric onto the paper so that it's a little wrapped up, like an unfinished Christmas present."

Auden peered closer at the hexagon, a little smaller than her palm. "How does the fabric stay folded over the edges like that?" he asked.

"Great question! You can either glue it down with fabric glue that comes out when you wash the finished project, or you can use a running stitch that you remove later." Auden seemed far more comfortable with what amounted to a fancy glue stick than the idea of a "running stitch," so she went that route, which she preferred anyway. "Okay, now make another hexie. Then you get to stitch them together, following where the hexies meet up. And once a hexie has other hexies on all sides, you can remove the paper. Eventually, you'll have an entire quilt top made out of them, all connected to each other.

Auden nodded without much enthusiasm. "It just seems so . . ."

"Slow?" Clark offered. "It is. Really, really slow. But that can be a good thing. So much of what we all do is fast. It's nice to slow down, to let your mind zone out a little. Plus, this is sewing you can do anywhere. On a plane? Sure. While watching TV? Do it all the time. Sitting in a house on the top of a mountain wondering if another person will get killed tonight? Doing it right now."

Leave it to Clark to address the elephant in the room. They couldn't stay awake forever; that much was obvious. Mary had already dipped her head down to Martha's shoulder. Heather was curled in the corner of the couch like some sort of upholstered marsupial. Clark's hexies lay untouched in a heap on the side table.

"Actually."

That was it. One word. But they were so surprised to hear Amy speak that the whole group stopped talking and turned toward her.

"Clark has a point. We don't know who killed Fran, and frankly, Lydia, I'm not sure why we should be following your orders. Maybe you did it." And with that pronouncement, Amy lapsed back into silence.

Cynde hissed at her friend quietly. "Amy, that is absurd!"

"Is it? Why? Cynde, you told me she bought the shop from Fran. And she's living in Fran's apartment! What if she owed her money? What if the deal soured? We're all just sitting here listening to her talk about hex things, and for all we know, she killed Fran, and she could kill one of us next!" Amy was red in the face, from emotion or maybe just from saying so many words at once. Then, as if landing a killing blow, she added, "I. Don't. Trust. Her."

No one spoke. The only sound was the icy crash of the storm against the roof and the windows, with an occasional pop from the embers in the fireplace.

How long had they stood there, as if frozen in place?

"Well." Lydia felt like her entire body was tightened like a spring about to pop. "That is an interesting perspective, Amy. I'm . . . um . . . I'm sorry that you feel that way but . . . um . . . you bring up a great point." Lydia looked up at the ceiling, trying to get the right tone in the fraught atmosphere of the living room. She fiddled with her hair, tucking away the strands that had escaped her messy bun, more to buy time than anything else, and then forced herself onward: "We should call it a night. I think that we should all go to bed at the same time and lock our doors from the inside. And I think we should all agree to get up and leave our rooms at the same time and come right to the kitchen tomorrow morning. Say 8 AM?" Lydia exhaled and waited.

"Perfect," Clark sneered, "Everyone knows you can't be murdered in your own bed before 8 AM. Them's the rules." Lydia could see a bit of his top row of teeth as his nose wrinkled in disdain.

Lydia realized she had been standing in front of the fireplace, addressing them like she would a classroom full of children. It wasn't that far off, to be honest.

Suddenly Auden stood up and joined her, facing the rest of the group.

"Listen. I think Lydia is trying to be helpful. And I, for one, think she made a great suggestion," he added, in his quiet but sincere way. Clark shrugged his shoulders, unimpressed, but Mary and Martha both moved forward a touch, and straightened their spines. It was their natural response to a man assuming authority.

Auden continued, "Amy, I understand you're scared. We all are. But I think locking the doors at night is a really good idea. Hopefully, we can all agree that, if nothing else, I had nothing to do with this terrible tragedy. If you remember, I was trying to fix the garbage disposal the whole time."

Mention of the egg debacle brought a little color to Mary's face, and Lydia saw Mary quietly sneak a few jelly beans from her blazer pocket.

"The ice is too bad for me to head back to my own cabin, so I propose I sleep out here on the big couch. I will keep watch. Does that help?" and he pointed at the largest couch in the room. It faced the fireplace and ran perpendicular to the front door. If he slept with his head toward the large glass windows, he'd be able to see the front door and the staircases that led both upstairs and downstairs and connected to the hallway of main-floor bedrooms.

She scanned the worried faces in front of her. Clark was still trying to look annoyed, but his shoulders had dropped, clearly relieved. Heather was curled up in a large armchair with her legs draped over one of the padded arms. With her arms crossed on top of her slight torso, Heather's face was turned against the back of the chair, her eyes focused on some distant point ostensibly outside the windows. But there was nothing to see out there. Just the reflection of their weary assembly and the sounds of the storm. Lydia wanted to offer a penny for her thoughts, but she had a feeling the cost was far dearer.

Amy nodded. The rest of the group clearly agreed with Auden's plan, and yet no one moved.

Auden cleared his throat and added, "Since the hot water is powered by the generator and not the gas line, we will only have the hot water that's left in the tank. Until we get power back, of course."

Still, no one stirred.

"If you want a shower, I would take one now. There won't be any hot water for another one tomorrow morning," he elaborated. "And make sure to take a flashlight."

That worked. They stumbled toward bed, each grasping a flashlight, hoping a last shower could rinse away some of the grief that clung to them like the ice that coated the tree limbs now creaking in the dark.

Lydia stood up as well, looking down the hallways at the closed doors. At some point in all the chaos she had gotten used to the sound of the sleet and had turned it into a kind of white noise. Now she paid attention again. Willing herself to ignore Amy's accusation.

The ice was building; she could hear branches creaking under the weight. She remembered her first ice storm, when she was a teenager, still living up North. School canceled and a whole day staring out the window at a world that looked like it was made out of crystal. She had loved it. Until it shattered. Every tree was full of potential danger. As soon as the roads melted, they were back in school, but the danger lingered.

Lydia walked a little faster than necessary back to her room, and Charlie trotted out of the living room and followed her, jumping up on her bed the moment he entered the room. She closed the door, locked it, sat down on the bed, and lowered her face to the white whiskered face of her dog. Charlie resettled himself, sighing his wise dog sigh.

Graham had wanted a fancy dog as a "practice baby." But she had insisted on Charlie, a rescue dog with sad eyes. Charlie was a terrible practice "baby," as it turned out. He didn't really give Graham the time of day, and it wasn't long after bringing him home that Graham looked at her one night while they were watching *Game of Thrones* and said nonchalantly, "I don't think I actually want kids." It wasn't Charlie's fault. The best, purebred Goldendoodle in the world wouldn't have saved her marriage. Sometimes, though, it felt like Charlie was saving her.

She stroked his soft ear and whispered her fears out loud for the first time that day. "Charlie, I can't stop thinking about Fran. And I don't know why I'm not crying. I should be crying, right? I want to cry. I want to. I want everything to be okay. If we could just prove that someone else did this, some outsider, maybe everyone would just see this as a tragedy. Measure Twice wouldn't have to be lost, just because Fran is gone. Because, because if someone in this house killed Fran, the retreat, the shop, will always be tied to that. They'll have killed Measure Twice, too."

Lydia whispered the last sentence, embarrassed to admit, even to Charlie, that her motivation to solve the mystery had such a selfish kernel at its heart.

It *had* to be someone outside of the house. Now, she just needed to prove it. That meant alibis. Figure out where each person was, cross them off the list, and she would be one step closer to saving the store each time. But that was the problem. While someone had been murdering Fran, the rest of them had been distracted. They were all so absorbed in the deviled egg drama. Would they have even heard another bear over the racket of the garbage disposal? She stopped to think. No. It was the perfect cover. No one was off the hook. Well, not no one. Auden never left the sink. She trusted him.

So that left six people. And whatever mystery person was in that car. So, seven. Nodding to herself, Lydia got up from the bed, shifting the soporific dog, and walked over to her half-unpacked bags. The same impulse that made Lydia hoard more fabric than she could probably ever sew also led her to buy new notebooks even though she had blank ones waiting, expectantly, at home. Lydia was pretty convinced that the right notebook would solve all her problems, so she just kept buying them.

For the retreat, Lydia had stashed a favorite in her bag: a deep orange bullet journal with a nice stiff cover that closed with wrap-around elastic. It was, of course, completely blank. Notebook and pen in hand, Lydia went back to the bed and pulled the quilt around her for warmth.

It was time to make a list.

# Chapter Eight

Lydia wrote Mary and Martha's names down on the first page of the journal. Underneath she wrote, "Motive?" Lydia chewed on the cap on the end of the pen. What had Mary said in her toast? "To Fran." What a harsh toast. And Martha hadn't said anything at all. That was really surprising. Lydia wrote down a note about the toast. Maybe there had there been a fight? An argument? It was hard to picture those women going so far as to actually confront someone. They were more likely to give an outfit a long, measured look and then declare: "Well, would you look at that figure." They took the backhanded compliment to the next level. But Fran was dead, and Lydia had to consider all the possibilities. Maybe she could imply she'd had an argument with Fran? Encourage them to confide in her? For a moment, she felt a twinge of excitement.

Then Lydia looked at her notebook and suddenly felt a hot wave of shame wash over her. This wasn't an episode of a TV mystery. And she was no bumbling British local about to solve a crime. She ripped out the page of the journal and crumpled it up, then got out of bed and buried it in the bottom of her duffle bag. She wasn't a detective. This wasn't a puzzle. What was wrong with her? Back in bed, she turned off her flashlight and tried to close her eyes. Surely it would be less daunting in the morning. The power would come back on, the phone would be working, and they could call the police. Let the professionals handle it.

Sleep eluded her. She thought about turning on the flashlight, trying to read a book. Since they had scheduled personal time, Lydia, ever the bookworm, had brought a few different options with her to the Laurels. She had no interest in learning about how to make hand-sewn stuffed animals, so she quickly dismissed that option. Poetry was good for a quiet hour looking out at the mountains, but she didn't have the capacity to consider metaphors at the moment. That left the murder mystery she had brought, set in the gorgeous and brooding Shetland Islands. Nope. She shuddered at the thought of reading a fictional version of her very real, very current, nightmare.

Besides, the flashlight she had taken to her bedroom would have made it feel like she was at summer camp, up reading past curfew. She had to go to sleep. There was nothing else to it. But no matter how strictly Lydia commanded herself to fall asleep, it wasn't working. She decided to try washing her face. Earlier, she had been so overwhelmed, she had simply gotten straight to bed.

In the little Jack-and-Jill bathroom that connected to her room, she tried to wash her face like they did in commercials, with large splashes of water. But she had been afraid to wake the M's by bringing in her flashlight, so instead, she got soap in her eye and water all over the sink basin. The M's would not stand for that: Slovenly—that is what they would declare a mess like that. In the dark, as she was trying to wipe up the water, she heard voices.

Lydia wasn't trying to eavesdrop, but she couldn't help hearing Mary and Martha through the wall. Or, being a little more honest, she couldn't help hearing them through the wall once she moved to the other side of the bathroom and pressed her ear against the wall, crawling through the darkness. Either way, she was too curious to be ashamed.

"She was our friend!" Mary mumbled.

"She defrauded us."

"She didn't mean to; you know that, Martha. She thought she could pull it off. She didn't know the long-arm quilting wouldn't work. She couldn't have known she'd get sick. We had a choice. . . ."

Lydia stopped listening for a second. Fran had been sick?

"A choice! She knew about the money. She said she was desperate. What were we supposed to say? Remember how she started that conversation: 'Mary, love. Martha, dear. I know you need to be thinking about your future. What if I had an answer?' 'Mary, have you ever thought of your legacy? Martha, how do you want to be remembered?' Who talks to their friends like that?" Martha stopped to breathe, so angry she seemed to have forgotten all about it, and then continued, "I'll tell you who: a fraud. A cheat. Someone from that *Dateline NBC* show.

"And now we have nothing. Seventy-five years old and I'm looking for a job!" Martha started to raise her voice but caught herself. "Measure Twice was going to be ours. Majority shareholders or whatever nonsense she threw at us. A chance to decide on inventory, set the class schedule, discounted yarn whenever we wanted it. That was the promise. She should have told us. She should have said how much trouble she was really in. The debt."

Martha continued. "I know, I know. You think I'm heartless. Especially now. But her death changes nothing, Mary; it just makes it all that much worse." At that, Martha struggled to continue, audibly fighting back tears. "We've lost all the money we invested, Fran isn't here to even try to make it right, and I don't know what we are going to do next. Lydia has no idea, and honestly, she's useless. . . ."

That stung to hear.

"We can't, we simply don't have the damn money for Lencreek," Martha added, barely audible through her tears that had become loud, breathless sobs.

Lydia realized Mary and Martha were done talking. She could hear murmurs, comforting noises. The loud sobs quieted to soft tears.

She had never seen either woman cry before. She had never heard them swear or lose their tempers. It was the emotion, more than the admission, that floored Lydia.

Gingerly, she unfolded herself and snuck back to her own room. She hoped she was just imagining the look of disappointment on Charlie's face as she got back under the covers. She hadn't *meant* to hear all of that. Besides, what did it even mean? The name Lencreek sounded familiar. Lydia wracked her brain. Yes. She had been invited to give a sewing demonstration there and bring a sort of trunk show of goods and supplies for participants to purchase. It was a high-end retirement home on the outskirts of Peridot, one of the places that was a weird hybrid of a hotel and what she secretly thought of as an old folks' home. She had been impressed, at the time, by the size of their sewing club, not to mention the club's readiness to buy all manner of fabrics and tools. They sure seemed to have some disposable income.

Is that what the M's wanted? A fancy place to retire? She knew they each owned their own house, another reason she figured they weren't actually related. That said, she had never been invited to visit either lady at her place of residence. All socializing was done at the store. Though they did invite Lydia, pretty much every Friday, to join them at Peridot Baptist every coming Sunday.

She had to give them credit for their tenacity. Why did she have a vague recollection of Mary's house, then? The charm pack, she suddenly remembered, relieved to have found the hazy memory. She had delivered the bundle of pre-cut fabric to Mary's house after work one day and had been shocked to see how overrun and rundown the small house had seemed in the early evening light. Feeling like she had seen something private, she had put the charm pack in the mailbox and left quickly.

No wonder they were crying, she thought, pulling herself out of the memory and back into her cold bedroom in the Laurels. She couldn't imagine that Martha's life was that much different than Mary's. If Fran really had defrauded them, that had closed the door on Lencreek. Where did that leave them? Growing old in their houses, as the weeds grew taller and the paint chipped. Dusting useless clutter at Blessed Again. Waiting for Sundays and the chance to pretend everything was fine. What had Fran done?

She shook her head. The killer had to be an outsider. What if she lost Fran, the store, and even the memory of who she thought her kind, fairy godmother of a friend had been?

Sleep did not come. Instead, Lydia was wide awake, thinking about Fran, both the Fran she thought she knew and this new Fran. Fran wasn't dishonest. She wouldn't con somebody. Would she?

Lydia tried listing fabrics like a lullaby. And it actually started to work. Just as she repeated Miss Matatabi Nani Iro Double Gauze to herself, on the edge of sleep, she heard a door close. She jerked awake. Everyone had been told to lock their doors. They had all agreed to stay put, to stay safe. So why had she heard a door shut? She knew the best thing to do was stay in bed. Obviously.

But it was her retreat. She couldn't let someone else get hurt. Feeling like the dumbest character in a horror movie, Lydia slowly opened the bedroom door and stepped into the hallway. The fire was still glowing in the living room, so she clutched her flashlight but left it off. Then she looked at the line of shut doors and reality hit her all over again. Fran was dead. Someone was out of their room. As her eyes adjusted to the dim glow of the fire, she turned the corner and walked right into Auden.

Lydia swallowed the yelp in her throat just as Auden reached out and placed his hands on her shoulders. Startled, they stared at each other. Lydia blushed, a lifelong weakness, as she remembered her T-shirt emblazoned with a spool of thread and a needle under the bright pink words: SEW OVER IT. Forty years old and wearing a shirt with a catch phrase. But what was worse was Auden's T-shirt: UVA class of 2006. With holes in the sleeve, the shirt looked almost transparent, clearly loved. And, well, in a way, sort of revealing. The shirt clung to his shoulders but hung past his hips. Auden might be strong, but he was still more skinny than ripped. Lydia tried not to notice he was wearing plaid boxer shorts.

Cheeks still hot, she stepped back, broke the almost embrace, and whispered fiercely, "What are you doing?"

Auden looked at her, the bright pink phrase on her shirt, and then back to her still red face, and answered, "Water?"

"Is that a question?"

"No, no, I meant . . . I . . . I needed to get some water; it's hot sleeping so close to the fire. . . ."

Lydia couldn't stop blushing. He looked like a runner. He looked like her first real crush in college. Oh, God, thought Lydia, he looked like he would put his hands on your face when he kissed you. And he was still talking!

"I'm glad I ran into you, actually," Auden said. The word "actually" hung awkwardly in the air for a moment, as if they could both see the letters in neon. If her face was red before, now it was positively scarlet.

"Before she . . . before she died, did Fran tell you . . . she had big news. Did she tell you?"

Lydia reeled. The hallway promise, just the night before: *We'll have time to talk*. But they never did.

"No." Lydia looked at her bare feet. "She said she had something she wanted to talk to me about. And then. And then. . . ." Lydia felt the tears leaking out, even as she closed her eyes, willing herself to stop crying.

"I think you should know. Why don't we talk in the living room for a minute?" And with that he walked back to the long couch facing the glowing fire.

He folded up the blanket he'd been using and sat down. When Lydia did the same, he turned slightly to face her and said quietly, "Fran was dying."

Lydia sputtered, "What? I know! I found her. What on earth. . . ."

Auden interjected, "No. Fran had cancer. And it was terminal. She found out just a few weeks ago. She'd already sold you the store. But I think she was starting to worry about how to say goodbye, how to get her affairs in order. She came over to my cabin on Friday, before y'all got here, and told me. We were supposed to talk about what would happen to the Laurels later this weekend. But now . . ."

Fran had cancer? Auden knew and she didn't? Why hadn't she noticed her friend was sick? Why hadn't Fran said something sooner? Did the rest of the group already know? Why hadn't anyone said anything? Lydia felt faint. Auden waited for her to make some sort of reply, but Lydia had no idea what to say.

Charlie had followed her out of her room and settled in the living room while they talked. Even though Charlie now looked half asleep on the floor between them, Lydia suddenly announced, "Charlie needs to go out," and then turned and walked toward the door next to the picture windows that led out to the closest thing the Laurels had to a yard. She needed a moment to think. But then she stopped at the door, remembering the bear warning from her first night. She looked back at Auden, worried.

"What's wrong?" he asked, seeing her wrinkled forehead.

"Bears."

"Bears?"

"Bears."

"No, I heard you, I just don't understand why you're worried about bears," Auden elaborated.

"Fran already told me about the bears. That I shouldn't take Charlie out to pee in the middle of the night because of the bears. That it wasn't safe. I had just forgotten for a second. He's housebroken. He can hold it. Beats getting eaten by a bear," she added, lamely.

"Um, we do have bears here. But this is the middle of February. The bears are hibernating. Now, if this were May? It might be a little risky. But not now, especially not in this weather." Auden looked a little disappointed that he had to clarify for Lydia that bears hibernate in the winter.

"But last night. I heard this ruckus on the front porch, and Fran said it was a bear. . . . Why would Fran have said that?" Lydia asked, trying to keep her voice light. What she really wanted to say was, "Why did my friend keep lying to me, even about the little things?"

"Lydia, did you ever really talk to Fran about Hillside?" Auden asked, softening his voice like he was talking to an upset child.

Lydia stared at him. Hillside? What on earth was Hillside. Was this yet another secret she had no idea about?

"The rehab center?" Auden prompted Lydia, still lost in her thoughts.

"Oh, right, yeah, Fran mentioned that. Someone had been mad at her about her resistance to the center. I guess she wanted it to be a nature center? It really didn't sound like a big deal." Well, it hadn't at the time, she thought to herself.

"Was that all she said?" Auden frowned. "What about the vote?"

"The what now?"

"The vote. Lydia, do you understand how this mountain works? When the Dalton kids decided they wanted to sell the place, the fate of the house went to a vote—all the original families on the mountain got to have a say. Three bids made it to the final stage: the rehab center, the nature center, and . . ."

Auden fell silent. They sat in the darkness, looking at the fire. Lydia thought about a professional development course she had taken once as a teacher. Something about "active listening." Lydia tried to listen. Actively.

Auden continued, "You know, Fran was an amazing woman. I loved her. Honestly, Lydia. Like a bonus mom/grandmother, if that makes sense? And she looked after me, hiring me to be a caretaker, all that. But you can't . . . I can't . . . be a caretaker forever. It's not a career. It's not a long-term life. I want my own space. Right now, I live in a converted barn on the Ermentrout property, the one house higher up than this one. Again. It's fine. It works. But it's not a life. When the Dalton house became an option, I could see it. I could see the future in a way that finally made sense. One of the bids was mine, Lydia."

Lydia managed to say, "Oh."

"Fran and some of the others wanted to turn the house into a nature center. There was a coalition in support of Hillside. And then I put a bid in to turn the house into a split commercial and residential property. I would live there but also have my wood-working studio there. And sell the furniture I made."

"Oh. I am so sorry that didn't work out, Auden. That sounds amazing, but I don't really see . . ."

Auden cut her off, speaking with more passion than she had seen from him yet, "It's money, Lydia. Money and dreams. She convinced me she had the majority backing her nature center. I lost the money I'd spent trying to get the place zoned for residential and commercial use. But I believed in the nature center. But she didn't. She didn't have the vote. Lumpkin County Wildlife needed a sizeable donation to make the center work. She told people she would give the money. But she didn't. And now we have Hillside. She should have told you. Things like that have consequences."

And with that, Auden opened the door and let the poor dog out into the stormy night.

Charlie was a lazy dog, so he happily took care of business quickly and ran back in to sit by the warmth of the fire.

Lydia scrambled for the right response. It had all felt so . . . raw. He seemed exhausted by the conversation, with nothing left to say.

"Thanks, Auden. And thanks for telling me. For telling me about Fran. About Hillside. Thanks for keeping watch tonight." With that, Lydia started toward the hallway to her bedroom.

"I'm here if you need anything," Auden answered as she walked away.

She had never had that "important" talk with Fran. And now, even though she knew what Fran had wanted to tell her, she couldn't help but wish she'd found the time before it was too late. She crawled back into bed. There was no point in rattling off a litany of fabrics. No point in counting. Turning off the flashlight, Lydia stared into the darkness. Fran was gone. The retreat was a disaster. She'd been invited to her ex-husband's wedding. Amy thought she was a killer. There was no more lasagna. Some part of her recognized these problems were on very different scales, but it just felt like opening a hall closet and getting hit by an avalanche of crap. Worst of all, somehow, Lydia feared the worst was yet to come.

Sleep evaded her. Had Lydia made a mistake not confiding in Auden about the M's? Was Auden right about "the vote"? Was a crushed dream enough to drive someone to murder? Charlie snored away, oblivious to her turmoil. Throwing her quilt off again, Lydia grabbed the flashlight and headed back to the living room. He had been honest with her. She owed him the same. She'd tell Auden everything.

It took Lydia a minute to realize what she was seeing. Her late-night confession to Auden died on her lips. There he was, the too-handsome caretaker she had expected. But sitting next to him was Heather. Heather.

Heather's red hair shone in the firelight. She perched on the couch that Auden had been using as his bed, her whole body turned toward him in the half-dark. Lydia didn't mean to spy, but she found herself at the edge of the firelight, watching the whispered conversation, unable to force herself forward.

Auden nodded his head as Heather tucked her hair behind her ear, multiple cartilage piercings sparkling. Heather said something Lydia couldn't hear, and then Auden patted Heather on her knee.

Lydia had no right whatsoever to be jealous. None. But she did feel a small prick of satisfaction when Auden's hand left Heather's knee the minute Lydia stepped into view. She wasn't above ruining the moment.

"Oh, Lydia," was all Heather said.

What had they been talking about? Why was Heather out of her room? Hadn't they agreed to stay in their rooms until the morning?

"Hey, Heather. Hi, Auden. Sorry to interrupt you guys." No, she wasn't. "I couldn't sleep so thought I would get a glass of water, so, um . . ." Lydia forced herself to walk past them to the kitchen, using her flashlight to illuminate a path. She filled a heavy clear glass with cold water, took a sip, then steeled herself for the return trip past the strange tête-a-tête in the living room. Glass in hand she walked back toward her room, trying to act naturally.

"I'm going to hit the hay. See you two in the morning," she said, flatly. She sounded like a mom at a sleepover party.

"Good night, Lydia," Auden replied, awkwardly standing as he said it. He turned to Heather, who was still sitting on the couch, "Heather, I'm glad we got to talk. But it's getting late. See you in the morning?"

Lydia hid the smile she felt at his polite but firm dismissal of the young woman.

"Thanks for listening, Auden. Thanks for . . . everything. Sorry you can't sleep, Lydia," Heather added sharply, as she stood as well and turned to leave the room and head upstairs.

Lydia took another sip of her water, trying to find an excuse to linger until Heather was gone. Auden seemed to do the same as he walked over to the fireplace and grabbed the poker and jabbed at the dying embers, stirring up a little more flame.

"Everything okay?" Lydia asked, hoping she sounded concerned rather than nosey, when in reality she felt equal amounts of both.

"Heather's just freaked out. She'll be all right." Auden waited, seemingly unsure if Lydia wanted to talk or head back to bed.

"Good. That's good," Lydia replied. "Are you good?"

"I'm good," Auden said and paused again. "Did you want to talk about anything, Lydia?"

"Me? No. I'm good. Good night!" and, flinching at her dorky response, she headed back to her room.

Back in bed, again, Lydia wondered what Heather had meant when she said, "Thanks for everything." She wondered why Auden had put his hand on her knee like that. She wondered why she was wondering. Even sleep, when it finally came, felt tangled and heavy.

# Chapter Nine

**Sunday**

The morning air felt like a splash of cold water as she turned in her sleep and her face came free from her quilt cocoon. Auden had kept the fire going in the main room, so it wasn't exactly freezing, but there was no doubt that the generator was still out. The day before came rolling back to her, more brutal than the cold air.

Fran was gone. Murdered. The M's, crying at Fran's betrayal through the thin wall of the bathroom. The whole nasty story about "the vote." Heather and Auden in the firelight. She still hadn't said anything about the M's to Auden, which was surely the right call. Surely. Did she really believe the M's could commit murder?

No. Fran's death had nothing to do with the M's. Which meant she hadn't solved anything yet. Did knowing about "the vote" change anything? Lydia couldn't be sure. They had to get help and they had to get out of that house. Lydia untangled herself from her bed and threw on yet another pair of black leggings and a T-shirt; this one read, COFFEE FABRIC THREAD. Which were her essentials, more or less in order. The first thing she needed to face the day was coffee. True, she had told the group not to leave their rooms until eight. But glancing at her watch, she realized it was only seven. She couldn't spend an hour in her room, waiting and worrying. Wanting coffee. If she got up early and made coffee and breakfast, that just meant that she was being thoughtful, not reckless. Surely. Besides, she really, really needed coffee.

After Graham, Lydia had ditched most of the traditions that had marked her married life. She couldn't remember the last time she had been to a tapas restaurant, much less ordered a wine *flight*. But Graham had gotten her hooked on good coffee, and she still couldn't bring herself to go back to the pumpkin spice instant coffee pods of the long-gone past.

The house had a French press, and she had brought ground beans from PeriDOUGH, the local donut shop, so she was prepared, even without power, to start her day the right way. Coffee was truly an addiction, but this morning she needed the comfort of the ritual as much as anything else.

Thankfully, although the cabin was far up the mountain, it was still on the municipal water line, so she had tap water and a kettle on the stove to use, even in the ice storm. And she had always liked her coffee black anyway. The pan of cinnamon rolls from the morning before still had a few scraps that she piled onto a plate.

Blue-and-white mug steaming, she sat down facing one of the huge picture windows. Auden was still asleep on the couch. She noticed how long his eyelashes looked against his cheeks. She willed herself to look out at the mountains. Early in the morning, with the sleet still falling, most of the long vantage was lost to haze. But the closest ridge line still offered the texture of winter, the promise of more mountains and more forests just behind it. She willed the sun to rise bright and hot, but she knew it was hopeless. It was already seven in the morning, and it felt more like late afternoon as the icy rain slashed down.

She knew she had to get breakfast ready for everyone else, but she gave herself just a little longer in front of the window, even though her coffee cup was empty now. She wanted to pretend yesterday hadn't happened, just for a moment more. Suddenly, as if it had simply materialized there, a deer appeared on the grass. It was small, but not exactly a baby. Surprisingly more gray than brown. Lydia had always loved deer. Growing up in New England, she had seen them all the time, but since her family didn't hunt, they felt more like forest friends than anything else. Her general response was to say, "Aww!" each time she saw one, even though down in Georgia that tended to make people laugh, even sneer a little. It felt like the first good omen, that slender pale deer on the small yard—something gentle and wild and not a threat. But why was it out in the storm? Not such a good omen, after all. As if in response to her fears, the deer started and darted back into the dark woods. Lydia shook her head.

Auden was up, rubbing his face, and she tried not to notice how cute his disheveled hair looked. It was time to get breakfast ready, she reminded herself, smiling at him and standing to head toward the kitchen. Surely that small deer had shelter somewhere?

"Hey, Lydia, could I get your help?"

She started. She had been so engrossed in that small deer, and that handsome man nearby, that she had completely failed to hear Heather walk up and stand beside her chair. Heather looked at her expectantly and then repeated herself, "Lydia. Can I get your help?"

Lydia brushed the crumbs of day-old cinnamon rolls off of her shirt and simply replied, "Sure. What do you need?"

"Do you mind coming up to my room?" Heather asked, but before Lydia could answer, she had turned and started toward the staircase. It seemed that everyone had tacitly agreed that staying in groups for nighttime, not daytime. The wan light coming through the windows did help to make the house feel less menacing. She would be fine with Heather.

Lydia shrugged her shoulders and followed. Breakfast for the others would have to wait. When they went upstairs to the Rainbow Room, Heather ushered her in and then closed the door and started to whisper.

"Listen," Heather hissed, "you need to hear this. Last night, after dinner, after, well, after everything, I just couldn't fall asleep. This room has its own fireplace with a gas starter, and I thought a fire would make me feel . . . well . . . safer, I guess. But when I went to turn on the gas to start the fire . . .," Heather pointed at the pipe that fed the fireplace, ". . . that was unscrewed."

Was that why Heather had been talking to Auden? Why didn't Auden tell her that? Why didn't they tell her that in the moment?

Heather stared at Lydia, clearly expecting a shocked response.

When Lydia didn't offer the reaction she was expecting, Heather huffed in frustration and continued, "Someone opened this. Gas was pouring into my room. I had the windows shut tight because of the storm. If I had gone to sleep, with that valve open. . . . Lydia, do you see what I'm saying? I think someone was trying to . . . hurt me."

They were both silent. And they both knew the word Heather meant was "kill" not "hurt." Had whoever killed Fran tried to kill Heather next? Given Heather's white face and hands twisted together in front of her, Lydia could tell that was the conclusion that Heather had reached.

"But *why*?" Lydia sputtered. She knew she should have been comforting Heather, but it just didn't make sense.

"What do you think I stayed up all last night thinking about?" Heather sat down on the edge of her colorful bed. "Here's the thing, Lydia. I know you loved Fran. We all loved Fran. It's just that there was more to Fran than you knew. Does that make sense?"

Twenty-four hours ago, Lydia would have vehemently denied the idea that she didn't know everything about Fran, her fairy godmother, her magical life-changing friend. But now? After what Auden had told her last night? After what she'd heard from the M's? What else didn't she know?

Lydia nodded, and it was enough to prompt Heather to continue.

"Before you showed up, Fran was frantic to find a way to keep Measure Twice afloat. She'd been encouraging friends to invest in the store. And I'm not sure those conversations were always pleasant. I've been weirded out by Clark lately,"

Clark? Lydia had been sure Heather was about to mention the M's.

"It is a big leap to go from being weirded out by someone to accusing them of murder," Lydia pointed out, trying to adjust to the idea of Clark as a murderer.

"You don't know the whole story. You know how Fran would still come to help with openings sometimes, even though she moved out to this house? Well, a few weeks ago, it was just me and Fran opening the store. Before we were even technically open, Clark came roaring into the store, practically spitting nails. I was *so* curious, but Fran took one look at him and ushered him straight back to the break room." Heather paused, sensing Lydia was still unconvinced.

She continued. "That's when it got weird. I could hear raised voices, but I couldn't hear anything specific. I just chalked it up to Clark being hot and bothered about something pointless, and I went back into the storeroom to get the new needle minders. But they were still arguing when they walked to the front door. I heard Clark say to Fran, 'You have no right. You're playing with fire, Fran. This is the sort of business that gets people killed.'"

Heather stopped and looked at Lydia. Killed? Clark had said that to Fran?

"Heather, that sounds like a threat," Lydia admitted.

"I know, right? And if Fran had said something about it, laughed it off, I wouldn't have been so struck by it. But just as they got to the front door of the store, Clark noticed me. I had come out of the storeroom to set up the new accessories display.

Clark just looked at me and said, '"You heard me,' and walked out the door, got in his car, and drove off," and with that, Heather held up her hands, echoing her disbelief from the time.

"What did Fran say?" Lydia asked, shocked by the latest twist in the story.

"That's what I was trying to say before. Fran didn't say a thing! She just went right back to work, opening the store as if nothing had happened. Every time I tried to bring it up, she just changed the topic."

"Okay," Lydia admitted, "I see your point. I think there were things I didn't know. And Fran had been really desperate to find a way to keep the shop from going bankrupt. Somehow Clark got involved. But she sold the shop to me, Heather. . . ."

Was Lydia imagining it, or did Heather flinch at that pronouncement?

"So, why murder? Now? And even if I bought that idea, which I'm not sure I even do, how does that get us here, to Clark's trying to hurt you?" Lydia gestured back to the offending valve.

Heather put her head in her hands, her bold red hair horribly bright against her skin. The room felt dark and close even though it was technically morning.

Raising her head, Heather said, "Lydia, I don't know. But what if Fran knew something? Or did something? And Clark thought I was in on it? Maybe he thought I was in on it from the beginning; maybe he thought she filled me in that morning after their confrontation. Maybe he just knew I would suspect him and wanted to keep me quiet. I don't have all the answers. But I don't think we're safe here. And I had to tell you. You need to be careful. We both do. Don't tell anyone what I just told you. Promise me, Lydia," Heather added, staring straight into Lydia's eyes. Heather didn't say a word about Auden, and Lydia had no idea why, but she played along.

"Heather, I won't tell anyone what you told me if that's what you really want, but don't you think it would be better to get this out in the open? Tell the group about the fireplace, at least. Maybe even confront Clark?" Lydia offered. There were already too many secrets in the Laurels, and Lydia was starting to think secrets were far too dangerous. Plus, there had to be a good explanation for the scene with Clark, and they owed him a chance to tell his side.

"No," Heather hissed. "That just means he knows that you know, and you could be next. God, Lydia, I know you're such a sweetheart," but the way she said "sweetheart" made it sound like an insult, "but you need to be realistic. Don't. Tell. Anyone." With that, Heather stood up, tucked her flame-red hair behind her ears, and left the room, Lydia trailing behind, bewildered. How was she supposed to go about the day as if she were none the wiser about Clark? Lydia had a hard time keeping secrets under the best of circumstances, but now she felt overstuffed with them, worried that at any moment she'd blurt out the wrong confidence.

When they got back to the main room, Lydia realized most of the house was still asleep. Quietly, she went into the kitchen and put some muffins Fran had brought into the oven to warm and got another French press of coffee started.

Heather stayed in the living room, working on her EPP, seemingly her ordinary self. Lydia marveled at the young woman's composure.

The power outage had seemed to slow time itself. The light was always somewhere between dusk and twilight. The only sounds were the never-ending patter of the icy rain and the creaking of the old house in the storm, complemented by the even older grandfather clock, marking the hours. Lydia tried to pull together a sense of an agenda for the day, almost laughing when she thought of her printed-out itinerary from only a day before.

Lydia wasn't scared, exactly. And she wasn't angry . . . exactly. She just wanted it all to stop. She didn't want Fran to be dead. She didn't want Heather to be in danger. She wanted the stupid rain to stop. She wanted to go home. But that was not going to happen. And she needed to get herself together. She needed music. She went back to the Flower Room and grabbed her Sports Discman.

Walking back toward the kitchen, she saw Auden putting on a heavy winter jacket and raised her eyebrows in a silent question.

"I am going to try to at least walk the perimeter of the property. I'll be able to see if the ice is breaking up at all or if any trees have fallen down. It might amount to nothing, but I want to try," he added, shrugging as he pulled on a knitted winter hat. Lydia wondered briefly if Fran had made it for him. If he didn't want to tell her about Heather, she wasn't going to tell him she already knew. Instead, she watched him walk out the front door, and then looked down at the machine in her hands.

Her Sports Discman. The pride of her early college days, walking across campus with that jammed in a coat pocket (it never really fit) and listening to Dave Matthews Band and Dispatch and all the other "boys with guitars" bands she couldn't get enough of in the early oughts. It was bright, bright yellow and even had a sporty Velcro hand holder.

It had been quickly replaced by the iPod, the iPod Shuffle, the different iPhones that had followed. But Lydia was a pack rat, and somehow it had survived move after move, until finally landing in her little After Graham apartment life in Peridot.

When Lydia had started first dreaming up the SEW RELAX-ING retreat, she knew she wanted people to leave their "devices" at home. The Laurels had a landline, so she hadn't been worried about contact to the outside world, although now she knew better. At the time, it had seemed like a good challenge, leaving the clicks and posts and likes of daily life behind. But it posed a problem: music. Lydia *needed* music, especially after a hard day or when she felt overwhelmed, which was more often than she wanted to admit. Enter the Sports Discman! All the Discman needed to be operational was a few batteries and a total lack of vanity. Lydia had both.

Which was how she ended up in the kitchen of the Laurels, putting out breakfast food while jamming to "Satellite" by the Dave Matthews Band on a storm-filled Sunday morning. Even though they had all decided to get up at 8 AM, folks were still making their way to breakfast. Clark and Martha were sitting in the summer room, while Cynde was knitting next to the fire. Amy, it seemed, was still sleeping.

Lydia tried to just enjoy the nostalgia trip of her music, but then she heard voices from the summer room. She kept her eyes focused on the breakfast, but tried to hear the conversation happening nearby.

"Clark, she'll hear us," Martha hissed across the table to him. And in fact, in that moment, Lydia did hear Martha. Perfectly. The fatal flaw of the beloved Sports Discman was that it absolutely devoured batteries. And in that exact moment, the music had stopped, and even though she still had earphones in, headband earphones in bright yellow, she could hear them having what they clearly thought was a private conversation.

"No, she won't. Look at her. Listening to music on that prehistoric machine," and when he jerked his head in her direction, Lydia made sure to keep dancing around the kitchen as if she were still listening to music. She was being dishonest, but at this point, she wanted answers too much to care. This was her chance, without actually confronting Clark, to learn why he had argued with Fran and why, maybe, just maybe, he had killed her and tried to kill Heather. Surely the motive outweighed the means? Lydia left the headphones in, kept dancing and getting breakfast ready, and listened as hard as she could.

"Everyone thought Fran was such a sweetheart," Clark muttered, as he leaned across the table in the summer room with Martha. There was that word again. "I know you're not supposed to speak ill of the dead, but that doesn't mean we should have to lie."

Martha nodded, years of listening to her friend, Mary, having clearly taught her that silence was the best encouragement sometimes. Martha crossed her legs at the ankle and waited.

"I don't even know how she found out. They didn't press charges. They just said . . . it was implied that—maybe somewhere else would be a better fit. It's not like I was being greedy. I was just taking what was fair. . . ."

Clark continued. "I tried to explain that to Fran, but she could be so stubborn." Clark went on in an excellent mimic of Fran's voice: "'Stealing from a church, Clark; how could you?' It wasn't stealing!" Clark practically squeaked as Martha unconsciously shifted away from him. "They didn't pay me nearly enough to run all the finances. I was twenty years old and taking care of my whole family. My dad just drank away his paycheck. I needed to help my little brother. Besides, I just rerouted some funding. They didn't even notice for two years. Two whole years! How important could that money have been to them? We needed it. They didn't."

Martha finally entered the conversation, "But they did notice? And they fired you? And Fran found out? How?"

"Fran was just being Fran, knowing everything about everyone. I guess some old lady came into the shop to buy kitten-printed quilting fabric and they started talking," Clark said with a sneer. "Fran finds out this woman is from Smackover, Arkansas. Why did I have to come from a town with such a stupid name? Of course, Fran made the connection. And mentions my church."

At this point, Clark switched back to his eerily accurate imitation of Fran's voice: "'Oh Smackover! How fun is that! I wonder. You don't know the Cossatot Primitive Baptist Church there by any chance, do you?'"

Switching back to his own voice, Clark softly wailed, "Why did I ever tell her the name of that church? I didn't think it mattered. How was she ever going to meet someone from Smackover, much less my little church? But she did. And the woman was more than ready to gossip. The whole sordid tale came tumbling out, with this lady having no idea that Fran actually knew me!"

This whole time, Martha had barely moved. It seemed as if Clark had forgotten she was even there. "It could have ended there, but no, Fran took it further. She used it against me. This was before Saint Lydia arrived. . . ."

*Saint Lydia?* Suddenly she stopped listening so intently to Clark and Martha. Saint Lydia? Is that what they called her? It should have been a compliment, but the way Clark said it made it sound like—well, sound like she was a joke. If she wanted to find out what happened to Fran, she had to pay attention. She stored the insult away to deal with later and concentrated on the quiet words drifting from the sun porch.

"She wanted me to invest in the shop. Otherwise maybe the Botanical Garden would hear about my past. Maybe they wanted a board chair with a little more integrity. I told her it was blackmail.

She said it was encouragement." Clark paused, overwhelmed with anger for a moment, lost in the memory.

"She dropped the whole thing, of course, when Lydia bought the shop. She didn't need my money anymore. But she never let it go, my secret. It was just a matter of time. . . ."

# Chapter Ten

"Muffins!" Cynde exclaimed as she walked into the kitchen, startling Lydia, Clark, and Martha. Lydia made a show of taking off her headphones as Clark and Martha joined them in the kitchen.

"They're Fran's muffins, aren't they? Of course, they are; who else makes pumpkin muffins with this much sugar on top?" Then Cynde caught herself and said, "Made. Who else made muffins like these?"

She sat down heavily at the table, while piling three muffins onto a small plate. Amy, who must have woken up while Lydia tried her hand at spying, sat down next to her, after cutting one muffin in half and leaving the other half of it behind on the platter.

Lydia wanted to tell Heather what she had just heard—that it was blackmail; that was the secret between Fran and Clark, what they must have been fighting about that day in the store. She couldn't think of a way to break free of the group, so she decided to wait until later and do her best to feign normalcy in the meantime. The muffins helped. Cynde was right; no one made muffins like Fran.

They were soft but somehow not heavy. And then the sugar crunched just right, lightening the cinnamon spice blend. By now the whole group had made their way to the kitchen table.

Auden was telling Cynde and Heather about how Fran used to leave muffins at his cottage door when she came up to stay at the Laurels. Clark still sat with the M's, whispering conspiratorially. It would be too much to say the group was happy, but it was a far cry from the despair of the night before. Lydia thought back to her irrelevant itinerary. Last night was supposed to be a group game. And this morning was supposed to be the second sewing session.

If they even managed to have another sewing session, it would have to be hand sewing. That would take some time to set up. Obviously, there had been no game the night before. Looking at the table, now, however, Lydia thought it might work. A silly game with prizes to pass the time. Surely, the sun would be out by lunchtime, the ice would melt, and they would be able to call the police and get off of the mountain.

She decided to try.

"So. Okay. So, before . . . well, I mean, when we were planning. Me and Fran. Fran and I? God. Okay. We wanted . . . I still want a chance for us all to get to know each other a little better. We brought a game to play together this weekend."

She looked at the group in front of her, loaded down with muffins and coffee.

"I think it would be a great way to honor Fran to still play the game." She didn't miss Clark rolling his eyes. She may not have taught for years, but she still knew how to catch an eye-roll. She forged ahead.

"Growing up, my family used to play this game called 'Who Said What?'" Lydia smiled, recalling past summers of games at her family reunions. Oh, if Cousin Oscar could see her now, she wasn't sure if he would cringe or laugh. Knowing Oscar, he would probably do both simultaneously. "And we thought, or *I think*, it would be fun to play this morning."

She looked at the faces around the table. Who would be the first to reject the idea? Instead, the room was quiet but for the sound of the storm still lashing the house.

"Okay. Give me one second," she added, cursing herself for not having brought the supplies with her to the table that morning.

Lydia hurried back to her room and grabbed the tote bag of supplies from one of her many bins. When she had packed the bag, she had imagined making s'mores and laughing as they got to know each other better. The memory felt absurd now.

Back at the table, she distributed the supplies for the game: "There are three note cards in front of you. Okay, not in front of you, but coming around the table," Lydia amended as she handed out note cards pulled from the bag. Then she reached back into the bag and pulled out a handful of pens held together with an old rubber band. These got passed around as well.

"On the red card, write down your answer to the following question: What would be your last meal?"

"Last meal? Like I'm in jail? What sort of game is this?" Clark asked, his voice a little too loud.

"A get-to-know-each-other game. Your perfect meal. Whatever. Just write it on the red card and then pass all the cards to me."

Lydia had already messed up the directions. They were meant to start with a blue card. At least no one knew any better. As they finished writing down their dream meals, Lydia handed out the score sheet: a single sheet of paper with blanks for guesses and a score tracker for the end of each round.

Three rounds, eight chances to score in each round, with Auden standing in for Fran. Each round, each player had to guess "who said what." Each correct guess earned that player a point, so a score card was needed to keep track across the three rounds.

Lydia's family was full of academics and lawyers, smart people who were supportive if a little baffled by her recent life decisions. The family games of "Who Said What?" were legendary and always very, very competitive. Especially if players were allowed to choose the questions.

This time, Lydia preset *all* the questions. First round: last meal. Second round: one item you would take to a desert island. Third: a sewing retreat special—What fabric store would you choose to spend a thousand dollars in, Measure Twice excepted.

Lydia forced herself to focus as the red cards were passed back to her. Charlie had settled at Auden's feet. It wasn't a sign. Nope, definitely not a sign that Auden was a super awesome person.

Lydia read the cards they had passed back out loud to the group, not naming the authors, as each person at the table scanned the others, trying to figure out who belonged to what answer. Most were pretty obvious. Martha had the nerve to say deviled eggs. It was Clark who said Chateaubriand. Auden didn't even know what it was, and Clark clearly just wanted a chance to explain how refined his palate was. The only real curveball came from Amy, whose last meal request was Little Caesar's pizza and Crazy Bread. It wasn't gross; it was just sad.

"With his correct guess about Clark, Auden is currently in the lead. Now, the second-round question is this: What one item would you take to a desert island? Assuming that you have food and water figured out. Don't say a knife. Make it something interesting!"

The group looked at their blue cards and winced at Lydia's enthusiasm. But they filled them out and passed them in nonetheless.

Lydia glanced at the first card in her hand and then read aloud, "A sewing machine." Cynde laughed out loud, which was a relief to hear.

"A sewing machine? Where are you planning on plugging that in on your desert island?" Cynde asked, but kindly, with no edge. Before anyone could reply and give away who wrote it, Lydia steamed on to the next one, "The Bible." And then the next one, "The Bible."

"Well, how are we supposed to know which one said which Bible?" squawked Clark, pointing at the M's.

"Good luck!" Was all that Lydia could come up with as she read through the rest of the cards. Once they had figured who said what, she helped count up the points as she walked around the table.

"Auden, you have lost your spot. Heather is now in the lead!" Lydia announced. Auden took the disappointment well, simply reaching down to scratch Charlie between the ears. Heather looked unenthused, but then again, that was fair, wasn't it?

Heather had said she would take the Leonardo DiCaprio and Claire Danes version of *Romeo + Juliet* to the island with her. Lydia had seen that movie in the theaters, on a terrible high school date. It made her happy to think someone Heather's age loved the movie as much as she did.

All things considered, the game was going okay. She had just the question to end the game and bring a little more happiness into what would clearly be remembered as one of the worst weekends of all of their lives.

"You have a thousand dollars and one hour in any fabric store of your choice. Where do you go?" In a way, it was a selfish question, since Lydia just wanted another reason to daydream about the Cloth House, a small, luxurious store she had been to once in London with her best friend, Jes. She still dreamed about the velvet ribbons. Nothing in there was cheap, but everything was beautiful.

"Measure Twice is not an option, so no hurt feelings there," Lydia added. The cards, green this time, were passed up for the last time.

Again, it started out smoothly. Amy had said JoAnn's, which was just about as depressing as her Little Caesar's last meal. Cynde had said Fabric Universe, a beloved discount fabric warehouse south of Atlanta, which Lydia considered a perfect answer. A thousand dollars might buy you the whole Fabric Universe, displays included. Auden had answered, "Measure Twice, anyways," which made her flush red, much to her chagrin.

In a terrible echo of that embarrassing family round long ago, no one managed to guess Heather's answer: A Stitch in Time. The store had been closed for years. An out-of-the-way shop near Snellville, no one thought Heather would have even heard of it, much less list it as her dream shopping spree. When Lydia read out the right answers, Martha was the first to comment, saying, "'A Stitch in Time,' now that's a name I haven't heard in ages. Just ages. Right, Mary?"

Mary nodded. "What are you doing talking about a store for us old-timers? No instant picture for their classes!"

That set the room back. Instant picture? "Oh! *Instagram*?" Lydia asked.

"Yes, that thing," Mary replied sharply. While Mary and Martha had been talking and Lydia had been trying to think of what on earth an instant picture was, other than a Polaroid, Heather had remained silent, staring at the floor. But when Mary turned her gaze on her, she offered, "Oh, yeah, I never actually went there. Of course. But my, my grandmother, the one who raised me? I've told you guys all about her; she loved that place. So, yeah, it seemed like a good answer or whatever. I mean, this is all pretend anyways, right?"

Heather's reply was so tense that the group fell silent again. Lydia had no memory of hearing about Heather's grandmother. Come to think of it, Heather never talked about her past, never even really talked about her life at all, just ways to help the shop and new items to consider ordering. What did Lydia even really know about the bright, fierce young woman at the table?

"Well, I would have put down Measure Twice if I had known I could get away with it," Cynde offered, with a smile directed at Auden. "Fran always had such a good eye for fabric, and now that you," gesturing to Lydia, "are bringing in all these new patterns, I feel like I have a project wish list a mile long. If I can get the hang of this garment-making business, I'm not sure what I am going to want to make next."

It was a cheesy compliment, but Lydia could have hugged the woman. Nothing got crafters more excited than a discussion of yet-to-be-started, or still-unfinished, projects. Clark took the bait first. "When I finish the Tamarack, I know exactly where I am heading next. That Portside Travel Set by Grainline has been calling my name. I'm already thinking about a deep yellow leather."

"Really?" Heather asked, getting into the spirit of the discussion. "Not me. As soon as we get more of the Lady McElroy Faces in, in that green background colorway, I'm making a jumpsuit. Maybe the Yari by True Bias. Soft, simple, and mostly dark. That's my speed."

Exactly what Lydia had imagined when she first met Heather! At least that was more like the Heather they all knew and loved. No one else in the room really considered jumpsuits. Come to think of it, she wasn't sure she had even seen the M's in pants, much less a jumpsuit or a romper.

As if she knew Lydia was thinking about her, Mary offered, "Not me. And after this weekend? I'm just not sure I want to make any more garments. Ever." The statement seemed to knock the wind out of the entire group. No more laughter about a silly game.

The whole point of the weekend was to prove the concept. Then Lydia could launch regular retreats and solidify a needed secondary stream of income. Now the room was silent, and the silence told Lydia that not only had she lost a friend and mentor the day before, she had also lost the hope that her business would thrive. Who would want to shop at a store connected to murder? Connected. That was laughable. The store would become a curiosity. It had taken so long to really figure out what she wanted, who she was. And now it was all gone, in an instant. Selfish. *You're being so selfish. Fran died yesterday,* she told herself. But the pain was still there, the pain of losing her dream.

"What about a flannel shirt?"

Lydia was so lost in grief that she literally jumped at the question before responding, "I'm sorry, what?"

"You know, like what I'm wearing now," Auden added, gesturing to his sleeve.

"What about it?" she replied, still baffled by the change of topic.

Auden furrowed his brow and spoke a little slower, "Could I make a flannel shirt? You know, with stuff from your store?" Martha smirked at Lydia's noticeable, now all-too-frequent, blush as she answered with far more information than Auden could possibly need or want: "A flannel button-down, absolutely. You would probably want the Negroni Pattern by Collete. And then, we just got some Kauffman Buffalo Plaid in, which runs about twelve dollars a yard. You would only really need two yards. Plus, we stock Tabitha Sewer buttons. And the machines at the shop all have button feet."

*Button feet?* she thought to herself. She was worse than Baby from *Dirty Dancing*, "I carried a watermelon." She needed to regroup.

"Okay, everybody, hand in your score cards. I'll tally up the points," Lydia said, holding out her hands to collect the cards. "Head out to the living room, and I'll be out in a second. AND, once I declare the winner, we actually have some prizes. Fran and I picked them out, so . . . anyway . . . out you scoot. I'm going to clean up in here, and then I'll be out in a minute to declare the victor!"

One by one their sad assembly made their way back into the living room. Lydia had been telling the truth; she and Fran had planned the game and had brought prizes for the winners. There was nothing extravagant—just some fun sewing swag from the store. The small gifts hardly seemed to matter anymore, but Lydia thought maybe it would lighten the mood a little.

Just as Lydia wiped the last coffee mug, Cynde spoke up from the kitchen table. Lydia was surprised to realize Cynde hadn't left for the warmth of the fireplace with the others.

"Hey, Lydia, could we talk for a minute?"

Lydia put down the blue-and-white mug and turned to her friend. Did Cynde know that Fran had been ill? If Auden knew, it was entirely possible that Cynde did as well. Is that what she wanted to talk to her about now?

She began, "Did you know . . .," but stopped when Cynde said the same thing, just a beat behind her. Then both women started again, "Of course you know . . .," and stopped again, awkwardly chuckling. Lydia mimed letting Cynde walk ahead of her and said, "Go, you go."

Cynde winced a little and took a deep breath, "I'm sure you know. I mean, you and Fran spent so much time together. But I just. I wanted to explain why I had such a hard time yesterday. You deserve to know. I loved Fran."

Lydia was shocked. She had expected Cynde to tell her Fran was sick. It seemed like every time she thought she knew where a conversation was headed this weekend, she was wrong. But when she thought about it, it made a sort of sense. And she could tell that Cynde just needed someone to listen. She continued in a voice that was barely a whisper. The others, chatting about the game in the living room, would have had to strain to hear her. Lydia hoped they didn't, even though she had already learned that the Laurels wasn't a house built for privacy.

"I didn't want the others to know. I'm sure you know. Like I said, you spend, I mean spent so much time together. Well, anyway, I'm a little older than Fran and all but, well, it's harder for my generation. . . ." Cynde grew quiet again. "I loved her," Cynde repeated, speaking more to her own hands clasped on the table in front of her than Lydia.

Lydia replied, "Of course, I mean we all. . . ."

Cynde stopped Lydia with an upheld hand. "No, Lydia, I *loved* her. I have for years. I mean, that laugh, right? Did you ever notice how she always folded her hands when she was listening? Almost like she was praying. Like listening to you was as important as prayer?"

Lydia knew at that moment, as far as Cynde was concerned, she wasn't even in the room.

"And it seemed possible. Fran had been alone for so long. I've always been alone. We always joked we'd be old women at the care home together, park our rocking chairs next to each other and gossip about all the other old ladies. Why not start that now? We don't have to be alone. I don't. I didn't. We could have been together. I would have taken care of her. Cut back my hours." There Cynde stopped, looked at Lydia with one eyebrow raised.

"I know. I mean, she told me. That she was sick. But doctors can be wrong. Sometimes people have years, not months. Love can be a lot of things. I wasn't greedy. I just thought, why do we have to wait for those rocking chairs? I told her in a letter. Got a stupid card with two rocking chairs on it. Tucked the letter inside. I'm not ashamed of who I am. Just because I don't talk about it all over the place. Fran wasn't ashamed. I wanted any time with Fran I could get."

As she said it, Cynde dropped her head into her hands. Lydia rested her hand on her friend's back.

Cynde seemed lost to the world. Lydia looked past her, to the side of the fireplace, and saw Amy sitting on the edge of the sectional, awkwardly looking away. Had she been listening? Lydia cleared her throat. Amy sat up immediately and pretended to fix a loose thread on her sweater. It was so obviously fake, and Lydia couldn't understand why she would even try to create the pretense.

"I'm so sorry, Cynde," she offered, and squeezing her friend's shoulder one more time, she left the kitchen. It had cost Cynde a lot to be that vulnerable, and Lydia knew that if she tried to hug her, it would just be the straw that broke the camel's back. The rest of the group was in the living room, expecting prizes, so she walked quietly back to her own room, still thinking about those rocking chairs.

Had Graham ever talked about her like that? Not that Graham was much of a talker, but still. He golfed, which took forever, so he must have talked about something to his work buddies, his connections. No, Graham would never have talked about her that way. But she never talked about him like that, either. They were nothing like a pair of rocking chairs.

Back in the Flower Room, Lydia pulled out the bin of supplies and notions she had packed for the retreat. Somewhere in there were the prizes. Fran had put them in a bag of some sort. Probably one of the million Measure Twice tote bags that filled Lydia's entire world. She pushed aside the extra rickrack and spare sets of pins. There. Another Measure Twice tote bag, handles tied together with a cute ribbon. Fran's handiwork. Inside she found the prizes they had picked out and a packet of letters.

She smiled as she looked through the prizes: a ten-dollar gift certificate to Measure Twice. A leather wraparound bracelet that doubled as a measuring tape. Lydia had already snagged one for herself when the shipment came into the shop. And then finally a small pair of scissors, the kind that sewists call snips. They were little, spring-loaded, and fit in a tiny matching leather holder. She had also already grabbed a pair of those.

And then there were the letters. A stack of letters also tied with a cute ribbon. They hadn't said anything about letters. Fran had done this on her own. Lydia untied the ribbon and counted. Six letters, each with the name of someone on the retreat. The envelopes weren't sealed and there were no addresses or stamps, so Fran had clearly meant to give them out at the retreat. Lydia knew she should take the prizes, put the cards away, and go back to the living room. She knew it. She totally and one hundred percent knew that those cards were none of her business as she opened the first one and read it as quickly as she could.

Then the next and then the next. Before she knew it, Lydia had read every letter except the one addressed to her. They were all, every last one of them, apologies. Clearly, Fran felt like she had a lot of apologize for, which would have surprised Lydia two days ago but definitely didn't anymore. She was trying to make things right in the time she had left. It was Fran's handwriting, no doubt about that, as she looked over the short missives. To Mary and Martha, she had written, "I hope I can earn your trust again." This made sense, given what Lydia had "overheard" the night before. To Cynde, she had said simply, "Maybe we need to find some rocking chairs." In light of Cynde's admission, the note broke her heart.

Clark's card was a perfect complement to what Lydia now knew of his past, a card that just said, "I like who you are, now." There was no note to Amy, which was fair, since she had been a last-minute addition to the retreat. She couldn't bring herself to read the card Fran had written to her, not yet. Instead, she placed the card on her bedside table next to her water bottle and vowed to read it later that day, in the privacy of her room, with no one waiting for her to return to the living room bearing gifts.

She would give them all their cards. Maybe tonight at dinner? Maybe at breakfast tomorrow, if they were still trapped by then? But as she flipped back through the cards, she realized she hadn't read Heather's yet, and opened the card to begin.

"Heather, I should have told you sooner. I know. I know everything. I know you are my daughter. I don't know why you lied to me. We have wasted too much time. I have wasted too much time. But we don't need to anymore." Lydia dropped the note.

Fran was Heather's mother. Heather was Fran's daughter. And Heather knew Fran was her mother. But did she know that Fran knew Heather knew? The room started to spin. Lydia forced herself to count to six as she breathed in, eight as she breathed out.

The group was still waiting for the prizes, but they all knew how disorganized Lydia was. They were probably listening to Mary and Martha discuss the more appropriate parlor games of their youth, convinced Lydia was just having a hard time finding things, when really, Lydia was struggling with finding too much. Too many lies. Too much truth. At this point, she wasn't sure which of the two scared her more.

# Chapter Eleven

"Lydia! Lydia!"

The sound of her own name shocked her out of her reverie. "One minute!" Lydia called down, trying to sound nonchalant, as she rushed down the stairs.

She had to pretend everything was the same as it had been twenty minutes earlier. Facing the group, Lydia channeled her middle-school teacher voice: "Okay! Cynde, it looks like you guessed the most answers correctly, so you win our first-place prize: a ten-dollar gift certificate to Measure Twice!" The group groaned, unimpressed by Lydia's creativity. "Oh, that's not all I've got!" she exclaimed, dramatically drawing another prize from the tote bag. "In second place, we have Mary. You've won this stylish leather measuring tape bracelet!"

No amount of enthusiasm in her voice could distract from the fact that Mary was as likely to wear that bracelet as she was a miniskirt. But Lydia plowed on, "And finally, in third place, we have Clark, who wins these adorable snips from Japan!"

She passed out the prizes. All three looked at each other and quickly exchanged them. Within what seemed like seconds, Cynde had the bracelet, Mary had the snips, and Clark had the gift card. It was a nice moment of levity in what felt like a day that had already lasted forever. And it still wasn't even time for lunch.

Lydia had started to tune out the old grandfather clock, its ringing bongs a part of the scenery, just like the angry lash of icy rain against the roof and windows. But as the group gathered themselves for the next task of the day, a loud bong broke the momentary silence. Lydia counted along in her head: ". . . ten, eleven, twelve."

"Lunch. I guess we should go ahead and have lunch. Although, to be honest . . .," Lydia paused, uncertain how to end the sentence. She had no idea what they would eat. Breakfast had been easy. Coffee and baked goods. That was more or less what she had planned originally. Dinner could be canned soup from the pantry and the cornbread Fran had made, she supposed.

But lunch was "a whole 'nother kettle of fish," as her dad used to say when she was a kid. The silence stretched out. Lydia started thinking about Mary's jelly beans. Just how many of those were stashed away in various pockets? Had she finished all her Combos from the drive up?

"I'll fix lunch." It was Clark who had spoken up, shocking the group. "Y'all just stay in here doing whatever you feel like doing, I suppose. I'll call you in when it's ready." With that, Clark walked into the kitchen without waiting for a reply or reaction.

The group scattered. Heather went straight to her room. Lydia wasn't ready to confront Heather just yet, so she let her go. Cynde went downstairs to look over some trim for her shirt. Auden started playing the world's slowest game of fetch with Charlie, rolling a tennis ball up and down the hallway of the main floor bedrooms.

Mary and Martha took their hand sewing out to the summer room and studiously avoided making eye contact with anyone else.

Looking around, Lydia realized she was alone in the living room with Amy. Oh, well, time to give that friendship another try.

Surprisingly, it was Amy who spoke first, saying, "I shouldn't have said it."

"What?" Lydia asked, utterly confused.

"That you might have killed Fran. I'm sorry. I didn't mean it. I've never been involved in a murder before, and Cynde was so sad. I just lashed out. I'm sorry. I shouldn't have. . . ."

"Thanks," Lydia replied, meaning it. "I think this is uncharted territory for all of us."

They were both quiet again.

"Did you mean it about going to Shenanigans?" Amy asked, breaking the silence.

"What?" Lydia asked, utterly confused yet again.

Amy responded calmly, speaking slowly as if that, perhaps, would help Lydia understand better. "Shenanigans. On the ride up to the Laurels, you mentioned to Cynde the idea of doing a girls' night out and seeing a comedy show. Were you serious?"

A girls' night? That conversation seemed like it belonged to a different lifetime. But here was Amy, voluntarily having a conversation with her, so Lydia decided to go with it. "A little, I guess. I don't have a date or a show in mind, but I have really been wanting to see something. It seems a shame to live in Peridot and never have gone, you know what I mean?"

"March seventh?"

"What?"

"Would March seventh work?" Amy asked.

Lydia hadn't heard so many sentences in a row from Amy ever.

"Theo Von is coming to Peridot. I noticed it when we drove over to the shop to pick you up. I love him. I've seen him three times in Atlanta. Do you think the Peridot show will be good?" Amy asked

Lydia had never heard of Theo Von. In fact, she had only been to see a comedy show once, when she was in college up north. The comedian had been drunk. The audience had been drunk. And instead of telling jokes, the whole night had devolved into insults hurled from the stage to the audience and back again. She'd left before the second act, and she could still hear the heckling and taste the terrible buffalo wings they had ordered in a sad attempt to "make a night of it."

That was all she had as far as comedy show experience went.

She improvised and asked, "Do you think he works well in smaller venues?" since she knew Shenanigan's couldn't be the biggest stop on anyone's tour.

It was a Hail Mary, but the question worked regardless, and Amy was off again. "It depends, as I'm sure you agree, since it all comes down to the vibe. I've seen him about fifteen times, by now"—Lydia didn't have to pretend look impressed, or shocked, at the number—"and I think he really works best with Southern audiences, you know? Since he's from Louisiana," Amy concluded, smiling at Lydia as if they were at a Theo Von fan club meeting.

Huh. Lydia would never have expected such depth of emotion about live comedy from someone whose favorite food was Little Caesar's pizza. And Crazy Bread. It was weird. And kinda cool. Lydia hoped she could keep saying the right thing.

"My brother loved him," Amy added quietly

"Your brother loved Theo Von?" Lydia asked, surprised by the new revelation.

"He died. My brother, not Theo Von," Amy added, still barely above a whisper.

"Oh, Amy, I am so sorry."

"It's a disease, you know?"

"Was it cancer?"

"What? No! Jackson was an addict. Addicted to Fentanyl. It wasn't his fault. Not really. People act like addicts are bad people. They aren't. They are just sick. He needed it at first. A back injury on the job. The doctor gave it to him, for goodness' sake. People look down their noses, but addicts need help, not judgment. He was at Hillside. That's why I knew about it. Before. It's a good place. An important place. They really tried with him. After his first stint, the entire family was hopeful. But he relapsed. And he took what he was used to taking before he got clean. It was just too much. And it killed him."

Lydia was too stunned to speak.

"He didn't mean to kill himself. He just didn't realize his body couldn't handle it. I don't blame Hillside. I really don't. But I miss him every day. That's why I love going to Theo Von's shows so much, if that makes sense."

"When did you say it was?" Lydia asked.

"March seventh," Amy replied automatically.

"You know what, I'm sure I could ask Heather to close the store that night. When we get back to town and civilization, Wi-Fi, all those wonderful things, let's get tickets. We'll bring Cynde, get some drinks?" Lydia suggested.

Amy's face broke into a smile. Lydia realized it was the first time she had seen the woman smile. All she said was, "I would love that," and then Clark called them all to lunch.

When they walked back into the kitchen, the others following behind, Lydia had to wonder how many times one person could be completely and utterly surprised in one weekend. At some point, would her brain just refuse to compute new revelations? Lydia had hoped Clark had a secret line on some boxed mac and cheese. Even if it were some gluten-free, dairy-free abomination he had brought with him, she was ready to be grateful. But instead, he had made . . . well. . .

"It's salade niçoise," Clark declared triumphantly.

And indeed, it was. The French classic. Clark had boiled some new potatoes and some eggs and had sliced them up and added fresh green beans and olives that had been brought up with a hope of a charcuterie board that had long been abandoned. Canned tuna and some olive oil, salt, and pepper from the pantry rounded it out.

It looked delicious.

Clark had even set the table with Fran's beautiful blue-and-white plates. The group sat down to eat, and for at least ten minutes, no one spoke. Meanwhile, Lydia set about finding something to drink.

As the rest of them kept eating, Lydia rummaged through Fran's pantry and found what she had been looking for: instant iced tea. A big canister of the powdery goodness. She decided to forgo checking the expiration date. Sometimes ignorance really was bliss.

In a cabinet, she found a large pitcher in the matching blue and white of the plates, and she used it to mix the instant iced tea. Was it traditional? No. Was it shameful? According to the M's, it was on par with Clark's penchant for dairy-free mac and cheese. But Fran had once admitted, late at night in the store taking inventory, that she had grown up on the stuff. It was a comfort, even if it was a secret one, and she always had some in her cabin in the mountains.

"Ta-da," Lydia said, as she set the pitcher down on the table.

Mary perked up, thinking it was the real deal sweet tea that they had actually finished the day before.

"Oh, you found some, you clever girl. That is just what this lovely little meal needs, a touch of something sweet," Mary beamed.

Clark cut in, "Sweet tea? We finished that yesterday. I checked."

But it was too late, Mary had already poured herself a glass and taken a more than dainty sip.

She started sputtering before Lydia even had a chance to explain. Martha was right behind her, taking a sizeable sip as well, and then equally indignant and disgusted.

The whole table froze, and then Amy broke out in loud, raucous laughter.

No one, up until that point, had ever heard her laugh, much less uncontrollably. There was another long pause, as Amy kept laughing and the M's decried the fake iced tea, and then the laughter started to spread around the table.

Suddenly, Lydia felt like she had never seen anything funnier in her life. Her whole body shook with laughter. Amy reached across the table, still laughing, and poured herself a tall glass of the offending drink. After taking a huge swig, she almost choked, laughing even harder.

"They're actually right. This is *terrible*," and she went on drinking and laughing.

The whole table followed suit, gulping down the artificially sweet drink, declaring it was disgusting, laughing, and then drinking some more. They only settled down when the pitcher was empty. The room felt lighter, even though no one could explain, now, what had been so funny in the first place.

Once she had caught her breath, Lydia told the table, "Why don't y'all take a minute to yourselves and how about we meet in the library in about an hour for the second session? I know sewing seems ridiculous at this point, but I think it might be nice to have something to do, you know? At least we can hand stitch the bias binding even with no power."

Everyone nodded, rising slowly as if exhausted. Mary and Martha volunteered to stay behind and clean up, and for once, Lydia didn't meet expectation and talk them out of it. Instead, she stood by the fireplace, uncertain. She didn't want to take a nap. There was obviously no question of leaving the house for any reason whatsoever. Auden had reported back that the ice made it more or less impossible to go more than a few steps down the drive. Clark, Cynde, and Heather were debating the next steps for their quilt coats.

That left Amy. It had been nice getting to know Amy earlier, but the conversation had been intense, and Lydia was tired of intensity. What she wanted was to be alone, but that scared her. She had already fed Charlie and let him out. She didn't have the patience to pick her EPP back up. Then she remembered another project she had thrown in her duffel bag at the last minute. Sure enough, when she went back to her room and rummaged through her things, it was there: her first ever attempt at embroidery. Well, that wasn't quite honest. Her calico rescue cat, Baby Lobster, had more or less obliterated her first attempt. She just chose not to acknowledge the incident.

Sewing garments was Lydia's main passion, but she was a glutton for punishment when it came to taking on new crafts and hobbies. She had invited a local sewist to the shop to do a class on embroidery and had completely fallen in love with the painstaking craft. Although none of her attempts during the class looked anything like the instructor's, she was determined to figure it out.

Back in the living room, in a chair close to the fire, Lydia got to work. Her piece of fabric was actually the back of what would eventually become a loose linen jacket. The linen was a deep, bright pink and she had it stretched taut across the embroidery hoop and stiffened it with a stabilizing fabric ironed on to the back.

As she got out her needle and embroidery floss, Auden sat down on the couch closest to her chair.

"That doesn't look like PEP," he said.

"PEP? You mean, EPP? Ha! No, this is embroidery. Still needles, but a different outcome altogether," and with that she tilted the hoop so he could see her progress.

"Blackberries, blackberries, blackberries," he read out loud, looking at what she had written on the linen in washable fabric ink.

So far, she had only managed to chain-stitch her way through the first "Bla" with the dark yellow thread she had chosen to pair with the pink fabric.

Most people, including everyone on the retreat, had already looked at her project and asked why Lydia was so obsessed with blackberries, which she had to admit was an understandable response.

Auden, however, seemingly lost in thought, simply said, "'All the new thinking is about loss.'"

Lydia almost dropped her embroidery in surprise. Her heart felt like it had been replaced with a disco ball.

"You know Robert Hass?" she asked Auden, incredulously.

"'Mediation at Lagunitas' is my favorite of his poems."

When Lydia didn't reply, Auden continued, "Remember? My name is Auden? English professor dad? Poetry with my pancakes?" he prodded her, smiling.

"Oh, right, yeah, I remember. Yeah, clearly, I love the poem. I mean, I'm embroidering it on a jacket. It's just that most people think I have a weird obsession with fruit. Clark asked me if it was some sort of series and the next jacket would say, "Banana, banana, banana," she admitted, smiling back at Auden.

She went on. "I was an English major in college. I still remember the first time I read this poem. It just felt like it made sense." She felt embarrassed by the admission.

"I know exactly what you mean," Auden replied. "That's how I felt the first time I read Robert Hayden's 'Those Winter Sundays.' Living on a mountain, I just felt like I understood exactly what it meant when he said 'the blueblack cold.'"

They were both quiet for a moment, listening to the sound of the icy, unrelenting rain. It was Sunday, Lydia realized. In the winter. And she heard the last lines of the poem in her mind, "'What did I know, what did I know // of love's austere and lonely offices?'"

What did she know? So much less than she had thought at the start of the weekend. She wanted to ask Auden so many things. Why did he live alone at the top of a mountain? What other poems did he love? Did he like to hold hands when he walked with a girlfriend? Did he have a girlfriend?

"Fran never told me."

"What?" Lydia asked, confused.

Auden repeated himself, slowly, "How did you end up buying the shop? Fran never told me."

Lydia paused. How could she possibly explain the moment that had changed her whole life? She decided to try her best to be succinct, even though it had never been her strong suit.

"I used to live in Atlanta, and I had been spending some time up in Peridot, at the store, taking sewing classes," she offered, aware that the tricky part was coming up.

"I guess it all comes down to timing. Fran couldn't keep the store afloat, financially, and she was looking for a buyer. I had, um, recently parted ways with my ex-husband, and I was looking for a new start. It clicked. And then everything happened. I'm sure Fran told you about what happened in Peridot last summer . . . the murders . . ."

But at that exact moment, just as she gathered the courage to try even one of the questions, Clark shouted at her from the top of the stairs that led to the lower level.

"Lydia, I have all my button options picked out. When on earth is the second session going to start? Or have you decided to make the afternoon 'personal time' instead?" he scoffed, making air quotations as he said it.

She sighed. "Of course, we're still having the second session, Clark. Put the buttons on the fabric so we can do a compare/contrast, and I'll be down in a second."

Stowing her embroidery away, she turned to Auden and tried to say how grateful she was for a moment of beauty and quiet in the storm of that weekend.

Instead, she said, "Don't feel any pressure to come. I know you didn't sew anything yesterday."

He laughed quietly and answered, "Yeah, if it's all the same to you, I think I'm going to set about getting more firewood stacked and checking for batteries for the flashlights. I'd feel better knowing we had backups. I'm going to try the old radio, too, and see if I can get a weather report."

"Of course. Thanks for doing all of that." And with the momentary spell of a winter Sunday broken, she went downstairs to lead the second session, telling herself that gorgeous men who loved poetry weren't hard to find. But she remained unconvinced.

Shaking her head to clear the thought of a handsome handyman from her mind, Lydia addressed the group gathered in the library: "Okay, folks. Let's get this next session started. I know this has been really hard on all of us, but I think Fran would want us to keep sewing, and, to be honest, I think it's best we all stick together, so let's go." Lydia tried to say it with a smile, but she knew they were all struggling. Still, they all tried their hands at folding bias tape around the edges of their jackets. She was grateful. The work would be a bit tedious, using handstitching instead of the machines, but it was better than nothing.

Well, not quite everybody. "Hey, Cynde, have you seen Amy since lunch?" Lydia asked, starting to feel a now-familiar twinge of foreboding.

"No, I think she might want to take a break from sewing? I tried to check in with her last night, but I got the sense she's just completely overwhelmed by what's happened," Cynde answered.

Heather spoke up, surprising the rest of the group, "Don't you think we're all completely overwhelmed? I mean, I worked with

Fran. She was," Heather gulped for air, "she was like a mother to me. Amy barely even knows . . . knew her."

Cynde held up her hands, palms open, like she was trying to calm a scared dog.

"I know, Heather. I know. How about we just focus on our coats for now? I would love your advice on what color bias binding to use?" And with that question, Cynde coaxed the young woman back into the session.

Lydia knew why Heather was acting so strangely, but she wasn't supposed to know. She tried to tackle her bias binding instead. Some people hated bias binding. Lydia loved it, even though she sometimes got turned around and almost got started in the wrong direction. Bias binding was more or less just a folded strip of fabric, cut on the diagonal so that it could stretch. You sewed it first on the outside of the neckline, and then folded it over and sewed it into the inside of the fabric. It captured the raw hem and left all the edges of the coat looking smooth and polished. That moment of folding it over and enclosing the hem felt like magic to Lydia.

It reminded her of a photography class she had taken in high school. You put what seemed to be a blank piece of paper into what seemed to be a tub of water, and then you watched as a photograph materialized. It was careful work and Lydia was too on edge. She yelped as she pricked her finger on a pin, and then set her work down. She needed a distraction. Then she had it: Amy.

Maybe it would help if Lydia invited Amy to the session personally. It was hard watching Cynde comfort Heather, knowing so much that was unsaid between the two grieving women. If she went to see Amy, she could be thoughtful and get out of the basement. Perfect.

"Cynde, I'm going to go check in on Amy, see if I can convince her to give sewing another try," Lydia called out as she walked toward the staircase.

When she got to the main floor, she saw Auden walk in the front door. His arms were full of firewood. Setting the pile down by the door, he took off his heavy-duty rain jacket and shook like a dog.

"Hi," she said, smiling at his display.

It was finally Auden's turn to be embarrassed. He ran his hands through his storm-soaked hair and stammered back a quiet, "Hello." Marshaling himself, Auden continued, "I was just out getting firewood, like I said. I think we should keep the fire going."

Lydia nodded, "Thanks for taking care of that. Everybody is downstairs working on their shirts. Well, almost everybody, Amy's still upstairs. I'm going to see if I can convince her to come down."

Auden was still standing by the door, and Lydia hadn't started up the stairs to Amy's room. She wanted . . . well she wasn't sure what she wanted. Part of her wanted to tell him about Heather, but part of her felt like it wasn't her place. Did it have anything to do with Fran's death? She didn't know. But she knew she liked being near this kind, quiet, currently completely disheveled man. Reaching down to grab the wood, Auden broke the moment and Lydia, chiding herself, started up to Amy's room.

Lydia felt almost angry. They had all agreed to stick together. And that had barely lasted one night. But surely it was safer to stick with the group for the sewing session. It was fair for Amy to feel uncomfortable, but they had to think about their safety. How could she nap, anyway? With Fran's death looming over them?

Buoyed by her own frustration, she knocked quite loudly on Amy's door. Nothing. Embarrassed, she knocked again, a little more softly.

"Amy? Hey, Amy, it's Lydia. Can I come in? We would all really like to have you come join us downstairs for the second session," Lydia said to the door, trying to keep her voice light and welcoming. She couldn't help but think about when she had stood at Fran's door, just the day before. But there was no reason to be worried for Amy. Still. Better safe than sorry. Lydia tried the door handle, found that it was unlocked, and stepped into the room.

# Chapter Twelve

"Hey, Amy, why don't you come downstairs?" No reaction. Lydia took another step in and saw a shape in Amy's bed. Realizing Amy was asleep in her twin bed, Lydia let out the breath she hadn't realized she had been holding. Of course! She was sleeping. That was when Lydia saw the hand. Amy's hand was hanging limp at her side. Who slept like that? And with that question, time started to slow down.

Why hadn't Amy moved when Lydia called out to her? Why was her whole arm hanging like that off the side of the bed?

That was when she saw the pill bottle, bright orange, on the floor near the dangling hand. Pills? Even though some part of her knew it wouldn't make a difference, Lydia stepped farther into the room. Amy's eyes were closed, but Lydia couldn't see the quilt rising and falling like it should, like it would if Amy were breathing. She crossed to the bed and lightly touched Amy's neck, just below her jawline. Nothing. Her eyes went from Amy's neck straight back to the plastic orange bottle on the floor.

Instinctively, she knew not to touch the bottle, but she crouched down and read the label, careful not to disturb anything around her. Fentanyl? *Fentanyl?* What on earth was Amy doing with that? Amy had just told her that was what killed her brother. Lydia had heard about it on the news. The new OxyContin, but a thousand times stronger. A thousand times stronger than heroin. It was the new scourge of the rural South. What was it doing in Amy's room? Lydia had already dealt with a murder, and now she found herself face to face with . . . what? a suicide? An accidental overdose? Did Amy die the same way as her brother? It didn't fit. Nothing about Amy read as addict. If anything, she seemed so committed to preventing other people from experiencing what her brother had.

They would never go to Shenanigans now. Lydia hadn't cared about the night out before, but suddenly, the fact that Amy would never sit next to her, rattling off information about some random comedian, filled her with pain.

How was she going tell Cynde? What could she say? *You've lost both your friends. Something has happened to Amy.* Absurd. What had actually happened? Had Amy been murdered?

But when she stepped back, turning to leave the room and tell the group, she noticed something on the small table between the two beds. A note. In clear black letters, it read, "I'm sorry"—that was it. No punctuation, no signature, no explanation.

Amy was sorry. What was Amy sorry for? Lydia's vision flickered for minute as the ramifications of the note sank in. Had Lydia just read a confession? Amy killed Fran? Amy killed Fran.

Lydia stumbled out of the room and down the stairs, where Auden was still working on stacking the wood and tending to the fire. And drying off from his short adventure out into the still-raging storm.

"Auden, I need you to come upstairs; something has happened to Amy," Lydia said and then turned and headed back upstairs without waiting to see if he followed. He was right behind her as she opened the door and pointed to the pill bottle on the floor.

"I already checked for a pulse. Auden. She's dead. And I think she killed herself. That's fentanyl. And that, I think that's a note." Auden was already craning his neck to read the note on the small table.

"'I'm sorry—,'" he read out loud to himself. "Is this a confession?" Auden asked, turning to Lydia, eyes widening in shock.

"What do you think?" Lydia replied, honestly curious if he would come to the same conclusion she had.

"That's sure what it looks like. I guess I just don't understand what I'm missing . . .," he admitted.

"Well. I think I might know," Lydia paused. It had flashed in her mind as soon as she saw the note, a reason that tied it all together. She didn't want to break Cynde's confidence, but the stakes had changed. There was no more room for secrets. Not after a second death.

"Earlier, Cynde confided in me. She'd been in love with Fran. And well, I've noticed the way that Amy looks . . . looked . . . at Cynde. What if it was jealousy? Some sort of love triangle?" Lydia posited, looking to see Auden's reaction.

He whistled softly. "I guess we all had things we didn't know about Fran. I wish she had felt like she could have been honest with me. With all of us. I wish. Well, anyway, yeah, that could make sense. I've got to be honest, I could see a love triangle, but it's hard to imagine Amy killing anyone. She was just so. . . ." He trailed off, searching for the right word.

"Vanilla?" Lydia offered.

"Exactly. But I guess you never really know what someone else is capable of. You're going to need to tell the group. And we'll have to lock this door now as well."

"I know I have to tell them. I should be glad we have an answer. At least we know what happened, and we don't have to be afraid of anyone else getting hurt. But I just can't believe someone else is dead. Where on earth did she get fentanyl? That stuff is seriously bad news. Amy knew that. Her brother had been addicted to the stuff. It killed him." Lydia explained.

"Wait, Lydia, did you look at the pill bottle?"

"Yes. Didn't you hear me? I mean, I saw it and saw what it was," Lydia replied, feeling like she was being unfairly criticized. She crossed her arms across her body without even realizing it. He was supposed to be on her side.

Auden seemed to ignore her reply as he stepped gingerly toward the bottle.

"Look, Lydia. This is Fran's. It has her name right here on the prescription. She must have been in pain and just not wanted to say. This was hers. When Amy, well, when it happened, Amy must have seen this. Maybe she took it at the time? Hid it in her room for some reason? And then the guilt must have gotten the better of her. And she had a solution right there. Take the pills. And, well . . . here we are. She knew from her own brother that it would be fatal. I might be able to believe that Amy killed Fran, but if she did, I bet she felt horrible afterward. She just wasn't cold blooded," Auden concluded.

"Oh, my word. You're right. About all of it. Oh, Lord, this is going to crush Cynde. Don't touch the bottle. Let's just go downstairs and get this over with. I still have the master key, but maybe, I don't know, maybe Cynde will want to say goodbye or something before I lock the room up."

For the second time that terrible weekend, Lydia left a bedroom and went to deliver the worst possible news.

Lydia walked to the top of the stairs leading to the basement and called down. "Hey, everybody, let's take a break from the sewing. I need to talk to the group."

She could hear what sounded like Clark muttering complaints along with the sound of zippers as the others closed up their tool pouches and headed up to the main floor.

Again. She had to say it again. The sewists filled the living room, taking seats around the fireplace, exhausted. Everyone was trying to care about sewing, and she could have cried in gratitude for their effort. They had no idea how much worse things were about to get. They probably thought she wanted to plan for dinner. Lydia walked to the fireplace and stood facing the group, an eerie echo of the day before. Clark noticed and tried to make a joke.

"Oh, look, everyone, Lydia has to make yet another announcement. What is it this time, Lydia? A black bear in the bathroom?" His sarcasm only earned him a weak laugh from the women around him.

"Amy is upstairs," Lydia started, but then choked on her words and couldn't finish the sentence.

Cynde cut in. "I know. I'm the one who told you she was resting."

"Amy is upstairs, and I am so sorry to have to tell all of you this, but it looks like she has taken her own life."

Would Lydia ever get used to this? She hoped not, because she hoped she would never have to give this sort of news, ever again.

Silence met her words. Until.

"What do you mean?!" Heather yelled.

Heather stood, glaring at Lydia, as if Lydia had done something wrong. All of a sudden, the saying "Don't kill the messenger" made terrible sense. Lydia stuttered, caught off guard by the reaction, since she had only really worried about Cynde. It had never occurred to her that Heather would respond with anger. The others were equally flummoxed.

Mary reached out a hand to the young woman, who shook it off with a brisk jerk of her shoulders. Heather repeated herself, speaking slowly and annunciating each word with excruciating precision: "What. Do. You. Mean?"

"Amy is upstairs. She's dead. It looks like she killed herself, overdosed," Lydia said slowly, as kindly as she could, thinking of both Heather's anger and Cynde's inevitable grief. Lydia also knew that the group would think this was the worst part of it, but Lydia had more to say.

"And, um, next to her body was a note, and she said she's sorry."

For a moment it sounded like the ice storm was inside the house; somehow the noise felt next to them, inside of them.

"That is what I mean, Heather. I'm so sorry," and she let the M's turn in unison to comfort the young woman.

Lydia gave her full attention to Cynde, saying, "Cynde, I think Amy killed Fran and then killed herself." With that, she moved to Cynde, and grasping her firmly under her elbow, steered her around the fireplace and into the kitchen with its long pine table.

She guided Cynde, who walked as if drunk, to a chair and then sat down next to her.

She could hear the others talking in the living room, but she let stillness wash over the table for a moment. She owed Cynde a moment to catch her breath. As if a moment would be anywhere close to enough. Still, there was more to be said.

"Cynde, I am so sorry to ask this, but do you think, well, is it possible that Amy was in love with you? And um, well, is it possible she was jealous of Fran?" Lydia tried to keep her voice soft and gentle. Cynde was past crying. She looked empty. Lost.

She shook her head, "I don't think so. I don't think so?" She looked up at Lydia as if it were a test question and Lydia could give her the real answer. "We were friends. Amy was a little . . . timid. And I think she likes that I'm a bit raucous. I thought she would enjoy this weekend. Maybe relax and let down her guard. She never gave me any reason to think. . . . But if she really left a note, how could I not have seen it, Lydia? Am I blind? Am I just broken?" And at that, Cynde gave herself over to tears again. Quiet, seemingly endless streams of tears rolled down her face. For one absurd moment, Lydia thought of her beloved British murder mysteries and all the many offered cups of tea. Cynde needed sugar and caffeine.

"Cynde, listen. Go sit in the summer room and take a minute for yourself. I'm going to bring you some chocolate from last night and some tea," Lydia said, and she helped Cynde to the room at the end of the kitchen. With the kettle on, she searched for chocolate to put on a plate with the tea. She could hear the others in the living room, peppering Auden with questions.

Cynde held the door open for Lydia as she took the tea and chocolate out to the summer room. There was nothing to say.

Cynde had already confided in Lydia. She had already mourned the loss of a friend. This was something beyond grief. So, Lydia simply sat by her friend and looked out at the storm.

At least she could offer Cynde this, company in the silence. Then, as if on cue in some terrible mash-up of *Noises Off* and *The 39 Steps*, a new sound joined the relentless susurration of the rain. It was Charlie. Her normally sleepy dog was barking like the world was ending. To be fair, she thought, wasn't it?

Lydia rushed from the summer room to the living room, only to find Charlie facing the large windows, hackles raised and growling. She looked out into what was visible of the back yard, thinking maybe Fran had been right about the bears, after all. Using her softest voice, she tried to call Charlie up onto the couch for a snuggle, something he could never refuse, but the dog didn't budge. In fact, instead of relenting, he switched from growling back to full-volume barking.

Her shoulders scrunched toward her ears as she braced herself for Clark's inevitable complaint. He was hardly Charlie's biggest fan under the best of circumstances. Listening to Charlie unleash another volley of barks, she had to admit this was far from the best circumstances.

But it wasn't Clark who finally snapped and yelled at the dog. It was Heather.

"Shut up!" she yelled at Charlie, surprising the entire room. "Shut up!" Heather repeated, even more loudly.

It did work. The dog stopped barking almost immediately. Heather had always made sure to keep treats at the register for Charlie, and the poor dog couldn't seem to process that his benefactor had turned against him.

But that didn't stop Heather, she continued her rant, "What are you even barking at? There is nothing to see! And nothing out there!"

The scene had turned tragic, which worked like a superhero beacon for the M's.

Martha and Mary stepped forward, flanking Heather.

"Dogs can be such a nuisance," Mary muttered quietly to Heather. Lydia had noticed that they often started with a statement of agreement. In another life, Lydia thought, those women would have made amazing hostage negotiators. Or, actually, mobsters.

"Breeding really makes a difference when it comes to dogs, especially boy dogs," Martha added, as they herded Heather toward a couch.

"My cousin in Savannah had a spaniel. Now that was a hunting dog. . . ." Martha continued with the anecdote, which worked almost like a spell on Heather. Lydia could see the tension leave the young woman's body. Meanwhile Mary stepped toward Cynde and Lydia, who at this point had been joined by Auden as well as Clark, surprised as anyone that it was Heather, and not him, angry about the dog.

"Why don't y'all make yourselves useful and get dinner ready," Mary suggested sweetly. Lydia knew from experience, however, that it was not really a suggestion. It was a command.

They filed into the kitchen, leaving the three figures on the couch in the living room, a strange tableau of anger and comfort where no one actually touched anyone else. The M's didn't know, but Lydia did, just how much it might mean to Heather to be mothered.

Fran may have had great plans for that night's dinner, but the refrigerator could no longer be trusted. At least the stove still worked, and they had running water, even if it wasn't hot. Fran had wrapped up some cornbread tightly, and Lydia had every intention of finding some honey to put on it.

Cynde simply sat down and stared off into space, and by silent agreement, the other three let her be.

"I already made lunch, so I don't see why I should be expected to pull off another miracle for dinner," Clark huffed.

"That was a lovely lunch," Lydia offered, "but I think the M's are trying to comfort Heather. The day has just been too much for her. While they talk about the Westminster Dog Show, the least we can do is make ourselves useful."

As if in response to her statement, Charlie circled and then flopped into a pile at Cynde's feet. Following her gaze, Auden asked, "Why do you think Charlie was barking like that?"

"Because he's a dog. And not the best trained dog at that," Clark answered before Lydia could even open her mouth.

She ignored him and answered Auden anyway, "I don't know. That's really unlike him. You've probably noticed; Charlie is more of a sleeper than a fighter. Maybe there was some sort of animal in the yard that he could hear and we couldn't?"

"Could be. Though I don't see why an animal would be out in a storm this bad," Auden countered.

Clark joined in again, "Maybe it was the same person that tore through the driveway yesterday. You can't convince me that wasn't Amy, too."

Lydia's stomach dropped. Suddenly she wished desperately that Charlie would start barking again. Or that Martha would demand Lydia listen to her thoughts on why water spaniels were superior to hunting spaniels. Anything to get out of the conversation unfolding before her.

Clark, however, was warming to his subject, "Think about it. Somebody drives past the house like a maniac. Then two people die. Now the dog is going berserk at an empty window. Are you trying to tell me there is no connection?"

Lydia thought back to Heather's accusations. That was another incident to add, even though she didn't mention it out loud. Then she remembered Amy's face, breaking into a smile as she rambled on about some comedian Lydia had never heard of. She couldn't believe that same woman was a murderer.

"We've been thinking this whole time that this has been about Fran. Why? Maybe this is about Amy. Maybe it was her fault someone hurt Fran and she killed herself out of guilt. Guilt that it was her fault, not that she actually committed the crime," and with that Clark stopped talking, like a lawyer in a courtroom resting his case. Lydia wondered if he knew about Amy's connection to Hillside.

He seemed oblivious to Cynde, still sitting at the other end of the long, wooden table. But Auden wasn't.

"I don't know about you guys, but I'm getting really hungry. How about we try to figure out this dinner situation? Easier to solve a mystery when you aren't hungry, right?" Auden asked, standing up and moving toward the pantry, guiding the conversation away from the death and grief just above them in the house. He opened the pantry doors and let out a disappointed sigh.

"We have . . . more instant iced tea," he said, trying to capture some of the mirth from earlier. The attempt fell flat. But at least they weren't talking about Amy anymore. Lydia was grateful Auden had steered them clear of those rocks. She stood up and joined him at the pantry, leaving Clark and Cynde to their thoughts.

Lowering her voice so that only Auden would hear, Lydia whispered, "I need to talk to you."

# Chapter Thirteen

"Auden, do you think there's something we are missing, some connection between Fran and Amy? Besides Cynde. I keep thinking about "the vote" you told me about. Amy's brother was treated at Hillside. Could that be a connection? How much did Amy know about Fran's opposition to the rehab center? What if whoever has been driving past the house is involved, too? I know it seems all tied up, but I don't feel safe, Auden. I don't."

"Lydia, the storm won't last too much longer. We'll be able to call the police soon. They can figure it out. In the meantime, I'll keep you safe, I promise," he added, and they both quickly glanced out to the living room, to the couch, and to the gun only they knew was hidden beneath it.

"Let's figure out dinner," Auden said, trying to distract her. And Lydia had to admit, she wanted to be distracted. Since Lydia had no intention of opening the refrigerator twenty-four hours into their power outage, they raided the pantry again, and dinner was a weird mix of what could be heated up on the stove and what was just easily at hand. When the group reconvened at the table, the days of salade niçoise were clearly over. Instead, they faced a variety of canned soups, heated and displayed in Fran's beautiful white-and-blue bowls. Fran's cornbread, a bowl of fruit left over from breakfast, and a massive plate of cookies Cynde had brought rounded out the mismatched buffet.

They ate quietly. Morale was so low that Mary and Martha failed even to comment on the faux pas of serve-yourself soup and a simultaneous dessert offering—not even to say "how daring it is of Lydia to try something so unexpected" or whatever elegant, backhanded compliment they normally would have managed. Instead, the two women suddenly looked old, not because of anything so superficial as wrinkles, but because they seemed, for the first time, terribly vulnerable.

Lydia chose a questionable cream of tomato soup and a massive wedge of cornbread. Auden followed suit. Cynde put a piece of cornbread on a plate and pushed it around. The M's had settled for chicken noodle soup, and they ate it daintily, one well-formed sip after the next, never bending their faces toward their bowls. Heather crumbled up her cornbread on top of some lentil soup, and Lydia couldn't decide if she was intrigued or horrified by the combination. They had finished the wine Saturday night and not found any other bottles in the house.

Lydia had been almost tempted to see if she could raid whatever secret source of gin the M's had squirreled away, but they weren't drinking at the meal. Besides, Lydia thought, she didn't need anything clouding her thinking or impacting her judgment. Too much had happened.

Even Charlie seemed subdued, curled up next to Cynde's chair. He hadn't finished his kibble and had made no attempt at begging scraps. What dog would want soup, she supposed, but she still felt like the dog understood how the group felt. Lydia struggled to name the emotion that lingered in the air, muffling any attempt at conversation, leaving only the sounds of the rain and the grandfather clock.

On the one hand, the terrifying question of who had killed Fran had finally been answered. They were safe. Surely? On the other hand, yet another death hung over their small group. They weren't close to Amy like they had been to Fran, but each one of them clearly still felt rocked by the senseless tragedy of it all.

Then Lydia remembered they had cookies on the table. Not just any cookies, but cookies that Cynde had made. Fran made the best cinnamon rolls and muffins, that was undisputed. But when it came to bringing treats to the shop, nothing beat Cynde's cookies. They were the stuff of legend. Thank God for cookies. Lydia had a lot of awesome slogan T-shirts, but she realized in that moment there was a gap in her collection. She needed a nice, semi-fitted T-shirt with a fun font that just read THANK GOD FOR COOKIES. Or would it be THANK GOD FOR COOKIES, with a capital G? Lydia shrugged to herself and focused on the cookies. Cynde had outdone herself. As if reading her mind, Cynde looked at the plates and started to list off the flavors of cookies for the group, as if she were a dessert sommelier. Lydia hardly listened. She knew these cookies well.

Lydia had already tried the snickerdoodles on a Stitch and Bitch Night the previous month. And the chocolate chip cookies, while tempting, were a little too mundane to get her attention. Oh, but at the other end of the platter, new flavors beckoned her. Cynde was still listing off the flavors: ". . . cowboy cookies, midnight indulgence, and, um, what was it called? Confetti? Funfetti. The rainbow one is Funfetti, whatever that means."

Lydia looked down at her hand-knitted socks, one a splatter of pink, purple, and blue, while the other one was striped in red and green. Her sense of fashion could best be described as a directive: *More color.* For a short time in college, she had even dyed her hair bright pink. Graham had hated it when she would bring out pictures to show their friends, but Lydia had thought it looked great. She'd even considered doing it again. In other words, Funfetti was the easy choice. Lydia tried to remind herself she was hosting, but she went straight for the rainbow cookies and put three on her plate. She caught Martha's barely concealed disdain, but she was not about to forgo carbs in the face of the second death in two days.

She shouldn't have worried. Everyone else followed suit. When Cynde mentioned she had tried a new recipe, key lime pie thumbprint cookies, it was enough to break the resolve of even the M's. Lydia was relieved to see them eat the cookies. They started to look a little more like themselves. She was tempted to rest her elbows on the table just to give them an excuse to scold her. Which, knowing them, would be an even sweeter treat than the baked goods.

Cynde also mentioned she had made gluten-free chocolate oatmeal cookies for Clark. He took five and ate them, one after the other, until his plate was empty. Maybe, Lydia thought, she should give up on the idea of sewing retreats entirely. Maybe the real winner was a baking retreat. No deadly equipment. No need for power, just in case she got cursed with another storm. They could just bake and eat and bake and eat until they fell asleep. What could go wrong?

But the sugar high was starting to wear off, and Lydia just shook her head, even though no one in the room was privy to her internal debate. If people got murdered over sewing, who knew what would happen with bakers. She should abandon the idea of retreats altogether before she had a case of poisonous cupcakes on her hands. She almost started to laugh. She was exhausted; they all were. When only a few cookies were left, the group shifted to the living room. They made the pretense of getting out their EPP projects from the night before, but it was just an empty gesture.

Cynde, however, was still in the kitchen, tucking the last remnants of cookies back into the boxes and tins she had brought with her up to the mountain. Lydia tried to find a reason to stay in the room, even though, with no power, there wasn't much to do. She grabbed a sponge and started cleaning the already-clean kitchen table by the light of the electric lantern.

Cynde put down the chocolate-chocolate chip cookies she had just picked up from the platter. Lydia put down the sponge.

"Listen, I can't. You can't expect me to . . . I can't sleep in that room tonight," Cynde confessed, her face lost somewhere between grief and despair. Lydia looked up to see Martha standing near the kitchen table. She had drifted over from the living room but hadn't announced her presence. Lydia was too tired to wonder why.

Then Martha spoke up, "Of course you can't, honey. Of course you can't. Lydia can handle the dishes. Come sit by the fire. This must be such a dreadful shock for you. I don't know how you are bearing up so well, considering."

Lydia didn't bother to contradict her and set about picking up the last of the plates and wiping down the table. She watched Cynde practically stagger to the living room and sit on the longer of the two couches, lit by the glow of the ever-burning fire. Auden never stressed about it, but somehow, the fire never went out, constantly fed just the right number of logs throughout the day.

Soon, Lydia joined them, as Martha offered empty platitudes to Cynde and Clark pretended to be fascinated by his hexies. Lydia had more or less forgotten Heather was even in the room. But now the young woman (Lydia needed to stop thinking of her as that), suddenly offered her room to Cynde: "Cynde, why don't you sleep in the spare bed in my room? I don't snore, I swear," she said, smiling feebly. The anger from earlier was gone, but Heather still clearly felt invested in what had happened to Amy, and what was still happening to Cynde.

Cynde practically crumbled from relief. "If you're sure, Heather, that would be great. Thank you. Honestly, if it's okay with you, I would actually love to head to bed now. I just need this day to be over."

"Absolutely," Heather replied. "I think I'll join you. Haven't done a great job of staying in groups, but there's no reason for you to be alone, either," and turning to the room, Heather added, "Good night, everyone. We'll see you at breakfast."

With Cynde and Heather walking upstairs to the Rainbow Room, Lydia wondered if it wouldn't be better if they all followed suit. She didn't feel in danger anymore, but she did feel completely depleted. An EPP session by the fireplace would be hopeless. That much was obvious.

"I think we should all just call it a day," Lydia offered, as Cynde and Heather disappeared from view. "We could all use an early night. Maybe the weather will be better in the morning. We still have some of Fran's muffins. I'll heat them up for breakfast around 8 AM again; does that sound good?"

Clark simply nodded and went to the stairs that led to his lower-level room. Auden offered Mary an arm as she rose from the couch and then did the same for Martha. It was an endearing sight, Auden standing thin and tall, flanked by an older woman on either arm. He managed to make it look like they were moving at his preferred pace, even as he shortened his stride for them and dipped his head down to hear their comments. Lydia wondered what the M's were saying. Maybe they would find out if he was a bachelor. The M's would ask to see if he needed casseroles dropped at the door of his mountain cabin. Lydia wanted to know because. . . .

Charlie pushed his nose against her, nudging her up from the couch, saving her from having to finish her own thought. Charlie padded to the back door and sat, expectantly, even as the rain continued.

Lydia opened the door to the small backyard and Charlie rushed out, peed, and ran back in, shaking the icy rain off his coat with indignation. "Charlie, if I could make it stop raining, believe me, I would. C'mon, boy. We'll get nice and warm in a minute," she offered, smiling at her beloved rescue. They crossed the living room, and when she turned down the hallway to her room, Auden was just leaving the M's at their door.

They stopped just short of bumping into each other, and Charlie moved to stand near Auden. *Traitor.*

"We have to stop meeting like this," Lydia quipped. To herself, she wondered if she had said a single cool or even normal thing to the man that entire weekend. "How was your evening stroll with the ladies of the house?"

"Once Martha realized I have people from Macon, she was ready to talk to me all night. That woman has an encyclopedic memory. She was asking me about my mother's cotillion as if it were yesterday. As if I had been there! I kept trying to tell her I don't put much store in that stuff, but . . ."

"She just kind of steamrolled over and kept talking? As if you agreed with her?" Lydia offered, completing his sentence.

Auden chuckled, "Exactly. I didn't really mind. They remind me of my grandma a bit. We never actually called her Grandma; she insisted on Lady Lee. Lee was her first name, and just because she was my mother's mother, that didn't mean she had to ever condescend to a term like Grandma. She died a few years back at the impressive age of ninety-two, and I still miss her.

"We'd see her for Christmas and have to slick back our hair, put on a tie. I used to hate it when I was a kid, but I still loved getting to see her anyway. She used to slip me a twenty-dollar bill in my Christmas card. Back then it felt like a million dollars. And you wouldn't believe it, but she always had these candies. I never saw her buy them; I don't think I've ever seen them in a store to this day. They were like something between a butterscotch and caramel? Have you noticed how Mary always seems to have jelly beans?" and Lydia nodded, impressed that Auden had noticed such a small detail. "It really reminds me of those candies. Lady Lee would have loved the M's. She would have loved . . .," and he paused, suddenly looking right into Lydia's eyes. "The Laurels," he finished, weakly.

All at once Lydia realized she hadn't showered that day. They had used up all the hot water the second night. Everyone had felt the need to shower after they found out Fran was dead. And with the power out, there was no more warm water in the tank. Why couldn't she meet gorgeous men with brown eyes . . . why couldn't she meet a man with stubble and a strong, sharp jawline, a man like that . . . anywhere but this nightmare of a weekend.

"I wish I could have met her. She sounds amazing."

Charlie moved toward her door and looked back at her as if to say, *You promised me a warm, cozy bed.*

"And you're right; the Laurels really is a special house," she replied. "I don't know if you noticed, but I think maybe the rain might be letting up a little. Do you think we might get power back tomorrow?" She knew he wouldn't know for sure, but she wasn't ready for the conversation to be over, even if it meant talking about the weather. Standing so close to him, in the dark hallway, with only the flashlights in their hands, Lydia would have been willing to talk about calculus if it meant the conversation didn't have to end.

"I'm hopeful. It's still raining, but not as hard. We just need the sun to come out in the morning, warm things up. If the ice loosens, Cherry Log is pretty good about getting things back to normal. You have to be, if you want to live here year-round," he replied.

She had so many questions. Would he stay on the mountain forever, now that his dream of a woodworking business had been dashed? Was he lonely? How did he feel about dogs sharing a person's bed rather than sleeping on the floor? Without realizing it, she had let the conversation lull again, and he spoke into the long pause.

"Good night, Lydia. I'm just down the hall if you need . . . anything. Anything at all." With that, he turned and headed back to the living room and the couch he had claimed for a bed. The couch with a loaded gun quietly stashed beneath it.

# Chapter Fourteen

L ydia curled up under the pink-and-purple flowered quilt on her bed. Charlie had already snuggled up to her feet. When she was married, Charlie had slept on a nice, monogrammed, L.L.Bean dog bed in the corner of their master bedroom. But once she had her own apartment, Charlie could sense the rules had changed. That first discombobulating night, he had hopped right up, turned around twice, and flopped into a pile of fur on what had once been Graham's side of the bed.

Lydia couldn't seem to help thinking about the house's own "love triangle" as she reached out to the bedside table and turned off the flashlight she had brought in with her. Icy rain hit the roof and made a hissing sound in the dark. She realized she was holding her breath. She forced herself to exhale. What had happened was a tragedy, a terrible tragedy, but it wasn't a mystery. Not anymore. Lydia certainly wasn't in any danger. So why couldn't she seem to breathe normally? She played back the tape in her mind, the explanation for all the death and sadness.

A love triangle. Amy loved Cynde. Cynde loved Fran. Amy killed Fran, and then, realizing the horror of what she had done, overdosed, leaving only her apology behind. It was nothing that Lydia could have prevented. Then why didn't she feel any real sense of closure?

She pulled the quilt up higher. Then she ran her hand across the quilt binding Fran's grandmother had clearly sewn by hand. So much of sewing was an expression of love. Sure, she loved wearing her pink sushi shirt. But it never ceased to amaze her how some time-intensive act, hand-sewing a quilt binding, could still show love generations later.

Fran always knew that. She knew that sewing something for someone was a tangible way to love them. In fact, that had been the last thing she had worked on, a hand-sewn, English paper pieced quilt for Lydia's new apartment. "So, you can feel right at home," Fran had said, as she worked cutting out the hexies. Lydia could still see the tiny pieces of fabric that had been piled so neatly on her desk, now bloodstained, scattered across the desk and floor, when she had found Fran's body. So much violence. Charlie shifted in his sleep, his old feet moving, chasing after dream rabbits. Amy had been mad enough to come into Fran's room, grab the sad iron, and bash Fran in the head? Why would she have even thought that Fran would have something like that in her bedroom. Until recently, Lydia hadn't even know what a sad iron was. Lydia's hands tightened on the quilt as she continued to list her lingering doubts.

Where had the passion come from? Even if Amy loved Cynde that much, Fran wasn't really an immediate threat. With Fran out of the picture, Cynde hadn't immediately thrown herself into Amy's arms. There may have been deep emotion, but no one was acting on it yet. So why the crisis? Why the drastic, terrible decision to end a life? Lydia might have joked about wanting to throttle Emma-Grace, but she never meant it. Heartbreak was horrible, she knew that better than most. But worth taking a life?

No. Not one life, Lydia corrected herself, two. Lydia wanted to accept what the others found so convincing. It meant they were safe, no murderer in the house, trapped with them until the ice melted.

But fentanyl? Amy? Lydia felt that pressing queasiness again. Amy wouldn't even take aspirin. At the time, Lydia had just found it annoying. Who doesn't take aspirin? But now Lydia knew about Amy's life, her brother, and she grappled with the idea of someone avoiding aspirin but overdosing on fentanyl. Amy had been so excited about the future. About a girls' night in March, just a few weeks away. What had happened in the small space of time before her death that changed all that?

And what about the murder itself? Lydia remembered Cynde's desperate attempt to hide the evidence of their avian hit-and-run, shoving her hands into the mess of feathers threaded into the headlights. What had Cynde said? Amy wouldn't even cook meat she was so squeamish. That same Amy attacked someone? Brutally? Without hesitation? And then had the presence of mind to clean herself up and act naturally, so naturally that no one had any idea she had just murdered someone with an antique iron? Were murderers ever squeamish?

None of it fit.

Cynde loved Fran. Lydia believed that. Amy might have loved Cynde. That was possible, maybe even probable. It would explain the weird tension between them that had haunted the weekend. Still. She remembered finding Fran, the grimace death had fixed on her friend's face. How much anger and force would it take to hit someone like that, just once, right on the side of the head? She was thinking in circles. It didn't fit. She was missing something.

She reached to get her water bottle on the bedside table and saw the note Fran had written her. Waiting. She couldn't put it off any longer, so she turned on the flashlight. Lydia held the closed envelope in one hand and rested her other hand on Charlie's back. It hurt to see Fran's tight, careful handwriting. She opened the card and read:

*   *   *

"Lydia, congratulations on your first successful sewing retreat. It is the first of many, I have no doubt. I hope you have loved this time at the Laurels. I keep wanting to tell you, but it never seems like the right time. You need to know that my health is" here some words were scratched out and Lydia couldn't read them, "not great," the note continued. "You know I like to pretend everything is fine, but it isn't. I'm dying. Cancer. And I need to be realistic. I first dreamed up the idea for Measure Twice while sitting in the large leather armchair by the main windows at the Laurels, looking out at the mountains. To me, the house and the shop have always been connected. I hope I have some time left. But just know, I have changed my will and left the Laurels to you. I had thought I could find some long-lost family, but then I realized, you are my family. But I still won't let you be in charge of teaching bias binding! How you keep starting backwards will always be a mystery to me. There is a mortgage on the house, and I have had to rent it out much of the year just to meet the costs. I don't know if it will feel like the gift I want it to be. But if anyone can make this work, it's you. You brought Measure Twice back to life. I hope you'll do the same for the Laurels. I wish I could be around to see you do it."

*   *   *

The card was signed with a simple dash and her name, Fran. No hearts, no warm wishes. Just the gift of a house. For the first time that weekend, that horrible, horrible weekend, Lydia let herself quietly cry. Fran wouldn't have wanted Lydia to make a fuss, but Lydia would have anyways. At least a hug. She wanted to hug her friend. Lydia had been wondering about the Laurels. Fran was the only child of two only children. The cousins she had played with as a child were distant and had drifted out of her orbit. And she had never so much as married, not even a Graham-length marriage. Lydia had assumed the house would be auctioned off; maybe the bank would buy it? She didn't know the details of those sorts of contracts. Now, here she was, the new owner of the Laurels, holding yet another piece of the puzzle in her hands.

Sleep was a long way off, and she knew it. Instead, Lydia switched the flashlight back off and lay in bed, moving pieces of information around in her mind the way she would move around pattern pieces on a length of fabric that threatened to be just a bit too small for her project. There was a way it all fit. She knew it. She just had to keep shifting the pieces until they clicked.

Mary, Martha, and Clark all had reasons to hate Fran. Cynde certainly had strong emotions. And Heather? Heather had a secret . . . a secret that might mean more than Lydia could seem to understand. A secret that Fran already knew. Did Heather know that Fran knew? She rubbed her temples, trying to dispel a growing headache. It all felt like a deadly version of "Who's on first?"

But Lydia had to be honest with herself. She just didn't buy that Amy had killed Fran. Which meant someone else had killed Fran *and* Amy.

She forced herself to consider Auden. Maybe he had wanted Fran to give him the house? To make up for ruining his chances with the Dalton house? Was it punishment for the loss of his dreams? Maybe Amy knew he did it and had to be silenced? She tried to picture Auden, pointing the shotgun at Amy, forcing her to take the fentanyl. It almost made sense.

But Auden had been with her when Fran died. And if he had wanted to kill Amy, someone would have seen him with the gun heading to Amy's room, surely. Maybe he had an accomplice? The car in the drive? Someone else mad about Hillside? But how would an outsider know how to get around the house? No, Auden didn't fit. Her gut told her that she was on the right track, though. What if the murder was really about the Laurels? She moved the pieces around again, and all of sudden, it clicked.

If Lydia was right, then there might be another murder. If she was right, the next step would require help. For the next step she would need Auden. But that meant she had to be sure, sure enough to risk her life on it, that she could trust him.

Lydia swung her feet off the bed, pulled off the quilt, and quietly left her room, Charlie trailing only a few steps behind. She left her flashlight in her room and navigated the house in the darkness, moving toward the glow of the still-burning fire in the living room.

Seeing that Auden was still awake, Lydia thanked every god she could think of that she wouldn't have to wake him, easily imagining a million ways she could embarrass herself in the effort. Clearing her throat, she sat next to him near the fire and tried to explain what she had come to understand: "Auden. Fran gave me the house."

Lydia waited for him to reply but saw that he was simply too shocked to respond, so she plowed ahead. "I didn't tell the group, but Fran wrote notes for everyone. I was going to give them to everyone at the end of the retreat, let people have one last touch of Fran in their lives. I read mine tonight. She did tell me she was dying. She just did it in the note. And she told me she is leaving the Laurels to me." With that, she paused, offering Auden a chance to interject. Nothing. She suddenly understood the cliché about being able to knock someone over with a feather.

Lydia plowed on: "Auden, listen. There's more. I was nosy. I read everyone else's letters. . . ." At that revelation, Auden's mouth tightened, but he stayed quiet, still willing to listen.

"There wasn't a letter for you, obviously. Fran didn't think you would be playing the game. And there wasn't a letter for Amy. Fran must have written the letters before Cynde told her she was coming. Anyway," she paused. Auden still looked shocked. Worse, he looked disgusted.

"I know. I shouldn't have. But maybe the ends justify the means? Maybe not, I don't know. The letters weren't that scandalous, really. But they got me thinking. What if Amy didn't kill herself? What if she was murdered, just like Fran was murdered?"

Auden sputtered to life, "Lydia, we talked about this. Who would murder Amy?"

Lydia, relieved he was at least participating in the conversation now, rushed to explain her theory: "I think Amy was murdered, not because of who she is, but because it meant we would stop looking for a murderer. She was just a scapegoat. I don't think this was ever about a love triangle; I think this whole terrible thing is about the Laurels," and with that, she stopped, pleased at her explanation for once.

"You think this is all about the Laurels? Are you saying I killed them?" Auden asked, his face reddening. "I didn't have to tell you about my plans, Lydia, about my woodworking, what I wanted to do with my life. I told you because I trust you. Not to have you throw it back in my face as a motive for murder."

Lydia reeled back, and she rushed to clarify, whisper-yelling, "*No!* Sorry. No. I'm saying, listen, I need to tell you about the other letters. And well, the things I have, um, overheard this weekend." It was a loose definition of "overheard," but she didn't want to admit to Auden how much she had been intentionally eavesdropping.

"At first, I thought this was all about Fran and the store. She'd been pressuring people to invest in the store before I bought it. I think she really rubbed some people the wrong way," which was putting it mildly, she added silently, "but then I thought I must have been wrong when Amy died. That was just a love triangle. But that didn't hold water, either. Cynde might have been in love with Fran, but they weren't together. Amy gained nothing in killing Fran. And the fentanyl? She wouldn't even take aspirin for a headache, and then suddenly she takes the strongest opiate on earth, the one that killed her brother? It never fit. Nothing about Amy being a murderer made any sense. You said so yourself when we found her body. So, then I wondered. What if it was about Fran, her life *before* Measure Twice? I still wasn't sure until I read the letter and learned about the Laurels. And if I'm right, Auden, I need to do something a little risky. And I need your help."

She took a deep breath and went on. "Because if this is all really about the house, then I'm the next target. At least I will be, when I tell everyone at breakfast that she left the house to me. And when I tell them . . . when I tell them I read the letters she wrote to everyone else," she added, still a little ashamed she had read them and had to admit as much to Auden.

"You're going to tell everyone you read their private notes from Fran?" Auden asked, forcing himself to keep his voice steady but clearly flabbergasted at her plan. Little did he know how much more absurd it would get.

"Yes. As soon as everyone is in the kitchen in the morning. I am going to tell them about the notes, that Fran left the house to me, and that I read the rest of them. But I don't want you to be in the kitchen when it happens," she added.

"Lydia, I said before, I really don't think we should be splitting up, and if people are going to be upset with you, I would . . . well, truth be told, Lydia, I would rather be there to keep you safe, just in case," he finished, looking down at his hands.

Was he blushing?

Since the night she'd discovered Graham and Emma-Grace and spilled her diet lemonade all over the bedroom carpet, Lydia had only been on one date. Set up by Fran. She had gone to dinner with her neighbor, Brandon, only to find him murdered not long after. After that, and her own escape from death, she had put all thoughts of dating firmly out of her mind. Firmly.

It didn't matter if Auden was maybe blushing a little bit. It didn't matter that she loved the idea of him keeping her safe, of him even wanting to keep her safe. Now he was looking up, right into her eyes.

They were lit by the fire, and Lydia suddenly felt too aware that they were both in their pajamas, even though Auden still had a blanket, one of Fran's quilts, draped across his lap. If she wasn't there to talk about a murderer, it might have even felt romantic. She suddenly realized how close they were sitting. They must have moved closer as they whisper-argued about the letters and her absurd plan.

He was looking at her now with an intensity she wasn't sure how to decipher. There were no distractions, the house quiet but for the ever-present storm. It felt beyond surreal, to be sitting in a dark house, by a fire, in the middle of the night, with a handsome man. As if no one else existed, as if the whole weekend had never even happened.

Just how he had been sitting with Heather the night before.

Lydia broke their gaze, looking at the dark window that only dimly reflected the light of the fire, leaving the storm-filled world outside impossible to see clearly. Auden was gorgeous; there was no way around it. And in the moment he looked right at her, she felt a nervous giddiness that she hadn't felt in more than months—that she hadn't felt in years. All she could do now was hope—hope that, when the storm ended, he would still want to look at her that way. Hope that, after he heard the rest of her plan, he would still want to help her. Hope that her plan would work.

"Thank you," Lydia said quietly, officially ending the moment. "Thank you for wanting to keep me safe. I do need your help to stay safe, but not in the kitchen. I need you to hide in the bathroom."

The grandfather clock chimed its longest run, all twelve loud bongs to mark they had reached midnight.

Lydia repeated herself, "I need you to hide in the bathroom."

"Excuse me?" Auden asked, shifting away from her as he said it.

"If I'm right, and I understand that is a big 'if' right now . . . if I'm right, then the person I think is responsible for all of this will want to hurt me next. We need to catch them in the act. Which means I set the trap in motion, by telling the group about the Laurels, and you wait in the bathroom that connects to my room to catch them in my room."

"You think this person is going to head straight to your room?" Auden couldn't hide his incredulity.

"Yes. I'm almost certain. And Auden?"

"Yeah?"

"We're going to need your gun."

# Chapter Fifteen

**Monday**

When she woke up, rested, she suddenly noticed that the rain had finally stopped. Lydia took a moment to soak in the quiet—the real, rain-free, quiet—of the morning. Thankfully, the night before, Auden had agreed to her plan. All of it. She flinched, remembering how awkward her good night had been. She had stood up, and then he had stood up, as she had leaned down to hug him, she caught him sort of around the waist as he rose and then he had patted her head since he couldn't hug her back from that angle. Terrible. It would have been funny in any other context, but when you're planning how to capture a double murderer, it's hard to keep your sense of humor.

She hadn't even said anything after that train wreck of a hug, simply straightened up, turned around, and headed to bed. At least for once she had actually fallen asleep quickly.

No nightmares. Instead, the real nightmare was just outside her room. Lydia was surprised at how calm she felt. Maybe calm is the feeling left on the other side of fear. No matter the reason, she was relieved to not be shaking. She needed to act natural. Everything depended on nothing seeming weird.

Shifting Charlie from the bed, she got up and grabbed black leggings and a shirt that read I HEART CRAFTING in pink letters on a black background. Slipping into the bathroom she shared with the M's, she brushed her teeth and splashed her face with the frigid water. She looked in the mirror and told herself to breathe.

She was ready. Hair in a messy topknot, she made her way quietly into the kitchen. She needed coffee. It was time.

Just like the day before, Auden was still asleep, and the house was silent—truly silent now that the sleet had stopped. With a steaming mug of coffee, she quietly tucked herself into the large leather chair that faced the enormous windows in the back of the house. Her house. It seemed impossible that she owned the Laurels. She wanted to be excited, but the loss of Fran flooded the extravagance of her gift with grief. How many times can one person change your life? Now she would never have a chance to tell Fran how much it mattered, how much it all mattered.

The mug in her hand was a twin to the mug Fran had kept in the Measure Twice break room. It seemed impossible to live in a world without Fran. She realized she was crying, almost silently. There wouldn't be any more moments where Fran changed her life like a fairy godmother. But at least there was one thing she could do for Fran. And she had to start now, so she peeled herself from the deep, comfortable leather chair and went back into the kitchen to warm up the leftover muffins.

Auden joined her, pouring himself a mug of coffee. She pulled the baking tray of warmed-up muffins out of the oven and set them on top of the stove. As she transferred them to a blue-and-white platter, she heard the rest of the house waking up. One by one, the rest of the group wandered in, filled heavy white-and-blue mugs with coffee, put muffins on matching plates, and sat down. The kitchen was filled only with the sounds of muffin wrappers being removed and the muffins themselves being consumed, a little more quickly than normal.

They all seemed in silent agreement that one thing was needed that morning: sugar. As they ate in silence, the beautiful silence left in the wake of the storm that had ended overnight, the sun shone into the summer room. The ice hadn't melted, but it was a promising start to the day. Maybe they could go home soon. Lydia, knew, even if they didn't, that one more thing had to happen before they could be free.

"I know you all think I had a bit of a blind spot when it came to Fran," Lydia announced to the table, with no segue whatsoever. Clark looked like she had just declared it was raining frogs. Everyone stopped eating.

"You were right. There was a lot I didn't know. Or maybe I didn't want to know. But I am coming to understand things a lot better. Yesterday, when I went to get the prizes for the game, I found something else, something important, something I should have told you about before now. You see, in addition to the prizes, Fran wrote each of us a card. And, I . . . well given what had happened, I . . . I read them. The cards. I read all of them," Lydia admitted.

No one spoke. Even Cynde looked appalled. And Clark, well Clark looked livid. Lydia pressed on.

"It was none of my business, and I won't mention your cards again. I'll give them to you in a moment. But before I do that, I need to tell you all what was in my card."

This shift surprised the group further.

"In her note to me, Fran told me she left me the house. The Laurels belongs to me, now. The house is mine, and. . . ." Lydia wasn't sure how to finish the sentence, but it didn't matter. It had worked. For a moment. Lydia thought ice had slid off the roof and crashed next to the window. But instead, Heather stood halfway to the table, staring at her empty hands in shock. The white-and-blue plate she had just been holding lay on the floor, shattered. Mary got up to help, but Heather had already turned on her heels and left.

Mary turned to Martha, muttering, "Poor girl; this has all been too much." Lydia grimaced, but waited, and passed out the cards to those still at the table.

It had to work.

Lydia prayed that on the other side of the house, Auden waited, just like she had told him to, in the Jack-and-Jill bathroom with the door cracked open. If she was right, just now, as Lydia passed out the cards to the stunned sewists still at the table, Heather was opening Lydia's door and stepping into the Flower Room. Auden would be watching as Heather reached into her pocket and pulled out the orange bottle she had tucked away, watching as she grabbed Lydia's water bottle on the bedside table, unscrewed the cap, added in two small pills, screwed the cap back on, and shook it.

In the kitchen, Cynde, Clark, Mary, and Martha were opening their cards from Fran and reading them, silently, angled away from each other as if there were any secrets left to protect. Lydia had expected Clark to be the first to complain that she had read the cards, but it was Cynde who spoke first:

"Lydia, what on earth possessed you to read these cards? Fran was a private person. She deserved to say what she wanted to say, privately," Cynde said, stressing the last word. "We've all gone along with your ideas on this trip, but you're acting like you are the only adult here. This isn't some summer camp, Lydia. You had no right to read the cards."

As she had fallen asleep the night before, Lydia had tried to prepare herself for exactly this reaction. It was unavoidable, but knowing that didn't make it any less painful.

She had practiced her excuses, but the words failed her now in the face of her friend, who clearly felt betrayed.

"You're right, Cynde. I was out of line. I hope, in time, you can forgive me. Ever since . . . ever since we. . . ." Lydia paused, trying to find the least hurtful word. "Ever since we lost Fran, I have wanted so badly to believe that it was some stranger, some outsider, who did this. Fran loved all of you, and she loved Measure Twice, and I guess I just thought, if I knew everything, I could keep us, the store, everything safe." Lydia hoped, as she apologized to Cynde, that the woman didn't notice how she also kept listening so keenly toward her bedroom.

Cynde clearly found Lydia's apology lacking and was just about to make it clear to her exactly how lacking, when Lydia heard the noise she had been waiting for: Auden's voice, saying loudly enough: "That's enough, Heather."

Lydia got up from the table and without saying anything further, ran to her bedroom.

The door was closed, and she waited for a moment, straining to hear the conversation inside. It was too quiet. Lydia opened the door to her room. Even though she had expected the scene in front of her, even though she had, in a way, planned it, she was still shocked. She was right.

# Quilty as Charged

Heather was sitting on Lydia's bed, her hand clenched around something Lydia couldn't quite see, and Auden was standing near the bathroom door, shotgun raised and pointed at Heather. Lydia knew absolutely nothing about guns, but clearly Auden did. He knew how to hold the shotgun and, with his lean body taut, with the gun raised, even Lydia felt a frisson of fear.

Heather turned toward the door, gasping, "Oh, Lydia, thank god you got here. I was right. There is a murderer in the house. Bu it's not Clark! It's *Auden*!" and at that she pointed at the gun, seemingly hysterical and afraid.

Lydia, however, knew better.

"Heather," she said sadly, "it's over."

Heather aged ten years in that moment. The bright red hair that had once seemed so rebellious and fun looked stark and harsh against her snarling face. The sharp angle of her chin, that had seemed impish before, suddenly looked cruel. It was not a quirky face now, but a bitter one. But before Lydia could say anything, Heather lunged, dropping the pill bottle in her hand and picking up Lydia's seam ripper from her bed. Before Lydia even reacted, Auden had stepped forward and pointed the shotgun at Heather, stopping her in her tracks. But that didn't keep her quiet and she didn't drop the seam ripper. Standing completely still, she shouted at Lydia.

"*Over?* You're going to try to tell me it's *over?* What do you know about *over?* What do you know about me? Do you know how long it took me to find her? And when I did? *You!*" she spat the word at Lydia. "Just when things were working, you showed up . . . traipsing all over her life—my life—our life! You. Ruined. Everything. It was my turn. For all of this! And the worst part?

I was going to tell her. I told her. I mean, I was telling her. You were busy running around giggling about weather alerts, and I was ready to have a mother. I was ready!"

Heather stared at Lydia with hatred in her eyes.

"Do you know what she said? She said, 'I know.' She already knew. She knew I was her daughter. She'd hired someone to find me when she found out she was dying. I had waited for so long. And all she had to say to me was that she knew? Then she said, 'Don't worry, nothing has to change.' Can you believe that?' Heather screamed.

"I had been dreaming of that moment ever since I tracked her down and found that stupid shop. It wasn't easy, moving to Peridot, learning to sew, hiding who I really was. But I learned the hard way that you can't just assume people are good. I had to *know* who she was before I told her. You can understand that, right? Why I had to lie? And now all the lying could stop. I could live here, in the Laurels. She told me, you know, late one night as we coded inventory. How she had wanted the house to stay in her family. That she was hoping to find a long-lost family member. *That was me!* She must have been talking about me!"

"And then she got sick. I knew she was sick. You can't hide terminal cancer. It was now or never. And then she could die knowing the house had come to me. Her daughter. *Me.* Just like she wanted. I told her everything.

"Then she had the nerve to . . . she actually. . . ." Heather stopped for the first time, gulping air like a swimmer in rough water. "She said nothing had to change. As if I should be thankful she wasn't mad at me, wasn't going to chuck me out. HER mad at ME?"

At that point, Heather looked at the seam ripper still in her hands. "You have to understand: The plan was never to hurt her. She decided. She decided that we couldn't be a family. That was her choice, not mine. I didn't mean. . . . It was never the plan. She said she forgave me. She was *smiling*. I had to make it stop. So, I did. It all has to stop."

"This house is mine, Lydia. This life is mine."

Suddenly the room was silent. All three of them looked at the water bottle on Lydia's nightstand, the fentanyl pill bottle on the floor.

Lydia had known she would be next. If she was right, if her plan worked, then Heather would do anything to keep the house from going to Lydia. That had been Lydia's whole plan, to scare Heather into trying to kill her and have Auden catch her in the act. Why was she still so surprised? No one spoke. Auden kept the gun trained on Heather.

"But why try to kill me? You could have contested the will." Lydia finally asked, breaking the silence.

"God, how stupid are you? Because of your stupid socks. Because of your stupid T-shirts. Because you actually like pom-pom trim. Because you are *not* her daughter! And this is not your house! Because the damage was done; there was no going back, and no one had any suspicions. Except you. It wouldn't have hurt, Lydia. I'm not a monster. And everyone would have understood why you had to kill yourself. You felt guilty. About Fran, about the house, about so blatantly stealing her whole existence. You were already apologizing to us. I would just explain to the group that you had taken the pills from Amy's room and killed yourself. It wasn't perfect, but I could have figured something out. You just needed to die. You just need to die."

At that point, Heather looked wrung out, like all her rage had drained her to a shell of her former self. If Lydia hadn't just heard the confession, she would have pitied the weak, vulnerable woman in front of her. But she didn't pity her, and the confession wasn't over.

"Okay, Heather, I get it, you hate me. It wasn't just me, though, was it? What happened to Amy? It wasn't an overdose, was it? You spiked her water and staged the overdose, just like you were going to spike mine. Why? What did Amy ever do to you? I don't understand," Lydia asked, her voice close to breaking. It was all too much.

Heather let out a soft laugh. "Of course, you don't understand. What have you ever understood?!" Lydia winced at the edge in Heather's voice. "What do you even know about Amy? She's Cynde's friend. What do you actually know about her? Did you even talk to her?!"

Heather stopped to get her breath, and Lydia had to admit she had a point; Lydia didn't know really anything about Amy, just Theo Von and Crazy Bread, and the sad loss of her brother. Before Lydia had even started to castigate herself, Heather was back at it. "Amy worked in the Peridot court part time. That was how she knew Cynde. She told Fran the truth about me. She even knew about Fran's plan for a new will. She told me as much after Fran was dead, tried to console me. Stupid, useless woman. She was thrilled she had something to contribute. Something that would make her interesting. Mentions over cookies, *Oh, Heather, did you know about Fran's will?* It was too easy to keep her talking, to tell her of course I knew all about it. So, then she says, *Oh, so you knew she was thinking of changing the will? Crazy, huh? I took the minutes*

*of the meeting about it, but for some reason she just acted like we'd
never met before, when I got here.*

"That was how she said it, *think of changing*, not *changed*. How
was I supposed to know Fran had already made it legal? It should
have ended with Amy.

"She didn't suffer. I just needed the will to stay the same. I'm
owed this. Why can't you see that? Once I realized Amy had to
die, it all made sense. A 'suicide' would solve everything. I could
tell that you didn't buy my story about someone trying to kill me
with carbon monoxide poisoning. This tied up all the loose ends
and might *finally shut you up*. Why can't you ever just shut up?"
Heather whispered.

There was nothing more to say.

# Chapter Sixteen

Auden was still holding the gun. He gestured from the seam ripper to the floor, and Heather dropped it, a soft thunk against the rug. The seam ripper wasn't much of a weapon, but it still felt better to see Heather empty-handed. Then Auden pointed to the bed. Heather took the hint and sat down. While Auden kept the gun pointed at Heather, Lydia took the pills and the seam ripper and then tied Heather's hands behind her back with leftover bias binding. It wasn't a perfect solution, but it was good enough. Auden lowered the gun, and they walked out together, leaving Heather alone in Lydia's room. Then he locked the door and sat in front of it, legs crossed, hands shaking ever so slightly.

"I'm going to wait here until the power comes back on. Then we call the police. You should tell the others," he added, gun laid across his lap. Auden said it with such authority that Lydia just nodded, placed the pills and the seam ripper on the floor next to Auden and went back to the kitchen.

Heather's broken plate was still on the floor.

The group had clearly heard yelling, but they just as clearly hadn't heard the actual words.

"Poor girl, she's just overwrought, that's all," Mary offered, assuming Heather had been yelling at Lydia about the cards.

Clark added, "I don't blame her for being mad. You had no right reading those cards, Lydia."

"I know, and I'm sorry. Like I said, I was scared of what was happening. It just didn't make sense to me that Amy would kill Fran. I had to keep digging. The cards were too perfect an opportunity to pass up. But that doesn't mean I was right to read them. You've all read them now. You know they don't say much. Heather isn't mad about the cards. We all have secrets that need to come out."

"Then she's mad about the house," Clark interjected, "and honestly, I can't blame her. I mean, really Lydia. What makes you so deserving of the Laurels? Why did you get a house when the rest . . . after the way she treated us . . . when the rest of us just got pathetic apologies? You just admitted you've been keeping secrets from us; who's to say there isn't something else you're keeping back?" Clark stopped himself, realizing he had started yelling at Lydia in front of the rest of the group. He blushed with anger or shame; she couldn't tell which.

Lydia wanted to scream right back at him to stop being an ass. That, she knew, was a battle for another time. She wasn't done telling them all the truth. Lydia took a deep breath. At least they were all still sitting down. Lydia then tried to explain the impossible, again:

"Heather killed Fran."

Oooof. Okay, her delivery still hadn't improved. She started again. "Heather lied to us. She isn't twenty-five." She could tell the group was lost. Why was Lydia talking about age? The girl was young, end of story. "Actually, she's thirty-five. And it matters because she's Fran's daughter."

She may as well have said Heather was the new Queen of England. Lydia kept going, "Fran got pregnant when she was a teenager and gave the baby, a girl, up for adoption. That girl was Heather. Heather tracked her down and lied to get close to Fran. When she revealed herself, something went wrong in the conversation, they argued, and Heather hit Fran. Then," and at that moment she turned to Cynde, "then she killed Amy and framed her to make it look like Amy had killed Fran and then herself."

Cynde looked strangely relieved, and Lydia thought she knew why. True, she had still lost her friend, but at least Amy was who Cynde believed her to be, not who Heather had tricked them into thinking she was. In short, Amy was Amy, not a murderer. Lydia kept going; there was still more to explain.

"It was never about you, Cynde. It was always about Fran. And about the Laurels. I read Fran's card to Heather, where she admitted to being her birth mom. Then, I read my card from Fran last night, and when I realized that Fran had wanted me to get the house, it raised questions, doubts. I wasn't sure, but I started to wonder if Heather was involved. I wanted to be wrong, I really did, but there were too many unanswered questions, too many loose ends. I told Auden my suspicions last night, and this morning he helped me set a trap."

Lydia realized she had to tell them about the gun. Sigh.

"I asked Auden to wait in the bathroom next to my room with his gun and catch Heather if she tried to do anything. Because Auden has a gun. A hunting rifle. It was Fran's. He knew where she kept it and has had it hidden under the couch the whole time."

If Lydia had expected a sharp reply from Clark, she underestimated how overwhelmed he would be with the new information. Grateful for the silence, she plowed on:

"I was right. Heather was so mad about Fran leaving the house to me that she went into my room and tried to poison me with fentanyl in my water bottle, just like she poisoned Amy. Auden caught her, and at first, she tried to come up with some excuse. But even then, even when there was still a tiny sliver of a chance I was wrong, Heather proved me right. She grabbed my seam ripper and tried to stab me. Auden stopped her in time. I'm fine. But she's tied up in my room with bias binding, and Auden is guarding the door. With his gun."

Still silence. Lydia couldn't blame them. She had known since last night, she had even laid the trap for Heather, and she *still* almost didn't believe it.

"Heather?" Cynde squeaked. "No. I don't believe you. Heather loved Fran, and she barely even knew Amy. Lydia, you've got this all wrong somehow. Because if Heather did this. . . ."

Lydia finished the thought for her friend. "It had nothing to do with you, Cynde."

Cynde started to cry, not a horrible gasping sob, like when they had found out Fran was dead, but a soft, steady cry that covered her cheeks in tears.

"It had nothing to do with me," she repeated to herself, and she stood up and went to sit, alone, in the summer room.

Mary, Martha, and Clark watched her go.

Mary was the first to break the new silence, offering, "I always thought there was something wrong with that young lady."

"Pish, posh," Martha replied. "Just yesterday you said she was a credit to her generation."

"Well, true, I thought she had good manners. But I also knew something wasn't right. Her hair? Those boots? She practically told us she was deviant. We should have paid more attention," and Mary seemed to aim that last comment at Lydia.

Surprisingly, Clark came to Lydia's defense, saying, "That's not fair, Mary, and you know it. Red hair and Doc Martens don't make someone a killer. We all loved Heather."

Lydia breathed in sharply, realizing they had all started to refer to Heather in the past tense. Heather wasn't dead. But she was lost to them. Should she tell Clark that Heather tried to make Lydia think he was the murderer?

"We all loved Heather," Clark repeated. "She should have told us. We've all done things we aren't proud of. . . ." He paused and made eye contact with Martha. "And we would have understood why she lied about her real identity. Fran wasn't her only chance at a family. We could all have been her family."

It occurred to Lydia, in that moment, that there was still so much she didn't know about Clark. True, she had "overheard" about his dad's drinking and a younger sibling. But why didn't she know more? Was he close to his family? Did he ever date anyone? She had let him live in her mind as a sort of caricature: fastidious Clark with his fancy snacks and sharp outfits. Clark was right about family. Heather couldn't be a part of it anymore, but they could all do better by each other, and she could take better care of the friends she had left. She could even treat the M's . . .

"I still say, it makes me think of poisonous insects," Mary cut into Lydia's thoughts. Insects? Why were they talking about insects?

"Insects have bright colors to warn people. Heather had that bright red hair. We should have realized she was dangerous," Mary concluded, pressing her lips into a thin line of righteous insight.

No one had anything to say to that. And then, blessedly, noise. The generator was back on. Who knew that the whir and thump of the old machine could sound so sweet? In that moment the digital clocks came alive across the kitchen. Sure, they were all blinking out of sync. Sure, they all had wrong times flashing. But clocks! Clocks meant . . . and before she could finish forming the thought in her mind, Lydia grabbed the phone, stretching the coiled cord to bring the handset right to her ear.

Lydia was quickly making a new list of sounds she loved. Generators. Now she added dial tones.

There was still so much to say. A million questions remained unsaid, unanswered. But in that moment, they all simply looked at the phone, the dial tone pouring out into the silence, as if an angel had appeared. Lydia raised her hand to the group, pointer finger up, in the classic teacher gesture of, "Class, be quiet." She didn't need to, no one was talking, but it felt right as she used her left hand to dial 911. She was so happy to hear another human's voice that she probably sounded *way* too chipper to be calling about two dead bodies.

"Nine-one-one, what is your emergency?"

"Two people have been murdered."

"What is the location of your emergency?"

"We're at 841 River Road, Cherry Log."

"Okay, ma'am, dispatch has been alerted and the police and ambulance are on their way. Is anyone hurt?"

"No. I mean. Two people are dead. And the murderer is tied up. But the rest of us are Okay."

"Have you checked for a pulse?"

"Yes, I am trying to tell you. They are dead. And we need the police. *Now.*"

"Ma'am, officers are on their way. Please stay on the line with me until they arrive."

Lydia nodded, sat down at the table with the phone pressed to her ear, and waited.

No one else moved. She was waiting for questions from the 911 operator. Everyone else was simply waiting. It didn't take long. Less than an hour later, Mary, Martha, Cynde, Clark, and Lydia huddled in the living room, clustered near the still-burning fireplace, as the uniformed men came in to take the bodies away. Auden was still outside the room, shotgun now unloaded, explaining his role in the whole affair to one of the many officers. Mary and Martha both turned away to face the huge windows as two stretchers were rolled out, each carrying a zipped-up black body bag. Cynde and Clark, strangely enough, sat together on the large couch, talking quietly.

More men and women in uniform streamed in. Lydia half wondered if they were setting up a crime scene recreation in the bedrooms. It seemed impossible. This was nothing like *CSI* or *Law & Order*. She didn't feel excited or even scared—just completely and utterly exhausted. She was staring into her empty white-and-blue coffee mug and standing by the fire even though she still felt cold, when she heard someone clear her throat.

"Ma'am? Ma'am? Are you in charge here?" the officer asked. Lydia wanted to snap, "No. You are. Look at your fancy badge and your fancy hat. I don't ever want to be in charge again." Instead, she nodded, saying nothing.

"Listen, ma'am," the woman continued, in a thick and soft Southern accent that made the "ma'am" feel earnest rather than snide. "They're saying you put the call in, and I need to know what happened here. Can you help me?"

Lydia finally looked her in the eyes. Encouraged, she continued, "My name is Sergeant Metcalf. What's yours?"

She looked nice. If that mattered. Heather had looked nice. . . . Lydia pulled her thoughts back from the edge. "My name is Lydia. I organized this weekend. It was supposed to be a sewing retreat?" She looked at Sergeant Metcalf, thinking maybe her grandma sewed, maybe she had some idea of what she was talking about. She didn't; she looked baffled.

She took a deep breath. "I own a fabric shop over in Peridot, and I organized a weekend of sewing for people who like to sew. People I know from my shop. It started on Friday," Lydia lost her train of thought. Friday? Only a few days ago? That seemed impossible.

"This is your house?" she asked.

"No, I live in Peridot. And the house belongs, belonged, to Fran. I mean technically it belongs. Oh, for goodness sake. Sit down. I'll start at the beginning," and without waiting, Lydia sank into a large leather chair next to the fireplace. Sergeant Metcalf took the chair facing hers.

"Yes, please, ma'am; start at the beginning if you would."

Lydia did the best she could. "We all came up here on Friday night to spend the long weekend together, sewing and relaxing." She flinched as she remembered her stupid slogan, and then continued. "Saturday afternoon we found, well, I found, our host, Fran, murdered in her room. She'd been hit in the head, with a sad iron."

Sergeant Metcalf began to speak, but Lydia kept going.

"A sad iron. It's a heavy plain iron people used to put in the fire and heat up and then iron their clothes with, before electricity. Fran used one as a paperweight. She had been hit in the head with it. They're heavy. And, well, we couldn't call the police or get to town because of the storm. So, we agreed to wait until it was safe or possible to contact the outside world. Then, on Sunday, we, I mean I, found Amy dead in her room from a fentanyl overdose." Lydia heard a small whistle escape from the sergeant, and she pushed on. "Amy was a member of the retreat. It looked like she had killed herself after killing Fran, and we thought maybe there had been a love triangle. . . ."

Lydia didn't elaborate. "But it didn't sit right with me. Then a lot of secrets came to light. I found out Fran wanted to leave this house to me. Um, she had cancer?" Lydia was already losing the thread of the narrative. "Fran was dying. She wanted to give me the house. But it turns out that another member of our group, Heather, was actually Fran's daughter that she had given up for adoption thirty-five years ago. Heather killed Fran when she confessed her secret and felt rejected. Then she killed Amy to frame her.

"I told everyone this morning that I had inherited the house, to see how Heather would react. I figured, if Heather was guilty, and I was right as to why, she'd want the house badly enough to kill me, too. I asked Auden to wait in the bathroom that connected to my room and. . . ."

She paused.

"He caught her trying to poison my water with fentanyl. She was going to try to claim I killed myself as well. And then she tried to stab me with a seam ripper."

Again, the sergeant tried to interrupt and again Lydia kept going, explaining, "A seam ripper is a sharp, curved blade used to tear out stitches. But Auden had his gun. So, she didn't."

"And that's who we found tied up in that bedroom?" Sergeant Metcalf asked.

"Yes. I tied her up with bias binding after she tried to stab me. Then the power came back on and the phone started working and I called 911 and here you are." Lydia, for the first time in her life, simply didn't have anything else to say.

Sergeant Metcalf seemed unperturbed by the absurdity of her explanation.

"You found both the bodies?"

"Yeah."

"And you engineered a trap to catch the killer?"

"Yeah."

"Who then tried to stab you?"

"Yeah."

"And someone has a gun?"

"Auden. Auden has a gun. Fran kept it here and he knew where to find it. He's the caretaker for the house. He lives in a cabin a little farther up to the mountain. But we had to call him because of the eggs."

"Excuse me, ma'am. What eggs?"

Sergeant Metcalf asked so earnestly that Lydia couldn't help smiling, even if she felt tears behind her eyes as she did so.

"Before the storm hit, we, um, there were some deviled eggs that clogged up the garbage disposal, so we called Auden, Mr. Williams, down to fix the sink. And then everything happened," she explained, her smile fading.

One tear leaked out and slid down her cheek.

Sergeant Metcalf saw the tear and had the grace to give Lydia a break, saying, "Ma'am, thank you for being so helpful. We'll need to interview the others. Also, we are gonna need the keys to the house and you'll need to make an official statement." She paused, taking in again how visibly exhausted Lydia looked from having told the whole terrible story of that weekend as another tear followed the first.

"But how about you get some food first, freshen up. We can call into Peridot and use an interview room at their station. We'll meet you there in a few hours."

It sounded like a good plan. Except. How was Lydia going to get back to Peridot? The others still needed to talk to the sergeant. Plus, she couldn't imagine those car rides: an hour with Clark debating whether or not the murders would impact his chance at being the chair of the Peridot Botanical Gardens. No, not an option. So?

Lydia had been quiet for too long and the sergeant was staring again. Ugh. Forty years old and about to admit she didn't have a way home. "Well, you see, Sergeant, I. . . ."

"If it's all right with you, sir, I'll take Miss Barnes back to Peridot," Auden interrupted.

"And you are?" Sergeant Metcalf asked, a little steel in her polite Southern drawl.

"Auden Williams. I'm the caretaker for the house. I had the gun. I already gave it to, I believe, your deputy?" he asked, pointing at the young man in uniform who was now examining Auden's rifle with gloves on.

"Did you give Deputy Weltner your statement?"

"Yes, ma'am, and all my information. But I know Lydia, Miss Barnes, got a ride up here, so I thought I could take her on home, if that's all right with you?" Auden said politely, but Lydia noticed a little steel had entered his soft voice as well.

"All right. That should be fine, Mr. Williams. It sounds like this Heather is who we really need to be talking to now."

Sergeant Metcalf stood up and addressed the larger group:

"Thank y'all for your patience. I can see this has been a horrible ordeal," at which the M's started nodding vigorously. "And now that I have talked with Miss Barnes here, we are just about ready to let y'all head on home. My deputy, Deputy Weltner, will be sitting right over there at that table, and if you could go over, one by one, and give him your statement, you can be on your way back to Peridot. But no leaving town from there, you hear? We'll be coordinating with the local Peridot police on this one, so make sure to leave your contact information."

Mary and Martha gravitated toward the deputy, drawn to the most distinguished man in the room, as always, even if a woman was actually in charge, while Clark walked to the kitchen to be the next to give his statement. To be fair to the M's, Deputy Weltner was a good-looking man, if you had a penchant for sideburns. She wouldn't swear by it, but Lydia thought she overheard Mary offer him some jelly beans. Even though Mary always had jelly beans, Lydia had never once seen her share them or even offer to do so. She looked over and saw the deputy's open, outstretched hand. And then she saw, miracle of miracles, Mary's tight hand drop red, green, and orange jellybeans into his palm. The sideburns on his face rose as he smiled.

Lydia wasn't a fan of sideburns, herself. She liked skinny guys named after famous poets; she liked. . . .

"Would you like to get some food back in Peridot? Then I can drop you off at your place. I remembered that you said you didn't have a car. I didn't mean to assume. . . . I can call a cab for you, if that's better. My friend, Tom, runs a really reliable service in Blue Ridge. He's got tires that can handle. . . ."

"Pizza?" Lydia interrupted.

"What?"

"Would you want to get pizza for lunch?"

"Oh, right. Sounds good. Is there a place you like in Peridot?"

"Frank's. That's my favorite. Have you ever had a Major Meat pizza?" Lydia asked in quick reply.

"No, but it sounds amazing," Auden replied, shaking his head with bemusement. "I'm going to walk up to my cabin and get my truck and come down and pick you up. The ice has melted enough. That work?"

Lydia could have sworn the top of his ears were turning a little pink. She knew for a fact her cheeks were red. "That totally works," she replied. "Charlie can come, right? And, I mean, is it safe?"

Auden reached down and rubbed Charlie's belly where he lay, stretched out by the fireplace. "Charlie can come. And it's safe now. You'd be surprised how quickly the mountain comes back to life," Auden said, as he grabbed his jacket and headed out the door.

She needed to say goodbye to the group. Were there even words for this sort of departure? Closing the door behind Auden, she looked back at her friends. They had lost Fran. Lost Amy. And, really, they had lost Heather. More than that, they had lost their façades. The secrets that had come with them into the weekend were no longer hidden.

Clark, Cynde, and Mary and Martha. Just three days ago, she had seen them as friends, but also, as she had just realized that day, she had seen them a little bit as caricatures, almost archetypes. It had been humbling to realize that each of them had deeper desires and fears than she had given them credit for. There was no way to apologize for her shortcomings. It was far too late to apologize for the ruthless way she had brought those secrets to light. Now it was time to go home.

"Sergeant Metcalf," Lydia asked. "Could I have a minute to talk to my friends? Just over there in the summer room? It won't take long."

"Summer room?"

"Oh, sorry, that's what Fran called the porch off the kitchen. I just want to say goodbye," she clarified.

"I suppose that's fine," she replied, perhaps a little frustrated with the M's unbending focus on her junior deputy. Lydia called them all over to the summer room, and Cynde joined from the living room and Clark from the kitchen, having just finished giving his statement.

"Auden has offered me a ride back to Peridot. I'm going to go to the station later to give a full, official statement. It sounds like the Peridot police will be following up with each of us, as well, in the days ahead. I guess I just wanted to say, before everyone went their own way. . . ."

What did she want to say?

"I'm sorry."

"What do you have to be sorry for, Lydia? We all know none of this was your fault," Cynde countered, sounding both earnest but also exhausted.

The others nodded, even Clark, which was a relief.

"I know it's not my fault. What happened. But I'm still sorry. I'm sorry we all felt like we had to keep secrets. I hope you will still feel like Measure Twice is your home, as well. I want to honor Fran. I want to keep alive the things she loved. She loved the store. I know she wasn't perfect," and at that Clark scoffed, which was also a relief. He was still Clark.

"Okay, she was far from perfect. Still, I know she loved all of you. I know because of the cards she wrote. I know because of how she worked to make this weekend perfect. Beyond that, I know because when I signed the contract for the store, she took me out to Frank's afterwards. She told me that the store wasn't the building. It wasn't the fabric and notions and kits. You all are the store. I hope, more than anything, I really hope we can keep that alive."

With that, she stopped talking. It was true. Fran had said that while Lydia had been scarfing down slices after the emotionally charged experience of officially taking over ownership of Measure Twice.

No one said anything. Lydia let her shoulders slump. It would be a little anticlimactic as far as endings went, but that was okay. If any situation called for grace, this was it.

Plus, Auden would be there soon to take her to pizza. Why did she always turn to pizza in times of trouble?

Then Clark broke the silence, "I'm going to head back to town now, too. Obviously. But Lydia, why don't you let us all know when the next craft night is at Measure Twice? We could use the time to talk about a memorial for Fran?"

Cynde added, "I'll bring cookies."

Mary and Martha nodded, and Mary added, "We could use some more time to work on our EPP. I know Peridot Baptist does a lovely flower arrangement, so we could discuss some options, too. Thursday, perhaps?"

That was it. No larger declaration of love or forgiveness. No enormous, cathartic reckoning of emotions. Just the offer to show up. To keep sewing. To honor their friend. It was perfect.

"Thursday sounds good. The new Dear Stella line should be in store by then, so we can do a fabric reveal, as well, and Clark, maybe you could help us think about some catering ideas for a memorial service," Lydia offered, unbelievably relieved. Relieved enough to pay to eat Clark's seaweed chips and his kale dip.

"Thursday, then. I'll bring some hors d'oeuvres to try out," Clark agreed.

Cynde stood to give her statement to Deputy Weltner, and Clark went to ask Sergeant Metcalf if he could have access down to the library for his "things." Lydia clearly heard the words "HEPA air filter," even though Clark was trying to keep the conversation hushed.

The police had already made it clear to Lydia that she would have to come back another time to get her belongings, since Heather was in her room, but they had given her permission to take Charlie back to Peridot.

Lydia grabbed the leash by the front door and clipped it to Charlie's collar. She looked around the living room of the Laurels. The sunshine looked so hopeful but also so alien. She only knew that house in darkness. She tried to remember the first time she had seen the Laurels, with Fran in the doorway, framed in warm light, welcoming her in. Fran knew then that the house would be hers. She had no way of knowing the tragedy that awaited her, Amy, all of them in a way, but she knew she wanted Lydia to have the house that she loved.

The house belonged to her. She would have to find a way back to that welcoming light. Before she could worry further, Charlie tugged her outside, relieved to be in a world that wasn't storming. Come to think of it, Lydia was too.

# Chapter Seventeen

Auden had said the mountain would come back to life, and he was right. She had opened the door into an entirely new reality. His pickup waited, idling at the start of the drive. Just the day before, the gravel had been trapped beneath a layer of slick ice. The emergency vehicles had brought salt and sand with them, and now she walked on pockmarked ice, easily keeping her balance.

Just the day before, the world had felt closed off and unwelcoming. Now she felt it releasing, relenting. Charlie trotted behind, lifting his nose to the new scents.

Petrichor, of course. Lydia could remember her surprise in college when she learned there was a specific word for the smell of the earth right after the rain: petrichor. Was there a different word for when it wasn't just rain but an ice storm? *There should be*, she thought.

When she reached Auden's beat-up pickup, Lydia opened the door and looked up at him and at the ridgeline behind him, listening to the gentle shattering of the ice as it fell from tree limbs and bushes. She knew what it was like to close a chapter. How many times had she told herself she was living AG, After Graham? As if his name had anything to do with her life now. She missed Fran already. But it felt right, to miss her here, on her mountain, as the storm lost its grip on the world. The police had asked her to leave her belongings at the house to keep the scene undisturbed, so she was leaving the mountain with only her purse and Charlie.

Climbing into Auden's car, Lydia declared, "Just in case you were worried. I'm not selling the Laurels."

"Oh," was all Auden said in reply, as they wound their way down the mountain, but he seemed lighter.

"We've all lost so much, you know? I obviously don't have a plan for the Laurels, but I want to hold on to it, at least for a while. Fran gave it to me because she didn't want to just sell it. I want to honor that. Fran gave me . . . Fran wanted . . . I just want Fran to know. . . ."

Lydia didn't start crying. She didn't.

They drove on for a while, listening to quiet country music, looking at the wreckage of the storm between Cherry Log and Peridot. Lydia had never been good at quiet, but it felt right, just being in Auden's company, watching the world slip past her window. The trip felt so comfortable she was actually surprised when Auden turned the pickup truck into the town square.

Even though everything had changed, Lydia still got what she secretly thought to herself as the Peridot feeling. As soon as she saw the old historic square, she felt lighter. This small cluster of shops and restaurants had offered her safe harbor from the disaster of her marriage, and now it waited in the watery winter sunshine, ready to offer respite from the nightmare weekend behind her.

Technically, it was the last day of a long holiday weekend, but the square was quiet. The storm had kept any weekend visitors at home, and locals were most likely out clearing debris and putting their yards to right.

As Auden turned his pickup into the square, Lydia pointed out Frank's, sitting at what she thought of as the bottom left corner of the square: "That's Frank's, but if it's okay with you, I'll run up to the apartment and drop off Charlie before we have pizza."

Auden nodded, driving slowly around the square, where traffic moved clockwise in one direction. Frank's was at the bottom, around 7 o'clock, and Measure Twice and the apartment were farther around, toward the upper left corner, around 2 o'clock.

Auden saw the store before Lydia could say anything and pulled up to an empty parking spot outside.

"I'm just going to take Charlie up and drop off my stuff, and I'll be down in a second," Lydia offered, flustered and talking a little too quickly. Auden smiled.

Once they got into the apartment, Charlie collapsed on the living room couch, all too happy to finally be out of the middle of the action, and Lydia went into the bedroom and stared at her closet.

When he had gone to get his truck, Auden had put on a clean shirt. True, it was an almost identical worn plaid button-down, but Lydia still noticed.

What she really wanted was a hot, impossibly long, shower, but Auden was waiting. Looking down at her T-shirt, the same "I HEART CRAFTING" shirt she had been wearing when they cornered Heather, the same shirt she had been wearing when Heather had tried. . . .

Lydia took her shirt off and threw it in the laundry hamper, taking a moment to wonder if maybe she'd just throw it out when she got back from lunch. Then she reached into her closet and pulled out one of the first shirts she had ever sewn.

When she hopped back into Auden's truck, he looked at her and smiled, a smile that lit up his brown eyes. He looked down at her shirt and then back up, simply saying, "Cool dragons."

Lydia looked down, too, at the Technicolor cartoon dragons that sailed across her handmade shirt. True, she could have tried to impress Auden, or even, God forbid, seduce him. But what was that saying? Begin as you mean to continue? Auden had already seen her slogan T-shirts; she might as well show him her handmades too.

Lydia realized the truck was still parked in front of Measure Twice. Auden was studying the store. Even though she knew she was being shallow, Lydia felt relieved that she had recently updated the store windows with new makes on the mannequins. Handwritten signs announced both the patterns and the fabrics available just inside for purchase. Heather had made those signs. Heather. . . .

Shaking her head, as if Heather were just freezing rain she could brush off, she needlessly declared, "That's Measure Twice," Even the specter of Heather couldn't completely dampen the pride she felt looking at the store.

"It looks really cool. I'd love to see inside sometime," and with that pronouncement, Auden started the truck and continued around the square until they were back at the bottom of the clock, parking outside of Frank's.

Lydia snapped into tour guide mode. "So, this is Frank's. Best pizza in Peridot. Only pizza in Peridot if you don't count the Pizza Hut we passed on the way in," and Lydia didn't count it. Chain pizza was, in her opinion, *fine*. Stuck at airport when your flight gets delayed for the third time? Pizza Hut can save the day. But Frank's was on a whole 'nother level.

# Quilty as Charged

The chime on the door announced their arrival, and for a moment, just a moment, Lydia considered putting her hand on Auden's arm to steer him to the counter, even though the setup at Frank's was pretty straightforward: a counter, with the menu above it, and the round tables scattered about the large main room, edged in slightly worn-down booths.

Auden walked straight to the counter, and Lydia followed, tucking her hands into her pockets, fiercely hoping she wasn't blushing.

"What was it you recommended?" Auden asked. "Super meat?"

The last three days of her life had been the worst. The honest, swear-to-God, worst days of her life. But, looking up at Auden now, backlit by the pizza menu, his earnest brown eyes radiating sincerity as he said the phrase "super meat," Lydia laughed.

It wasn't a long laugh, nor even particularly loud. Still, her shoulders relaxed and dropped down. Had she even realized that they were practically up to her ears, taut with tension?

Thankfully, Auden laughed, too, and then raised one eyebrow, waiting for confirmation or correction.

"You mean the Major Meat?" Lydia answered, in a comically serious tone, as if she were taking an order at an upscale French restaurant.

Auden picked up on the joke and responded, "Ah yes, the Major Meat, that sounds delightful," and with that he turned to the counter and ordered a large Major Meat and two drinks. At Frank's, the cups were large, red plastic ones, only one size, and you simply filled them with your choice of beverage at the machine. Auden passed Lydia her cup, and she immediately opted for too much ice and very sweet lemonade. Auden, she noticed, just filled his cup with water. They took the drinks and their table number, a playing card on a tall wire holder, and sat down at a round table close to the front window.

Lydia continued explaining the town square: "That right there in the middle is the courthouse, where Cynde works as a stenographer." They both paused, thinking of all Cynde had lost. Then Lydia barreled on, which was starting to feel like her signature move, and pointed to the part of the square they had passed between her apartment and Frank's.

"Over there is the Pampered Pantry, Clark's store, and next to that is Blessed Again, the church charity shop the M's run."

A waitress came over and placed a hot, fresh pizza on a stand on the table, took the playing card, and left Lydia and Auden to look at their lunch in awe.

"You weren't lying—that is major!" And with that, Auden took the spatula and served them each a piece, deftly twisting the stretchy cheese onto each plate. Lydia noticed he covered his slice in pepper flakes, but neither of them talked, too focused on eating the delicious, hot pizza that had nothing to do with the cabin, the storm, or the murders.

As if reading her mind, Auden put down his slice and asked her, quietly, "How did you really know it was Heather?"

Lydia put her slice down as well, a little reluctantly. It was good pizza, and she didn't particularly want to talk about Heather. At the same time, some part of her understood that it had to be said, that keeping it in would only make it worse.

"It comes down to love, you know?" Lydia asked, pushing the toppings that had fallen off her slice around the plate.

Auden choked a bit on his slice that he had resumed eating. "Love?" he asked, his voice rising slightly.

Lydia watched Auden take a large swig of his water and went on. "Yeah. Love. I know it's horrible, but I really did snoop into everyone's lives this weekend. I didn't want it to be one of us, I really didn't, but I had to be sure. And then it seemed like everyone had a motive," Lydia paused to eat a bite of pizza.

"It was horrible to realize that everyone in that house had a reason to be mad at Fran. Fran was always so good to me, you know? She wanted Measure Twice to thrive, but she didn't care enough about who it hurt. Still, I think anger isn't the strongest feeling; love is. Love is what really makes us irrational, not anger."

"Then I had to ask myself, who really loved Fran? When I realized that Heather had been lying to us about being Fran's daughter, I had to ask myself why. I think she was afraid that Fran wouldn't love her back, if she knew the truth." Lydia paused to take the last bite of her slice, relieved that Auden was already on his third. She always went for at least three slices when she ordered Frank's.

"It was finding out that Heather had been adopted that made you realize she was the killer?" Auden asked, giving Lydia a chance to put a second slice on her plate.

"Well, that was the start. But what really made it click for me was trying to imagine what would have happened if Heather had confronted Fran. Like I said, Fran was my fairy godmother, but she was also a little ruthless, you know? What if Heather had imagined a certain reaction, and well, Fran hadn't given it to her."

It was hard, still, to say out loud that she knew Fran could be cruel. But then again, no one was perfect. One moment of cruelty didn't mean Fran was a bad person, just that she was, well, human.

Auden looked at his watch but was too polite to say that he should probably be heading back to Cherry Log. Lydia knew the pizza lunch couldn't last forever. The police would be in touch before too long. She still had to pick up Baby Lobster from Jeff. Ugh, Jeff.

Interrupting her thoughts about creepy Jeff, Auden asked, "But you said it was about love. Not cruelty. I don't really understand."

"Once I realized Fran might have been cruel to Heather, even if it wasn't on purpose, that made me think about how much Heather must have been counting on love. She'd had so long to imagine Fran's reaction. That Fran would be thrilled and be *her* fairy godmother, like she was to me. Heather had seen that, you know? She must have assumed something even better for herself. The love she felt, and the love she *expected*. That was the strongest motive in the house," Lydia finished. She hadn't said it quite so clearly, at least not out loud. The simple waste of it all was enough to make the pizza taste like cardboard in her mouth. She certainly wasn't crying, but a large swallow of painfully sweet lemonade did offer a good chance for her to regain her composure.

"I hadn't thought of it that way," Auden admitted.

"Well, you were the one that kept her from killing me," Lydia added, in an attempt to lighten the mood, but instead they both blanched at the memory.

"I'm so glad you are okay," Auden responded softly. He looked at her across the remnants of their slices.

"Enough about Heather," Lydia declared, breaking the moment and cursing her own awkwardness. She plowed on, "Can I ask you something?"

"Sure. But I don't know anything you don't know."

"When we were . . . at the Laurels that weekend . . . the cars in the driveway . . . the way Charlie seemed so spooked. That wasn't Heather," Lydia winced realizing she had broken the brand new rule.

"Oh." Auden tidied up his plate, folding his grease-stained paper napkin. "The car was Collins's."

Lydia folded her own napkin, wishing she knew origami, even though she needed a new hobby like she needed a hole in her head. A hole in her head? Why were all those folksy saying so gruesome?

"He's my best friend."

"Who is?"

"Collins. We were going to open the woodworking shop together. He was, um, *displeased* with how Fran blocked our bid. So, he, made his displeasure known. He had no idea what was going on . . . he just thought it would piss Fran off, he's really sorry, I promise, it was stupid, he didn't mean any harm . . ."

Lydia looked at Auden looking at his napkin again.

"Scaring Charlie seems a step a too far, though." Lydia wanted to be forgiving, to let it slide for bestie Collins, but her loyalty to her dog came first.

"What? Oh no! Collins revved his car. He didn't stalk the property. There was probably an animal outside. Charlie was just being a dog. Defending his turf."

"Oh. Okay, then. That makes a lot more sense. It just bothered me. I'm not mad at . . . Collins?"

Auden nodded.

"But thanks for being honest."

"Of course." Auden forgot his napkin, looking only at Lydia. Some of his brown hair had fallen forward as they talked, and

Lydia felt an absurd desire to reach across the table and tuck the lock back behind his ear. This time Auden broke the spell. "I need to be getting home soon, but, um, I was thinking, I could help you with the Laurels, until you decide what you want to do. You could give me a call when you have a chance?"

His voice went up, turning the statement into a question.

Lydia steadied her breath, took the takeout menu on the table and flipped it over, writing down her name and cell number, and then pushed the paper toward Auden, adding, "Why don't you call me?"

# Chapter Eighteen

**Three Months Later**

D onuts seemed like a good starting point. Inviting Auden to dinner would mean . . . well, she wasn't sure what it would mean, which was the problem. Lydia knew she had chickened out by inviting him to come have late-morning donuts in the Peridot town square. But PeriDOUGH Bakery and Café's donuts were so good that it made it a little less of a cop-out.

They had settled on ten o'clock, a nice, civilized hour on a Saturday. Lydia asked Cynde to meet at the bakery earlier, at nine, so that she could have an earlier crack at the donut selection and a little dose of confidence. It was almost nine, so Lydia needed to get a move on.

This time, she left all her "sew amazing" T-shirts at home. She had briefly considered wearing her latest sew, a Zadie jumpsuit in the most gorgeous linen: bright yellow lemons and blossoms on a pale blue background. But a jumpsuit was a bold statement, and Lydia wasn't quite ready to make a *bold* statement. That morning she had rifled through her closet and decided on her recently made

Wiksten shift. The pattern had sold out at Measure Twice in less than a week, and she had felt a little guilty about putting one aside for herself from that first shipment. But now she knew that had been the right call.

It was a simple make, no buttons or zippers. But it had enough shape, enough details, to look intentional and pulled together. She had dug deep into her stash to find the right fabric for the pattern.

But she had found it: a saturated dusty pink linen with a heavy drape. It was a magical remnant find from her trip to the Cloth House in London with her best friend, Jes, years ago. It was just long enough to make the dress with almost no fabric to spare, and she loved how it looked when she was finished. Plus, it had pockets. Some of Fran's fairy godmother magic still lingered in Lydia's life.

It would have tickled Fran to see Lydia, nervously getting ready for Mr. Williams' visit. Not long after that pizza lunch at Frank's Pizza, Auden had reached out about looking after the Laurels. He helped her set the house up for rentals and ran the whole operation, checking in with her as needed. The calls they exchanged were short, but they were also frequent.

She tried not to think about how she felt each time she saw his name on her caller ID. Thinking about it would just trigger another blush.

She clipped Charlie's collar to his leash and headed out. As soon as she shut her own door, Jeff opened his. Lydia flinched. She felt guilty, even though Jeff had no idea she had briefly considered him a murderer.

"Oh Lydia, I'm so glad I caught you!"

Lydia mentally noted that four entire buttons were undone on today's silk shirt, a pink paisley print against a purple background.

"Hi, Jeff. Happy Saturday," and with that she tried to keep walking toward the stairs, but he reached out and held a box out toward her.

"Like I was saying. I'm so glad I caught you. This got delivered to me by mistake." Jeff watched her take the box, clearly expecting her to open it in his presence.

Instead, Lydia tucked the small box into her slouchy purse and tried again to escape.

"Need me to watch Baby Lobster any time soon?" Jeff asked.

"Nope. Thanks, though. No retreats planned anytime soon."

"Well, let's talk soon. I have a business proposition we need to discuss."

"Sure. We'll do that. Thanks for this!" and with that, she sped away before he could say anything else, or worse, try to hug her goodbye. A business proposition? What on earth could that be about? She didn't really want to find out. Jeff might not be a murderer, but he still gave her the creeps.

On the street, Lydia paused to open the small box. The package contained a jewelry box, and when opened, it revealed a small, sparkling brooch, the kind you would usually find pinned on a cashmere cardigan. Or use to secure a lovely scarf. The brooch itself was a cluster of three oversized buttons. The two larger buttons were covered in green and pink rhinestones. The smaller button had blue rhinestones. It was, well, it was perfect. Then she opened the small note that accompanied the thoughtful and mysterious gift:

"Dear Lydia, my mama always taught me that the best presents were the ones you were tempted to keep for yourself. I had her lesson in mind when I found this brooch for you. Please take it as a token of our profound thanks. And that will be enough said about that.

Yours in gratitude—Mary."

Lydia tucked the card and jewelry box into her purse, dropping the shipping box into a street side recycling bin; then she pinned the brooch to her dress. It matched perfectly. That was just like Mary. Lydia thought she understood the desire to say thanks, but also the desire to leave it at that. Well, Mary's secret was safe with her.

As she walked past Measure Twice, she waved to Delaney from the window. Delaney gestured for her to wait, so Lydia paused outside the shop. She still had a little time, and she always enjoyed talking to her newest employee.

Delaney stepped out of the shop and onto the sidewalk, immediately bending down to rub Charlie on the back of his neck. He stretched in appreciation. Lydia looked at Delaney. As per usual, Delaney was wearing one of her own makes, a Closet Core Elodie Wrap Dress in a soft Rifle Paper Company floral rayon. The pale green background and peach flowers looked lovely and summery, paired with Delaney's long brown hair that she wore loose down her back.

"Why don't I grab Baby Lobster and take her down to the shop?" Delaney offered, knowing the cat loved to nap in the sunshine of the shop window.

"Delaney, that would be great! Thanks! I'll be back to the shop around noon, we can do something fun for a lunch break," Lydia promised, turning to head toward the bakery.

"Sounds great. Just one more thing, Lydia. Could we talk later, maybe over lunch? I have an idea I really want to run by you," she finished, looking a little anxious.

"Absolutely, Delaney. We'll talk at lunch. I've got to run. See you later," Lydia assured the young woman. Whatever it was could wait. She hurried to the bakery, practically dragging Charlie along. He would be patient waiting outside the bakery, clipped to a bike rack, but he clearly had other ways he wanted to spend his time.

There were a lot of reasons she loved life in Peridot—big, important reasons like finding community and purpose. But also, donuts. That counted as a big reason to Lydia. More often than not Lydia started her day with a stop at PeriDOUGH Bakery and Café. The shop was all done in green and white, with a Formica counter and padded stools. To the left of the counter, a clear glass window let shoppers view the donut-making process. To the right of the counter were a few tables where the regulars sat with their morning papers.

"Bakery and Café" was a bit of an overstatement, since the owner, Kaleigh, really just did donuts. Well, donuts, quiches, coffee, and sweet tea. Coffee, not even lattes. Still, the offerings might be simple, but they were always delicious.

Pushing the swinging door into the bakery, Lydia went straight up to the counter and ordered six donuts: two cinnamon sugar, two glazed, and two of the special of the day, a new flavor called Miner's Gold that promised honey and vanilla in its yellow frosting. The donuts came in a bright green box with white lettering that she tucked shut as she turned to scan the bakery for her friend.

It was a relief to see Cynde, wearing her summer uniform of a sleeveless linen dress with bright appliqued flowers and orthotic sandals over socks, waiting at a table. She had invited Cynde to meet her at nine, a full hour before Auden was meant to arrive. They both knew that, had nothing terrible happened, it would have been Fran meeting with Lydia, calming her nerves and offering her advice. But Cynde had stepped into the role with grace and kindness.

Cynde already had two mugs of coffee and two Miner's Gold donuts sitting at her table when she waved Lydia over. As soon as Lydia sat down, Cynde took a big bite of her donut and mumbled through a full mouth, "I have some exciting news. I have a new job! You know *The Peridot Gazette*?"

Lydia nodded. Everyone knew the *Gazette*, the local paper as old as Peridot itself. Copies were always strewn around the bakery.

"I'm their new events reporter! It was time for a change. This way, I get to go out and see what's happening in the town and nearby, and I get paid for it!" Cynde laughed and ate more of her donut.

"Cynde, that is so great!" Lydia said, and she meant it.

"What about you?" Cynde asked, gesturing with a piece of donut. "How's the shop? How are you? When does *he* get here?"

"The shop is great. I hired a girl to help part-time. Her name is Delaney, and she's great. In fact, she's doing the opening today and offered to grab Baby Lobster and let her hang out in the shop while I, um, see friends." Lydia blushed. "And, well, there is something else." That was when she put the formal invitation down on the green Formica table. "It's actually happening, Cynde, the wedding. I think I might . . . well . . . I think I'm going to go," Lydia finished, blushing even more fiercely and looking down at her coffee.

Cynde actually spit her coffee out, back into the mug she had just lifted to her mouth. "Excuse me?" Cynde's jaw actually dropped, and then she just blurted out, "EGG!"

"What?"

"Their initials, Lydia, those stupid idiots, their initials spell EGG! Emma-Grace and Graham. You can't be serious about going to an EGG wedding!" Cynde laughed so hard it sounded almost like a wheeze.

Lydia found herself laughing, too. "I haven't made up my mind."

Cynde let Lydia off the hook at that, but she knew her friend would be checking back in about the EGG event. But for now, she played nice and changed the subject, asking, "When does the Brawny Man arrive?"

"His name is Auden, as you well know, and he is meeting me outside the bakery at ten. Then we're going to walk around the square for a bit. That's it, Cynde, just a walk," but even as she said it, Lydia knew she was grinning like a fool.

"It's almost ten, now, Lydia! I don't start the new job till Monday, so I won't report on your walk. But don't expect this special treatment in the future!"

Both women stood and then hugged. Cynde whispered, "You've got this," in Lydia's ear and then walked out of the bakery. Lydia gathered her box of donuts and went back to the counter to get two cups of coffee to go.

Lydia and Auden had agreed to meet outside the donut shop and walk around the square for a bit. Charlie waited patiently outside the donut shop. He knew the drill by now, and he knew good behavior might get him a little bite of donut, glazed, before the walk was over. Lydia untied Charlie, and holding his leash, sat down on a nearby bench to wait for Auden.

Lydia thought back to the first time she had seen him. The way she had awkwardly brought up "Musée Des Beaux Arts." She loved that poem, the way Auden described Brueghel's painting of Icarus's fall, this monumental moment in mythology. But in the painting, Icarus hits the water in the bottom right corner of the scene. Just a leg and water splashing up to hint at the body already underwater. The painting is really about how life goes on around it. Another line came back to her, as she looked out on her new life: "The dogs go on with their doggy life."

That wasn't to say that the loss of Fran, the senseless murders of Fran and Amy, weren't important. They were and they always would be. But Lydia also knew that Fran wouldn't want her to live in her grief.

Auden's white pickup pulled in just a few spaces down, and Lydia tried to look natural as she waited for him to get out of the truck and walk over. When she realized she was folding and refolding paper napkins, she gave up the attempt at looking natural, gathered the coffee and donuts, and walked over to meet him.

He hadn't changed. Actually, if anything, he had gotten cuter. His skin was a shade darker, the wrinkles at the corner of eyes a little more pronounced. Lydia caught herself wondering if it was a farmer's tan. She needed to focus and not stand there, drooling.

"Welcome back to Peridot!" Lydia declared, holding out the drink carrier with his coffee in one hand, while also trying to hold on to the donut box and Charlie's leash with the other hand. Charlie only complicated matters by fussing around Auden's feet, shamelessly begging for a belly rub.

"Thanks," Auden replied, taking the coffee and then crouching down to rub Charlie's belly. "What can I hold for you?" he asked, seeing her struggle to stay untangled.

"Would you mind holding the donuts? And grab whatever looks good to you. We can walk around, and I'll tell you all about Peridot," Lydia added, passing him the box after taking out another Miner's Gold donut for herself. He didn't need to know it was her second of the day. They set off, slowly, eating their donuts and letting Charlie sniff anything and everything that caught his eye.

While they were walking, she snuck a closer look at the care-taker from up the hill. Same Carhartt's. Same dirt-covered, nondescript work boots. But this time he wore a soft-looking chambray button-up, rolled at the sleeves and just barely tucked into his well-worn leather belt. Lydia really wanted to touch that fabric, but caught herself, and used the motion of her hand to gesture to the Measure Twice window as they walked around the square.

"Lydia, there's a cat in your shop window!" Auden exclaimed, pointing at the cat curled under the latest display on quilt jackets.

"Baby Lobster." Lydia replied, smiling at the cat soaking up the May morning sunshine.

"Baby *what*?" Auden looked at Lydia like maybe she had spent a little too much time with fabric and not enough with other human beings.

Lydia started laughing and couldn't stop. It felt like church giggles, and she knew she had to pull it together, but the harder she tried, the louder she laughed. She sputtered, "Baby . . . Lobster," which didn't make things any clearer for Auden.

She laughed, pointing back to the display, adding, "Baby Lobster is my cat. She hates car rides, and Clark hates cats, so she didn't come on the retreat. She loves the shop, though, and acts like she owns the place."

At this point she had gotten her giggles under control, but Auden still seemed baffled. "Is 'baby lobster' some kind of cat?" he asked, struggling to make sense of the conversation.

"Oh, right, sorry. She's a rescue. When I moved to Peridot and into Fran's apartment and started at the shop, I wanted Charlie to have some company. I'd never owned a cat, so I looked online at the local shelter, and there was a cat named Baby Lobster. I mean. BABY LOBSTER. Who on earth names a cat BABY LOBSTER? So, long story short, she had that name when I adopted her, and we've been a happy family ever since."

They both turned to look at the cat through the large windows. She was calico, with a white belly and a tortoiseshell-colored back. One ear was black and one ear orange. The splatter of color reminded Lydia of hand-dyed yarn. It was just another reason she had known Baby Lobster was the cat for her. As if aware she was being admired, the cat stretched, unfurled her tail, and then curled back up again, daintily licking one white paw. Lydia didn't mention that Baby Lobster had saved her life once, too.

Auden's wrinkled brow relaxed, and a wide smile spread across his face. "You can't help taking in strays, can you?"

She looked at him, trying to see if he was teasing her. And all of a sudden, she was a college freshman again, biting her lip and pushing her hair behind her ear, hoping a date ended in a good night kiss. Auden looked at her lips, then down at his hands, and then looked her in the eyes again.

"Lydia," Auden said quietly. She heard the insects buzzing around them, the distant call of a bird she couldn't name. She knew other people were strolling around the square, but for a moment, they all disappeared. There were a million things she wanted him to say next. Actually, she didn't want him to say anything. She wanted his rough, tanned hand on the side of her face. She wanted him to close the distance between them in an instant.

She wanted the smell of him: deodorant and laundry detergent and fresh dirt. Instead, he just said, "Lydia . . ." again, and before he could finish the thought Charlie saw a squirrel and yanked Lydia sideways, away from Auden.

Gone. The moment was gone. Lydia had an absurd urge to shake her fist at the offending squirrel. Auden chuckled and took a bite of his donut.

"So," Auden began, breaking the quiet, mouth full of donut, "what's happened to everyone? With everyone? You know what I mean." Auden concentrated on his donut and waited for Lydia to fill him in. They resumed their slow walk around the square.

"Well, Heather is still in custody. Last I heard her lawyer had pleaded mental illness, which, I mean, I guess? She seemed so clearheaded about what she had done, but that doesn't make her sane. She confessed pretty quickly, so I think they're just figuring out whether she goes to prison or an institution. To be honest, I stopped following the case. I didn't want her in my life in any way, you know?"

She added, "And we really heard it all, when she ranted about why she wanted to kill me, you know, back when . . . back when you saved my life."

"I was just trying to help," he replied.

"Nothing really came out that we didn't know. She had tracked down her birth mom. Gotten the job to get close to Fran, to find out what kind of person Fran was. She wanted the option to back out, but she found she loved Fran, and I think she just let the fantasy take over. She had seen Fran's fentanyl in her purse at the store one day, getting something Fran had asked her to grab. It was luck. Or whatever you call the opposite of luck. She dug around and found out Fran was dying, learned about the house, everything. She thought she would reveal her identity, Fran would weep with joy, and then Fran would leave the house to her."

"That's what you meant, when we talked about it at Frank's. That it was about love, not anger. Why didn't Fran just leave her the house? I mean, why isn't that what happened? That's what I never really understood." Auden admitted,

"I have had a lot of time to think about over the last few months. Why not just rejoice that you've found the daughter you thought you'd lost? Especially since she was sick. It could have been a chance for healing, for closure. Here's the thing I keep coming back to—we'll never really know what happened in that conversation. Heather can say that she was warm and lovely, but we'll never know if that's the truth. My guess? I think she dumped it all on Fran at once. That she was her daughter. That she was thirty-five, not twenty-five. That she had been lying all this time. And then I think she demanded things. Went straight to talking about the house.

"Imagine how Fran must have felt. It meant her daughter had found her and now just seemed to want payment. Heather had all that time to imagine a perfect mom, but I think Fran had also imagined a perfect daughter, and it wasn't someone with red hair and a bad case of resting brat face. I can see Fran being overwhelmed, sounding cold to Heather as she struggled to understand what was happening. That was probably all it took."

Lydia paused and ate some of her donut. The police told her, later, that there had been no sign of a struggle. Lydia imagined it had happened in an instant. Fran shut Heather down, and Heather, well, Heather just snapped.

Lydia shook herself and endeavored to get the conversation back on track.

"We don't talk about it anymore, really. But I do see the rest of the group. Clark is still around, still fussy. Maybe a little better? Fran had been, well, strongly encouraging him to invest in the shop. I don't want to say that she blackmailed him, of course, but she knew he had been involved in some scandal back in small-town Arkansas, and I guess . . .," Lydia trailed off.

She knew all the details by now, everything had come out during the investigation and the lead-up to the trial. Fran was her friend, and she just couldn't bring herself to really put into words what had happened between Fran and Clark.

Lydia realized Auden was looking at her, expecting to learn about Clark's fate.

"Right, so there was some scandal and he was so ashamed and once it was all out in the open, I think he realized no one cared. No one. I mean, don't get me wrong, he's still uptight enough to ask for the gluten-free menu at a barbecue joint, but he just seems lighter. More himself. He really wanted to be the chair of the board at the Botanical Garden in Peridot. And he got it. Right after everything that happened. Plus, business has been good at the Pampered Pantry, his store on the square that sells fancy snack food and whatnot. It's just over there," she added, pointing out the small but elegant-looking storefront.

"And get this. . . ." Lydia tried to pause to build suspense, but Auden was as patient and engaged as ever.

"He's been volunteering at Blessed Again, the church charity shop run by the M's!" Lydia pointed again, farther down the street to the charity shop.

Auden seemed underwhelmed, but to Lydia, it signified a deeper change. Clark had always been so . . . sharp. She was relieved to see him soften to offer help with no expectation of a reward.

"This is great," Auden mumbled, gesturing at his donut.

"Right?" Lydia replied, and then she paused, looking past him into the mountains. "What else? Cynde got a new job! She'll be reporting for the local paper, *The Peridot Gazette*. And she has started dating, which is just awesome. I think losing Fran was a real wake-up call, as horrible as that it is to say out loud. She comes to the store to get dating advice." As soon as Lydia said it, she started to blush. Desperate to stem the rising flush on her face, she kept talking, but even faster, "Not that I'm much help. Ha!" Internally, she flinched at her lame attempt at a laugh. So, she plowed on.

"Mary and Martha are still in classic form. Quilting, making deviled eggs, running a vast network of neighborhood gossip at Blessed Again. Though I have to say, they both come to my garment classes, which I really appreciate, you know? They had invested their retirement savings into Measure Twice, but when Fran sold to me, they got no real return on their investment. I don't know what the plan was, how Fran was going to pay them back. I like to think there was a plan. But I know that when we went on the retreat, Martha and Mary were terrified they had no way to live in retirement. I even, well, to be honest, I even thought that might have been a motive."

"Mary and Martha?! A motive?" Auden looked shocked. "But they're so . . . well . . . not sweet . . . but. They just remind me so much of Lady Lee, you know? Not harmless, exactly. Lady Lee would tell you what's what if you thought you could leave your dishes on the table. But murder?" He was clearly unconvinced.

"I know, I know," Lydia acquiesced. "I was scared, and willing to suspect anyone. Anyway, you wanted an update and there is some good news—it turns out that Fran also left me her apartment in Peridot. I had only been renting it before."

Auden looked at Lydia like he had no idea what that had to do with Mary and Martha.

"Right," she continued, noticing his confusion, "Well, since I moved into Fran's apartment, that, um, freed up my, um, ex-husband to sell the house we used to live in, and um, even though the divorce was final, he still owed me half of what the house sold for, so, um. . . ."

Why was she so bad at explaining difficult things?

"Let me try this again. Since I don't have to rent an apartment *and* I got a settlement from my ex, I gave that money from my old house to the M's."

Auden's jaw dropped. "You did what now?" He asked. The donut at this point completely forgotten.

"I already have a place. *And* I have the store. *And* I have rental income from the Laurels, thanks to your help," Lydia gestured at the whole world around them. "I don't need anything else. I have to believe Fran wanted to do right by them." She paused. "After the whole thing happened, Martha admitted that they had hoped on buying into a senior living community, but the capital just from their houses wouldn't be enough. They were stuck in houses they couldn't really manage anymore. With what I got for my share of my old place added to it, it worked out." Lydia was starting to feel self-conscious about how long she had been talking.

"I helped them move last weekend. They have a nice two-bed-room apartment in Lencreek, a pretty upscale senior community walking distance from the square so they can still run Blessed Again. The place even has a sewing club, which the M's have already taken over the leadership of," Lydia added, grimacing. She pitied whoever had thought they ran that group; there were defi-nitely new kids in town, as they say.

"They must be so grateful," Auden said, still floored that Lydia had parted with a chunk of her settlement so quickly. She looked down at the brooch sparkling on her pink dress and remembered Mary's note, saying, "And that will be enough said about that."

"They did stop by the store with a small token of their appre-ciation. And you'll never guess what it was," Lydia said, smiling mischievously at Auden.

Auden looked worried, "Deviled eggs?"

"No," Lydia laughed. "But close! It was a platter, you know the type with egg-shaped indentations, all the better to display your deviled eggs."

Auden and Lydia laughed together, and Lydia thought about inviting him up to her apartment to see the platter. But that would be too forward, surely. Although they were so close to her place. . . .

"What about you?" Auden asked, bringing her back to the present moment.

"What about me?" Lydia replied, embarrassed to realize she had been humming quietly to herself. "'When the morning comes, who'd you tell your dreams to. . . .'" She trailed off under her breath.

"I love John Prine," Auden added. Of course he did, she thought. He loved poetry and John Prine and had those beautiful hands, the type her mom would say belonged to a piano player or a surgeon. She was doing it again.

Auden was still talking. "You've given me an update on everybody else. What about you?" he asked, smiling.

What about her? Lydia wasn't sure she knew the real answer, but she started with the easy stuff. "Well, like I said, I own the apartment above the store now. I wouldn't say that it's great for a healthy work/life balance, but I really love it. I've been trying lots of new things with Measure Twice. I had really convinced myself that Heather knew what was cool and I didn't. Letting that go has meant that I'm having a lot more fun running the business. I've done giveaways. Scavenger hunts. Hired some part-time help. I even signed up to host the next Frocktails evening!" Lydia bragged, but when she realized Auden would have no idea what that meant she added, "Frocktails is like the prom for people who sew. Everyone makes incredible outfits to wear. There's a mini red carpet. A dance party. It's next month, right before my birthday. I'm super excited," she added, a little breathless.

"I want to make a Wilder Gown. It's this new pattern that just came out and it looks like a magical, floaty dress perfect for a special party. I even picked out this crazy deadstock organza I found to make the gown and then I'll layer it with a black slip, maybe a hack on the Ogden Cami. . . ."

Auden was clearly overwhelmed by the stream of sewing jargon she had just unleashed upon him, but he grasped on to one detail he understood,

"Your birthday's next month? I didn't know! Well then, let's toast to that!"

They paused at one of the benches that lined the sidewalk and sat down.

Lydia looked down at her empty paper coffee cup, uncertain if he expected her to raise it in a toast, but she shouldn't have worried.

Auden reached into his bag and pulled out two closed mason jars of lemonade—not the hipster jars that people buy but never use as a jar, but real jars full of lemonade. Lydia thought back to the night she had run into Auden in the dark, his worn-down, almost threadbare T-shirt. *He just keeps things. He uses them. And takes care of them,* Lydia thought to herself. And again, she came back to the present to find that Auden was already talking.

"The trick is to use fresh ginger. . . ." Auden paused when he realized Lydia was just staring at the jars in his hands. Auden took a noticeably deep breath and started again. "I make my own lemonade. And the trick, I was saying the trick is to use fresh ginger."

Lydia immediately formulated a million questions: "How long does that take? Where do you find the fresh ginger?" And once she tasted it, sweet but also hot in that hinge-of-the-jaw way that ginger is, she wanted to add, "Have you thought about selling it? Who else has tried this?"

He raised his jar and clinked it against hers. "Happy almost birthday, Lydia. Do you like the lemonade?"

She nodded, realizing he had let her talk the entire time. She blushed, yet again. "So, you make the best lemonade in the world. What else have you been up to, Auden? Enough talk about me," she added, as she took another sip of the sharp and sweet lemonade.

"Me? Right. Things on the mountain are good. Lots of renters for the Laurels, which of course you already know. I'm managing five other houses, so that keeps me pretty busy. I've been wondering lately if maybe . . . maybe the mountain is a little too isolated," and at that he paused, studying his lemonade.

What did that mean? If Auden left Cherry Log, where would he go? Did he want her to ask? Lydia wished the conversation came with an instruction manual. She was far too out of practice.

Just then, Auden reached into his bag and pulled out something even more miraculous than the lemonade.

Sewing. Auden had been sewing.

"I just wanted to let you know, I've been practicing. The PEP stuff you taught me."

He paused for a moment, both of them looking at the scraps of flannel in his hands. She didn't correct him. PEP sounded cuter than EPP, anyway. He must have been using his own shirts for practice. Then, looking back up at Lydia, he asked, "You still offering classes?"

And just like that first moment at the door of the cabin, when a handsome man in Carhartt's had said his name was the same as a famous, dead poet, Lydia was at a loss for words.

"Classes? Yeah, absolutely. We have a class coming up on rain jackets."

Did Auden seem a little crestfallen? She plowed on. He didn't want to know about rain jackets. "But if you mean EPP, PEP, we don't have any classes on that coming up soon. But I can always . . . I can offer a private lesson . . ." Why did that sound so sordid?

They both drank more lemonade, staring at the jars.

She wanted to see him again. Badly.

"Lydia, I haven't been completely honest with you."

Lydia's heart sank. For a second, she thought about the expression "my heart sank." It felt strangely literal in the moment, like her heart was beating from the bottom of her stomach, like a roller coaster had just dropped her and rearranged all of her whole internal organs. She tried to keep a neutral face but had a feeling she was grimacing. Just when she had started to imagine a romantic sewing lesson . . .

Auden rushed on, "I have a lead. On a space. For my shop. I hope it isn't weird for you, but I'm working on getting a loan, to, um . . ."

Lydia had really been working on her "active listening skills." She had. But this was too much. She had no idea what Auden was talking about and was too agitated to let him finish.

"A space? What do you want a space for?" She blurted out.

"I realized, with everything that happened, everything we talked about, seeing you be so brave about the shop, and you know . . ." Lydia realized she was holding her breath, forcing herself to be quiet. Would he stall out again? But Auden kept going. "Fran and Amy. What Heather did. I am no fan of clichés, but we aren't promised tomorrow, so I'm working on getting a loan to start my own shop. I'm planning on taking over Turn the Page, making it into a workshop and store combination for my furniture. I don't have a name for the shop yet, though. So, if you know any one good with names . . ."

Auden was smiling. Lydia realized she was smiling, too. She had a million questions. Would he move to Peridot? Or somehow commute from the mountain? How often would she get to see him? Was she at all part of what drew him to Peridot, or was it just about having a woodshop? What would be a good name for a woodshop? Wood World? Out of This Wood?

Lydia grimaced. Those were terrible names.

Auden saw her scrunched up face and rushed to apologize, saying, "I'm sorry I didn't say something sooner. It didn't seem important compared to what happened at the Laurels. But I didn't want to leave today without letting you know. If you think it is a bad idea . . ."

"What? No! It is a great idea. Sorry, I got distracted thinking about shop names. I'm guessing you're not looking for something like 'Auden's Oaks' or whatever?"

Auden laughed and Lydia joined him.

"Um. I will keep that suggestion in mind."

Lydia scrambled to think of what to say next. Then it came to her.

"Have you ever been up to Two Cousins? The vineyard just north of town?" Lydia asked, gesturing up past the town, and realizing too late she had again failed to explain the segue.

"Two Cousins?" Auden replied calmly. He seemed to be getting used to her drastic changes in conversational topics. "I've heard of it, but never made it over there for their wine or anything." His face twisted into a small smirk—fair, given that North Georgia wasn't really known for its wine anywhere except North Georgia.

"It's a really popular place for weddings," Lydia continued.

Silence grew. Why couldn't Charlie chase a squirrel now?

Lydia barged on, "I, um, I have a wedding I've been invited to out there."

"Okay?" Auden replied, still unclear as to where she intended to go with this line of conversation.

Lydia thought about the fancy wedding invitation hiding in her purse. Emma-Grace and Graham had decided on Two Cousins for their "big day."

Apparently, there was a perfectly good reason for her old life to be invading her new life. Something to do with Emma-Grace having family in Dawsonville and they all love Two Cousins . . . and so on. Lydia had considered making a stink, throwing a fit. Somehow, the idea of making it an issue seemed unfair to her new life. She loved Measure Twice. She loved Peridot. She even might . . .

Lydia looked at Auden's face, the crow's-feet at his eyes, the slight stubble on his chin. Such a kind face. She took a deep breath of the honeysuckle air, glanced at Charlie, asleep at their feet, oblivious to it all. And with her cheeks getting pinker by the second, Lydia picked up his EPP. She flipped it over to see that he had sewn the paper to the fabric.

She would need to find her seam ripper and start breaking the thread, but the new work would actually make the whole piece stronger in the end. She looked at Auden and smiled. He smiled back and reached his hand to hers on the bench, tentatively clasping her hand in his. Still smiling, she laced her fingers with his and asked, "So. Are you free on June fourteenth? And how do you feel about dancing in public?"

# Acknowledgments

To Gemma and Bowden—I hope you enjoy this new book. I can't wait to read the books you both will write. I so love being your mom.

To Andrew—I could never write a story as good as our life together. I love you.

To Bebop and Rocksteady—wait, am I Rocksteady? Rob and Christina, your friendships are lightning in a bottle. This muppet couldn't be more grateful.

To Jane Simpson—thank you for the trip to Cherry Log that started this whole thing in motion.

As always, my deepest gratitude to Dawn Dowdle and Faith Black Ross, and the whole team at Crooked Lane Books.

Thank you, Missy and Jes, for being my first fans and first readers.

To the Downtown house girls, my SOL peeps, the French House—you have made the mountain a second home. Thank you.

Thank you to my family and my friends literally around the world and here in Atlanta for keeping me sane and keeping me hopeful. Thank you, especially, to Pops, Lili, Gdad, and Gram for

# Acknowledgments

keeping my children so happy and loved while I typed away in the precious time you all gave me.

Sarah Gomel, thank you for reminding me to celebrate. All the things. And book releases, too.

To my SYWC students of 2023: Chris, Lily, Ashley, Ashlyn, Claire Louise, Lael, Bharathi, Chelsea, Venya, Evan, Justina, and Evie: tag, you're it! Time to go write a book!

And finally, thank you to the amazing women at Fabricate, Topstitch, the South East Fiber Arts Alliance, the Atlanta Sewing Center, Tiny Stitches Quilt Shop, Craft House ATL, and Fabric World. I wouldn't know sewing without you all. I can never thank you enough.